The Starling God

Tanya Sousa

forestrypress.com

~

For the animals who speak
although we don't always hear.

~

A Word From the Author

I want to prepare you to read about our world and to experience it from a non-human point of view.

When I composed that first sentence, I didn't notice until I was finished writing that I said "our world". Yes, we do think of this planet as our world. However, the truth is far different. We share *the* world with so many other creatures represented in a dizzying number of life forms. Please, then, allow me to start again:

I want to prepare you to read about the world and to experience our impact on it from another species' point of view. The world in this work of fiction will seem familiar in some ways and foreign in others, and you may have to think differently as you read.

Some readers who are staunch naturalists or sciencephiles may dislike that birds, the creatures looking in on our human behaviors and lives, are anthropomorphized. They aren't human, after all! They should be seen as different. I agree on one hand, but I would like to point out some of the amazing things we are discovering about our co-creatures every year, every month, every day. Dolphins have names. Elephants weep with grief and communicate in ways and tones we can't even see or hear. Prairie dogs have a language of sorts that we were unaware of until the tones were carefully studied. They utter sounds that seem basically the same to our ears, but are really full of subtle differences. They identify not only "coyote," for instance, but identify specific coyotes. They have one sound for a man, and another for a man with a gun and another for a man in a hat. This isn't fantasy; this is science. So why can't birds also share intentions and thoughts and even emotions through subtle sound variations and vibrations and body language? There are differences in all living things without a doubt, and we shouldn't expect them to have the exact needs or reactions we have. However, there is also a growing body of evidence that there is a certain undercurrent of sameness.

I wrote this story already knowing each bird species in the book after spending years observing them. Once I had the idea for *The Starling God*, I spent another five years researching each kind and actually writing. While the birds are speaking and feeling much like humans do, it was important to me that I had as much factual behavior represented as possible, although I do take artistic liberties in some areas.

The process is similar to what I imagine Richard Adams must have gone through to write his classic, *Watership Down*. I marveled when I first read that book because I had rabbits, and although his rabbit characters were also anthropomorphized, they had distinct rabbit behaviors and body language I recognized clearly, and I never lost the sense of "rabbit" in his anthropomorphized tale.

Adams only had rabbits to introduce to his readership, however, and almost everyone has a clear idea of what a rabbit is, how it moves and what it eats. I was faced with creating an understandable community of birds that people who don't observe birds or who live outside my own geographic area need to envision as clearly as those who already do know about them or live around them – yet there are so many species varying widely across this planet. "Robin" in England is not "Robin" in the state of Vermont, USA. Additionally, I had a reviewer from the southern United States read the manuscript, and he had no idea what kind of animal a "fisher" was since those mammals don't live where he lives. Therefore, to bridge the experience and information gap, I've provided a glossary of characters and important terms.

Writing a novel is always a journey. When I took this one, I ended up with much more information than I bargained for, and in complete wonder. I hope that's what you, the reader, enjoy as well.

Prologue

I need your help! He's going to kill them if you don't come. He's going to seal them inside the eaves and let them die!

How far are they with the project? When will that happen?

It's happening now. The carpenter is taking a lunch break, but he said he couldn't wait. He's already behind schedule.

Can you get to them and put them in a box with a towel until I get there? I'm almost half an hour from where you are.

I can do that.

In just under half an hour, a woman wearing a flower-print dress and long hair drove into a trailer park driveway – a tidier place than many of them – to the specific address where the caller lived. It was easy to find since there was a well-muscled man in the yard along with a truck, sawhorses and scattered tools.

She got out of the car and saw another woman appear quickly at the trailer door, waving her in with quick flits like a bird herself, words bubbling hastily. "I don't know what kind of birds they are, but they're just babies. I couldn't let them die slowly like that."

The longhaired woman looked into the box and saw three tiny, naked forms with their eyes still shut. "They're barely hatched! Did you see the parents flying around?"

The little bird woman shook her head. "I see different kinds around here, but I couldn't tell which ones belong with these. I thought you'd know, being a wildlife rehabilitator and all."

"You didn't keep the nest?"

"No. It's sealed in there now. I didn't think to keep it – I just took them out and put them on one of my old towels."

Without egg shells or feathers or the intact nest to offer clues, it was hard to tell what the hatchlings were. "Thank you for taking the time to save them," she said, lifting the cardboard "nest" carefully. "I'll do my best to see they do well."

The little bird-like woman nodded and smiled, looking into the box one last time before opening the door and wishing good luck.

The carpenter was measuring and cutting lumber to continue work on what must have been rotting eaves. The woman holding the box considered a moment that the eaves had been where the nest was found. There were only certain birds that would choose a place like this to raise a family. "Did you happen to see any adult birds fly out of there before you found the nest?"

He stopped working and pushed a baseball cap back and then forward again. "Those nasty black birds."

"Starlings?"

"I don't know what you call 'em. Ugly. I say best thing would have been to just let 'em go. Too many anyway – like rats – and all they do is shit all over. Not good for anything from what I can see."

The woman smiled at the man and he grinned, seeming to broaden his shoulders before pushing his hat back and forth again.

The warmth of her smile took his own eyes up to hers, and he froze a bit when he saw the coolness there. "I like rats. And starlings," she said quietly. She made her way to the car and placed the box gingerly on the passenger seat. Two of the hatchlings already didn't look good. They weren't likely to make it, but one was moving his blind head around curiously and looked a healthy color. There was hope for that one.

The newly hatched starling knew nothing at first but waves of light – pinkish light through still closed eyelids – and a strange sensation against his skin. It was still warm like how he felt before when he was curled up tight and with almost no light at all, but there was a difference in this heat – a softness of what he somehow realized was

Mother. Suddenly the peace broke with a sudden chill and sound of wings as Mother disappeared, soon replaced by new sounds that were almost more than he could bear. They pounded into his brain and some screeched through every cell of his being. He tried to move away from them, floundering and tripping, landing neck and beak first.

That was when it came.

Something appeared in his new mind like another sound, but it was not unpleasant as the noises he was trying to escape. It was long, haunting and filled with joy. There was something so wonderful and full in it, and it spoke only of good things. "You've finally been born, little one! I've waited a very long time for you." The baby starling kept lifting his head and craning about to find the source of the pleasant sound, but He couldn't locate it outside of himself. He wanted to find it. He had to find it. That was all he knew.

Chapter One

Destiny Lands

Sometimes destiny lands in front of you with an obvious thud. So it was when a young starling fluttered his wings in a gangly attempt to fly, but plopped instead on lush green grass next to Dove L'al. The dove had seen the fledgling coming so he hadn't stopped reverently pecking for black oil sunflower seeds.

It was a brilliant day for a young one's trial flight. Sun warmed the seeds so the rich, nutty flavor came to the beak in a luscious wave. L'al ate slowly, giving silent thanks between satisfying cracks of the shells. He and his One were the only birds feeding now. The earlier fresh of a newly released sun had drawn redwings and adult starlings in a drove, and although the masses swept through the ground seeds where the doves also preferred to feed, Watcher Rem, robust leader of the redwing blackbirds, had made the usual gesture of raking his beak to and fro in the seed tray to scatter more on the ground for the dove pair. When the other redwings dared to keep eating, he flapped his wings and displayed fiery red marks. "I say we are *finished*! Time to take flight and posts!" The Watchers and even the adult starlings lifted from the grass nearly in unison like a great breath.

There was nothing more happening when L'al saw the dun-brown fledgling careening toward him for the first time. "Incoming, L'in," he said. His mate cocked her head as the starling crashed nearby in a befuddled heap. The dun-brown fledge stared wild-eyed at Dove L'al, who bobbed in a gesture of peace. "You'll get it, young one." L'al's voice and manner were soft as his mate's fair plumage – fit for his position of Teller – the one who kept peace and shared the wisdom of the Gods. The little starling's eyes grew even wider as he seemed to shrink deep into the grass.

"Who are your parents, young one?" L'al approached with more bobbing of his head. The bees worked on creeping phlox, late daffodils, and forget-me-nots that frothed and spilled around a nearby stone wall, but the youngster only opened his beak wide and pulled his neck back quickly.

"Dove L'al is your Teller, little one. He may be trusted. Speak the names of your parents," L'in said. The small bird pressed himself even closer to the ground. She cocked her head again. "He's behaving strangely. Where are his parents and nestlings?"

"Flower!" L'al cried, and flew a respectful distance away. L'in landed next to him on a cedar fence that stretched far in either direction while the God called Flower approached and kneeled where the starling huddled miserably in the grass. Suddenly, the fledge's head raised, and he cried out in recognition. Her featherless wings reached down to lift him – sounds bubbling from Her to the starling – and the youngster peeped back. "Mother," he said. "Mother, you're here!"

L'al and L'in remained completely still on the fence, and L'in swore she heard her mate's heart pounding in his breast. They watched the God carry young starling to a hill that rose up to meet a line of greenery that would burst with yellow blooms soon. Lines of color like this often announced a God's nest. The featherless wings rose and tossed the starling into the air for another practice flight. L'al never blinked as he watched this over and over until the young bird seemed tired. The dove barely dared to breathe, feeling his mate close to him as they experienced the wonder together. He concentrated on her presence, though he never took his eyes from the starling taking flight from the wings of a God. Only L'in's form beside him convinced him the moment was real.

The God lifted young starling a final time and disappeared into the nest with him, Her strange, multicolored feathers flowing colorfully behind like the very flowers She provided to draw insects and create additional fall and winter seeds. It was a power of the Gods to change plumage at will, so L'al learned to recognize the tones and bubbling sounds that came from the God he served. It was the natural way since recognizing sounds and music is every bird's strength.

Birds here called this God "Flower" since she more often than not chose plumage to reflect their shapes and colors.

The Teller couldn't speak until excitement suddenly burst forth with a shake of his feathers, nearly knocking L'in from her grip on the fence. "He's Chosen!" He fluttered to the ground where he felt more solid. "Within my lifetime, I may be able to teach a Chosen One, and who knows what he might teach me."

L'al walked dazedly to the gravel path nearby and absently pecked for bits to add to his gullet, necessary to grind together with the seed he'd recently eaten. He needed to decide what to do; should he share this event with one of the Praisers so an evening message could be sent to all? Should he quietly train the young starling and not let on about his special nature?

"L'al," his mate crooned, rubbing her beak affectionately against his neck. He felt his body relax, and he quickly returned the loving gesture with quick nibbles with his beak in the downy feathers around her eyes and throat. She laughed. "You need to think carefully about what to do, and the answer may not come tonight. Let it settle for awhile."

"If everyone knows what he is, he may be overwhelmed. Such privilege can attract the wrong attention," the Teller murmured, starting to pace fitfully. "But isn't it my place to spread news of the Gods? Could there be greater news for a Teller than this?"

"There is something *very* rare about this one," L'in nearly whispered. "We have heard of the lost or injured and then Chosen, but L'al, he called Flower *Mother*."

The realization struck him. The young starling wasn't Chosen, taken in and nourished, he was *of the Gods* – Equal. He had heard of this as well, but hadn't been sure if it was myth. In truth, he'd always doubted...

"The Gods *are* powerful," he whispered as Rem and another shift of his Watchers approached for a meal. "Had your fill, Teller?" He barked from habit of keeping strict order.

"I have, Rem. L'in and I will rest nearby." He tried to sound as natural as he could, but the alert redwing caught a tone in the Teller's voice. His black feathers shuddered as if a fox was near.

"Is there trouble afoot?"

"No," L'al felt he answered too quickly. "I can't seem to decide what message to have the Praiser sing tonight." *Not actually a lie*, the dove thought with relief.

"If I may make a request, we haven't heard "The Song of the Watch" in awhile."

"Consider it done." L'al bobbed.

His mind whirled as he asked the sweet-throated SLee, a young purple finch who had the range and heart of a much older bird, to sing "The Song of the Watch" for the evening praise.

As the sun prepared to meet the black, SLee flew to his place on one of the thin, taut metal limbs that ran from one strange God-formed branchless tall tree to another and then another – found near all Gods' nests and running along the sides of the Gods' paths. It was an especially sacred singing place, and some birds believed the even, taut metal limbs could heal. SLee perched and felt the vibrating force beneath his feet. He concentrated, letting it fill his being before facing God Flower's nest. Most birds fell silent, and he filled his lungs to share the song:

"Gods – Watchers of all
Protect us from harm
And if it may come
Then sound the alarm
So much like a redwing
Be feathered or furred
Our enemies flee from you
Pain is deterred.
Watchers, Oh Gods,
Protect us from harm
And like stolid redwing
Then sound the alarm."

L'al and L'in snuggled close, listening. They hadn't finished their conversation while the others were anywhere near, and when the song ceased, the Teller finally dared to speak. "It's too early to share this news with the others," he said in a hushed voice. "I need to be sure the Gods intend to share Him with us. I need to be sure He really is born of the Gods and not only raised by Them." He sighed. "There's so much I'm not sure of."

"I think keeping it quiet for now is a good idea," L'in said. She was nestled in a sleep position, but her eyes were still round and alert.

"Why would an Equal come to us, L'in?"

"Perhaps because you're a gifted Teller, and it's thanks from the Gods," she answered proudly. She nibbled at his neck, and he dipped his head modestly. Normally, they wouldn't have the luxury of roosting at night together, but would be taking turns keeping eggs warm until they hatched, with a similar care arrangement until their own young fledged. But for the last two years their eggs had not hatched through no fault of their caretaking. This spring, L'in sensed no life in them again, and she had sadly pushed them out.

"Perhaps this is why the Gods have taken brooding away from us." He laid his head over her sleek back. "There's something greater meant – a greater purpose. Whatever the reason for this, there's change in the air, One. Things will never be the same if He lives among us."

"What will happen?"

"I don't know." He felt his heart beat faster again, and a strange dread washed over him. He ruffled his feathers to shake it off, startling his reposed mate. "It can only be good. The Gods provide. The Gods are good unless we are not. We have done things right here. I can only see it as a gift.

Chapter Two

From the Wings of the Gods

The young starling made more practice flights from Flower's wings, and L'al stayed as close as he dared to watch the progress. The God found insects in the grass and fed the fledgling where He could turn a curious eye sideways to see where food came from. All the while, the dove wandered nonchalantly among lily fronds and sometimes over pebbled earth, pretending to find his own meals there. The finches darted about, red and gold, too engrossed with eating seeds and tending young to notice the single young bird where one shouldn't be, and the Watchers, though always vigilant, were scanning for the flame of fox in the fields, looming hawks, shadowed cats or other Blooders that would threaten the Sacred Space; no one was looking for a miracle.

L'al thought how free the Sacred Space had been of marauders, but the Watchers remained on guard. Robins pulled at worms; swallows swooped in complex air dances, and L'al was amazed no one noticed the small one in the care of a God.

"It's as though no one *expects* to see it, so they don't," he told L'in. "Even the Seekers haven't noticed? How could it be?"

The day came when young starling flew from Flower's wings and made a beautiful landing on a mid-level maple branch. God Flower stood at the base and looked up, watching for a while, sounds bubbling from within until She finally turned and left the small bird on His own for the first time.

L'al kept some distance, but could see young starling looking about, first up at the leaves, then at the bark below His feet. He ruffled His new feathers and gave them a preening, pulling out bits of white matter that itched as His feathers and body grew. *What a transformation from the frightened little one just suns ago!* Dove L'al thought. A fly landed on the limb beside starling, and He turned His head sideways to take a closer look. He recognized it as food, and felt the desire to snatch for it. The fly felt the gaze and zoomed between leaves turned almost translucent by dapples of sunlight.

Now is the time, a voice seemed to pop inside L'al's head. He pushed himself from the ground with a whoosh of air from his wings and settled on the branch close to the starling. "Too long," was all he could say as he landed neatly. Starling only looked at him with surprise. "You waited too long, young one. You'll have to move faster than that if You wish to eat. I am Dove L'al," he added as an afterthought.

"Mother brings me food," starling answered.

"I believe Your Mother has set You on Your own. It's time to find Your own way. Didn't She tell You that?"

"Mother only sings sounds to me," starling said. "She brings me food and will return to take me back to the nest."

L'al was astounded. "God Flower – Your Mother – doesn't speak to You?"

"She speaks in sounds. There is no sound more beautiful than Mother's singing," young starling said, and squinted as if the very thought of his beloved Mother was a blanket around him. He envisioned her coming for him, her warmth folding around him and keeping him safe, taking him back to the nest where he would take most of his meals and sometimes roost on her to see what she was doing. He would learn to be like her by watching. He knew he must watch very closely to see how living was to be done.

"But You understand *my* speaking?" L'al persevered.

"I've always heard your kind from far away. At first it didn't make much sense, but then I heard something familiar. In time, I understood. Your voices aren't as sweet as Mother's, but the words you sing in evening do help me sleep."

Your kind, L'al tossed His words around in his head, then let them slow down to be savored. Starling looked like any fledge he'd seen in his years, but the words reminded L'al he was speaking to an Equal. He trembled inside, and the trembling made his body follow suit until he squeezed his eyes shut and meditated on the sounds of the rustling leaves and the feel of solid wood. It was one way Tellers could relax during stressful encounters or mediations – times when it was especially important to maintain composure. "What do You know of the world outside Your nest?" He finally asked.

"What do you mean?"

"What do You think life will be like now?"

"Life is warmth, and food, and Mother. And sometimes these new things!" He gave a chirrup. The dove felt anxiety threatening to bubble up again, but his sheer will forced it back down. He struggled to ask the right questions. *Gods, help me find the answers I seek.* He thought, and a flash of inspiration struck him.

"Do you know what You are?"

"I don't see why there is a you and a You," young starling continued to look around before looking briefly at the dove again.

The older bird stretched his neck. "The first is a usual form of *you*. The sound you are hearing in *You* is the same sound found in any word of importance. I am Teller L'al. Your Mother is one of the Gods. The sound of *You* I use has everything to do with who You are."

Starling turned his head slightly in L'al's direction, but then was distracted by an ant crawling on the limb by his toes. He reached down and gobbled it up. "I only know I'm the same as Mother."

The dove's heart thrilled. "You're right, young one. You are Equal to Your Mother, but there are differences You need to see. Do You notice the birds flying about?"

"Birds?"

"Like me."

Young starling looked through the leaves at a sky dotted with flying things arriving at and leaving the Sacred Space, diving to catch insects, trolling the grass, sailing by on patrol.

"You're special, young one. You're Equal to the Gods – to those like Your Mother – but we are Your people. I believe You've come to live among us as bird to do great things, but first You have many things to learn. I believe this is why You've entered my life."

"I am the same as Mother. I'm not one of you." Young starling turned his head away.

"The Gods have featherless wings, but we have feathers. *You* have feathers," L'al mustered all the courage he had and poked his beak at young starling's wing to stress the point. "Though the Gods have many powers, they choose not to fly. They gave birds the gift of the sky. Flight is not necessary for them. Your Mother has given You the form of bird to live among us. You fly. Your Mother is one of the Gods. She is one of Them who provides and protects, who is greater than all."

"I am not one of you!" Starling scuttled away from L'al to where the limb branched from the tree and huddled there.

"You should come with me, young one. You'll need to stay warm and safe tonight. There's a storm coming on the wind, and L'in and I would be happy to house You until You may be taught how to completely live on Your own."

The starling's eyes were wide now. "Mother will return for me!" L'al tried to bob closer to the fledgling to comfort Him, but the dun wings opened quickly and slapped the dove's extended head with surprising force. L'al jumped back and the starling hopped up and down, slapping the air with frantic wings. "Mother!" He cried. "Mother!"

Dove L'al left Him there, calling out for the God who wouldn't return this time.

"I failed," he told L'in. "I don't know how to make Him understand, and He's rejected me."

"Leave Him," she soothed. "He may have fledged from the Gods, but He is still a young one and is frightened. He *will* hear you in due time."

The rain began hours later, drowning out the starling's intermittent, plaintive calls. By the time the black was nearly arrived, the rain pounded even harder, and there was no evening praise. The

Sacred Space remained empty and still except for the rhythmic slap of water on leaves, grass and ground. L'in and L'al nestled tightly together against the torrent and wondered if the fledgling would survive the night. "There's no question He is an Equal," L'al told her before the rains came. "At least I can be sure of that now." There were so many days that he spoke to his mate, and she was so one with him he felt as if he was speaking in his own mind, as if there was no bodily separation between them. Her soft voice was like his conscience, always rational and true.

"The Gods wouldn't send Him to be taken away so soon," L'in reasoned.

"But if I was supposed to say or do something differently, and I lost my chance…"

L'in gave him a sharp peck. "You need to stop. You're a fine Teller. You've been given a great challenge, and you will not fail."

L'al drifted to sleep to claps of thunder, wishing he could be as certain as his dear mate.

Chapter Three

The Lessons Begin

The young starling didn't feel the first drops of rain that fell, sheltered by limbs and leaves. He only felt a swimming mix of relief that Dove L'al had gone, and fear that Mother had really abandoned him. He called for her more and more desperately until his throat was dry and hoarse and the torrent began. Black settled over the landscape as suddenly as a blanket pulled over his nest box. "Mother," he peeped, but more to himself now, and the drops became rivulets around him. His body ached with cold and exhaustion.

Lightning flashed through the leaves, making Mother's nest show for moments. The clear boxes on the nest's side were bright with the same light that plunged from the sky; the starling saw a shadowy form looking out. It never became cold and wet in the nest, and the bright light inside didn't flash quickly, but remained until Mother settled for the night. She controlled the very light in the sky, the starling thought.

A leaf above gave out from water weight, splashing the youngster on the right wing. He shook it away and wearily ran his beak through the feathers.

Feathers.

He sank into a horrible emptiness before finally tucking his head beneath his wing to shut it all away.

He wasn't able to sleep through the night, but woke to each sound and sense – and it was all so loud and miserable and horribly different. Once he startled to what seemed to be a voice: "*You will help them remember.*" He snapped awake and gaped with horror at the large eye that seemed to be looking back deeply into his. When he blinked again, it was gone. There was something familiar in the voice...

Just before the sun released in the silver mist, the liquid notes of a song cut the stillness:

"Cheery-Cheery – Cheerily!

Joy of morning: come and see

What dear Gods bring you and me

Sacred Space, shel-ter and feed

Cheerily I beckon thee!"

Starling had heard the song before through the clear boxes on his nest's side, but it had never been so vibrant. It entered his heart and lifted him for a moment, though the thought of the word "Gods" brought the weight back.

His belly gnawed with hunger, but he lost hope that Mother would come to feed him. The fluid, happy tones of the song repeated until other birds began to stir and call to each other in morning greeting and announcements.

"The rain is through!"

"Today, my Relm takes first trial flight!"

"The sky is clear of hawk shadow!"

"Beautiful morning greeting, Hralla!"

"The Watchers feed!"

"Rain has damaged Hmon's nest!"

There were many more messages strewn through the air, and starling wondered how they expected anyone to understand them if all spoke at once. He pulled back his head quickly as he realized *he* managed to hear each and every message with no difficulty. How? A vision of Dove L'al popped into his mind, the small head and longish neck bobbing strangely. *We are Your people.*

Starling's hunger pain lurched him back to the moment. With a deep breath, he jumped from the branch and flapped his wings, landing a bit less than gracefully on the ground where Mother brought him to feed several times before. It wasn't far from where the singer with the fluid, cheery morning song still perched upon a thin, taut branch that stretched across fields like some mystical vine. The singer, Hralla, starling presumed between snaps at crawling insects, sported a rust colored breast and charcoal wings and head. She looked absorbed in peace, and finally dove down in a single motion as smooth as her voice, to rest on the ground about twelve feet away from the fledgling. She nodded greeting and began earnestly hopping through the grass, turning her head this way and that until she could snatch bugs and worms. It seemed to starling that she ate an inordinate amount.

"How can you fly and eat so much?" he couldn't help but ask.

"Dear one!" She laughed. "I'm getting food for my nestlings, not just for myself, of course! How do you think your mother fed you before you fledged?"

She flew soundlessly away, then up under a form draped with clematis vines still far from blooming. The raucous cries of, "Mother you are here!" and, "my mouth first!" told him the nestlings were there. He felt the hollowness return although his belly was full of the good food Mother taught him to eat. She would be proud of him, he thought, finding the insects on his own. It would be what she wanted. This filled him a bit.

He lifted his head to look about and was amazed at the activity of so many birds – so many colors, sizes and different voices, and so much happy work being done. It was then Dove L'al landed beside the starling with the rapid *who-who-who-who-who* sound that apparently announced his comings and goings.

"If it's true, and Mother is a God of this, greater than all other creatures, then She is the *best* of the Gods," starling announced with no other greeting. He turned his head to survey all around.

L'al was amazed how L'in's clear mind always brought such wisdom. Once the fear had passed, the young one *was* ready to hear. How impatient he had been! *Be gentle with yourself,* a voice seemed to speak in L'al's mind. *You are working through a new and exceptional event few Tellers face.*

"I can't say one God is greater than another, but instead I can say that how birds behave within a Sacred Space determines how generous a God is willing to be. We have observed Law well here, and God Flower – Your Mother – is pleased. She provides us food, places to shelter, water to drink and bathe with and freedom from enemies."

"Sacred Space?" Starling's mind was whirling.

"Although the Gods have the power to travel quickly and far without flight, and though They certainly may exercise many other powers anywhere, They have domains – places where their unique powers are used. It is this domain we call "Sacred Space". Some of us dedicate our lives to living close to a particular God's Sacred Space, and assure that the God or Gods who dwell there receive adequate praise, that laws are kept, and young are taught the wisdom."

"This is Mother's domain?"

"Yes. And Yours as an Equal to Her."

L'al saw the starling's eyes shine as He surveyed the Sacred Space again with a new outlook. It was His Sacred Space! His Mother had placed Him among these birds to oversee it with Her. He savored the sound of how it was to be *Him* and not *him*. If Mother wanted it, then He would be sure to use it from now on.

"I call Your Mother 'Flower,'" L'al continued. "Since Law is kept here, She provides many things. All of this," L'al pulled his breast up high and spread his wings for emphasis, "is from God Flower's wings to reward us. See where robins, and starlings like Yourself, and cowbirds move through short grass? Flower keeps large spaces of grass short so they may find food there easily. The very flowers spread about are placed by Her will, and attract more insects in the warm months, offer nectar for hummingbirds, and put forth seeds in winter when many other foods have become buried in snows."

L'al walked toward the place where Rem and his sentries fed on sunflower seeds, always wary. Several jumped to attention from the dove's movements, then they returned to pecking when they saw it was only their Teller. "God Flower offers us sunflower seeds to sustain those who are faithful, and for those who travel through and require a place to feed."

Starling drank in every word, but hit upon a snag when the dove

16

mentioned 'Starlings like Yourself'. He raised the issue with His new mentor. "Which of the birds are starlings like Me?"

"The dark birds with bright yellow beaks."

"Mine isn't yellow!" Starling cried with concern.

Dove L'al chuckled. "See, it is, but it is darkening for now. When you grow and are ready to take a mate, it will become yellow again. Like Your God Mother, part of Your color changes, though not at will. Your feathers will also change."

"At least everything about us isn't plain," young starling said with a sigh. He had been disappointed to be compared with the starlings. They were so short and nondescript next to the colorful and graceful forms all about Him.

"There is nothing plain about starlings," Dove L'al said with a blink and popping of his usually calm eyes. "In fact, I am not surprised starling was the form God Flower gave You. There are myths about starlings, although most birds have long believed them lies created by starlings themselves to promote their own power. I am, however, at least somewhat familiar with the Lore."

"Do you believe the myths? And if you don't believe, why would you bother to learn the Lore?"

"A Teller's job is about sharing wisdom and information. We keep the peace, the Law and the harmony. I don't judge the Lore or the belief of others, young one. I need to be aware of the many different beliefs so I may help factions understand each other. One cannot mediate what one doesn't understand." L'al had never needed to explain his duties before. He preened. "I think this is important knowledge for You, fledgling from the Gods. I don't know what Your purpose might be, but my heart says this is a key idea."

The two sat together quietly, digesting the thoughts. Dove L'al nearly floated from the wonder of it. "It's wise not to judge another's Lore," he said again, softly, almost to himself. "It may take the lifetimes of many, and countless seasons to discover, but we may very well find that what seemed myth is truth, as I am seeing with You."

"Can you tell me the starling Lore?" the young one asked breathlessly.

The Teller felt a rush of something ill but brushed it away and considered a moment. "For Your purposes, I think You need to hear from one of the starling's Secret Keepers. They know the Lore at a depth they would never share with anyone but other starlings – special starlings. I know whom to ask, but first, I have to consider the possible consequences of any actions we take from now on. That's another important lesson to learn. Every action has a reaction. An action must result in greater good and not harm others for our own benefit. The only way to be sure to do this is to consider well before You take any path."

The starling nodded.

"I'll take You to meet my L'in. She will teach the more functional aspects of life as bird."

"Who is L'in?"

"L'in is my One – my mate. Someday, You'll find your One as well. May she be as sweet." L'al lifted from the ground with another rapid series of whooshes, and the starling pushed off less easily behind him, flapping his wings more quickly than the experienced dove. Luckily, they didn't have to fly far. They landed in a tree, about midway up, that L'al explained would be rich with red berries in early fall. "I chose the spot as a gift to L'in," he said.

"Did Mother place your tree as she did the flowers?" The starling asked.

"It was before my lifetime," L'al answered reverently, "but the Gods choose what remains and what leaves the Sacred Spaces. I can only assume Her will raised it."

The nest was a rather untidy pile of twigs, starling thought with surprise, but everything about the dove seemed simple and quiet. Perhaps this was another branch of that way.

"Tellers don't believe in adornment," L'al said as if reading starling's mind. "We put our energy toward the Gods instead. Others believe a fine nest is a thanks to the Gods. It is another of the places where kinds differ. You'll learn all these things as You grow."

Starling watched the Teller fill his throat with air and bend forward to call his mate. "L'in my One," he called. It was an eerie, soft sound that vibrated through the starling and made him shiver. In a moment, another bird like L'al appeared, but even gentler around the eyes and a bit smaller and finer. "This is the young one, L'in," the Teller announced happily.

"Young one?" She eyed her mate with mirth. "Surely He has a name!"

Chapter Four

All in a Name

L'al was so immersed in the idea of the Starling God that he hadn't even thought of asking for His name. The starling was likewise struck speechless; the other birds identified themselves each with a particular word, but it hadn't occurred to Him that *He* should have one.

"What is Your name, fledgling?" L'in finally asked, thanks to the male's silence.

"I don't know. I don't think I have one." The starling didn't feel very special now, especially when every other feathered thing had a word, and He had nothing.

"Perhaps there was a sound God Flower used for You, but it wasn't a word like ours," the Teller suggested. The starling closed His eyes and allowed the image of His beloved Mother's face hovering over the nest box and her featherless wings reaching in to fill His hungry belly. There *was* a sound she always made to Him in the same way these birds used a name!

"My name is – _____;" starling uttered the sound almost as flawlessly as from the face of Mother herself. L'al was shocked at how much it even resembled Flower's tone.

"Please repeat that?" L'in requested helplessly, and starling continued to repeat the sound as the doves tried over and over to say it.

"It's a sound of the Gods," L'al sighed. It may be Your true name, but our throats will never utter it."

21

"We can offer You a bird name," L'in suggested. "You may keep Your real name close to Your heart for one who might understand it."

The three began discussing the best choice. "Every profession has a first sound that usually represents them although this is not a hard and fast rule—"

"—All except the Praisers," L'in added quickly.

"Yes, all except the Praisers because there are so many who choose this profession that any beginning sound goes. Tellers usually begin with an L'. Watchers often begin with an R. Cleaners—"

"—They clear the dead from the paths of the Gods," L'in interjected. "A gruesome job to some, but it has to be done."

"Cleaners most often with a J," L'al continued, "and Seekers usually with an S."

"What are they?" starling questioned.

"They're similar to Tellers in that they remain open to all Lore, but they don't reteach it. They seek knowledge. They especially seek new knowledge about the Gods – study them – and share that information with Tellers. We then decide what information should be shared and how it should be shared," L'al said. "It's too bad I don't know what purpose God Flower intends for You," L'al said wistfully. "It would make naming You so much easier."

"I like the sound of both the Teller and Seeker," starling mused. "Is it possible to be both?"

"You're fledged from the Gods. I believe You're capable of anything… Although I've never known a starling to be any regular bird profession – they normally only have their Secret Keeper and teachers of various kinds. They also have names that are nothing like most other bird kinds I know of. Those names are similar to sounds made by the Gods, but close enough to normal that we are able to speak them."

"Is there any bird within this Sacred Space called SL'an?" Starling played with the name in His mind and liked the feel of it.

"SL'an is a good name. So it is Yours. You will meet another young bird, fledged before You but still in Your range, named SLee. He is the only other with the S and an L following."

"His parents desperately wanted their nestling to be a Seeker, or perhaps a Teller. They named him SLee because of these not-so-secret wishes," L'in explained.

"Fledges choose their *own* professions if they're to have any in particular," L'al added. "The name is then given or chosen before leaving the nest for first trial flight. How SLee was named is not...*usual*."

"Oh, were his parents beside themselves when he chose 'only' Praiser!" L'in's eyes squinted with a laugh. "Still, they were unwilling to change the name that showed their fondest wish--—"

"Death!" A voice screeched. "DEATH!"

"What's happened," L'in gasped. Bird-wing sounded everywhere; the Watchers scrabbled for order then darted to and fro to find the source of the cry. Swallows swooped and snapped beaks at invisible enemies, and Hralla came toward the doves and starling SL'an like a cannonball.

"Teller!" She wailed. "It's my sister, Hroo! Her nest has been raided! Two nestlings missing!"

"Missing?"

"Dead!" She wailed again. "Missing, but surely dead. There's blood, and an aura we don't recognize."

L'al was frozen for only a moment, then training and purpose spurred him. "What Blooder is responsible?"

SL'an wondered what a Blooder was, but held His tongue as His heart pounded wildly.

"No Blooder was seen! The Watchers witnessed nothing. Hroo witnessed nothing. She returned from gathering food to find two dear babies where there were four, and the horrid feel of death!"

"A message must be sent – panic has already taken hold." L'al drew himself up.

"I can't be the one to deliver this message!" Hralla cried.

"Bring SLee," L'al fixed Hralla with a firm but kind eye. "If you can locate him and send him here, that would be a great service to us all."

Hralla flew away as fast as she'd come, and within moments, SLee landed, a most tiny bird for such an important job, starling SL'an thought.

"Praiser SLee, there's news to send quickly – the first non-praise message you have ever sent. It must be accurate, and it must be well heard. You must repeat it many times before stopping. Do you understand?"

SLee was trembling. SL'an had the feeling it wasn't as much fear as a sense of excitement for a first imperative task. "I will not disappoint, Teller L'al. What's the message?"

"Two nestlings gone from Hroo's nest taken by an unknown Blooder. All birds on alert. All birds report any unusual activity to Watchers and Teller. All birds feed close to their nests until further notice. Now go!"

SLee's tiny wings carried him with striking speed to the taut limb where he immediately began the message. Activity ceased as the young purple finch delivered information, clear and true.

"We should go to Hroo," L'in said without looking either male in the eye. L'al's heart nearly broke for his beautiful mate. It didn't matter that L'in lost her nestlings from never hatching. The pain to her was as great as if a Blooder's jaws had closed. There was no better to understand Hroo's dilemma than her, but L'al knew that understanding such loss now meant reliving her own again.

"What is a Blooder?" SL'an finally dared to ask.

"Those who eat our flesh and blood. They are the fox, the hawks, the cats, and others in some places. The Gods protect us from Blooders when They can."

"Why didn't Mother protect Hroo's nest?"

"Sometimes we don't understand the Gods' ways. Sometimes the Gods choose to make an example of a wrongdoer or someone who doesn't uphold the Law," L'al sighed. "Hroo is nothing like Hralla, although they are sisters. Hralla chose to be a Praiser, but Hroo has completely rejected the wisdom. She is one who doesn't recognize Gods as greater than bird, and who refuses to give praise or worship."

"Mother wouldn't allow nestlings to die because of such a thing, would She?" SL'an's stomach lurched.

"Flower is a God, Fledgling. It is not Her fault that some birds bring tragedy upon themselves rather than upholding the Law."

L'in gave L'al a soft peck. "This isn't the time for a lesson, One. Hroo needs us now."

Without another word, the dove pair launched from the red-berry tree with young SL'an close behind.

When they reached Hroo's nest, they found her cowered, wide-eyed, with her young crying miserably for food. Each time one of the two tried to poke his head into their mother to rouse her, she only jiggled slightly, staring without seeing.

"Hroo, we're here," L'in said. "Your pain is consuming, but your babes need to feed."

When He landed, a horror filled SL'an's beak and ecked into His brain. His neck tensed, and His very feathers threatened to stand on end. *Death*. The aura whispered. *Blood*. It said.

"I…I will not leave," Hroo began to shake. "If I leave, I may return and find them gone – all gone."

"Dear one," L'in spoke softly, and with such sadness, SL'an wondered what had happened in her own life. "If you don't leave, your nest will be empty for certain. They'll die with no food."

"We're here," L'al added. "Go find food for yourself and your nestlings. We'll stay alert. I've put the Watchers and all birds on guard. Whatever Blooder entered the Sacred Space won't do it so easily next time."

L'in nodded, and Hroo looked sideways at her crying little ones and readied herself for flight. "I'll be close," she said.

"As will we," L'in assured her.

After Hroo was gone, L'in whispered to L'al and SL'an, "Oh! Can you feel it?"

"I did when we landed," the starling said, relieved He wasn't the only one experiencing the horror.

"It will go away soon, but Hralla was right; I don't recognize the kind. This is a Blooder we've never seen."

SL'an's flesh crawled again, and He shuddered visibly.

"We share Your fear, young one," L'al said, even softer this time so the remaining nestlings wouldn't hear. He would arrange a special Praise for God Flower tonight, a Praise asking forgiveness and protection from the unseen Blooder in their midst. After arranging this, he knew he must go alone among the flowers to meditate on what these recent events meant and what he should do next. He hadn't had time to announce an Equal among them, or to consider further if he should. He did know with every feather on his body that the appearance of this strange Blooder *now* was no coincidence. "Where there is great good, there is great evil," he murmured.

"What?" SL'an and L'in asked together. L'al was taken aback. He hadn't meant to speak! "We need to feed as well," he said quickly, aware that he was as hungry as the nestlings. "When Hroo arrives —"

She flew in to her screeching babes as if on cue.

"—L'in and I will take You to the feeder where Flower leaves rich sunflower seeds."

"Shouldn't I look for food elsewhere?" SL'an asked, pulling his head back.

"Starlings eat a bit of everything, young one – *SL'an*." The Teller corrected himself. "You'll enjoy the taste of this new food, I'm certain."

Hroo made one more hunting trip before the three ended up leaving. "Thank you," the robin said wearily.

"I'll request that Rem sends some of his Sentries to help you."

Hroo didn't answer, but L'al knew she was still in shock and took no offense. He, his mate and the Starling God made their way to the feeder where some Sentries were on break.

"Would Rem spare some of you to ease Hroo's mind?" He bobbed respectfully. "She's still in shock and fears leaving the nest."

One of the younger redwings hopped angrily toward Dove L'al. "Why *should* we? Isn't it what she's deserved?"

"Her nestlings have *died*!" SL'an burst out, and hopped back at the Sentry.

"Mind your manners, fledgling!" The Sentry spat, fluffing his wings so his bright red spots blazed. L'al suspected this bird had aspirations for Rem's position someday.

"Peace," the Teller flapped his own wings between the two. "This is SL'an, Sentry. He may be a fledgling, but he speaks the truth. The Law must be upheld, even when it means coming to the aide of one who has not upheld it herself. The Gods demand harmony first and foremost." SL'an was struck by the sudden '*he*'.

L'al turned to SL'an. "Though you speak the truth, starling, you must remember the point of view of others. This Sentry and his flock risk their lives daily to protect those who uphold the Law, and those who don't. It is a difficult seed to crack when your very life's work is undone by those who don't follow."

SL'an retreated and lowered his head. The Sentry lowered his head as well. "You are wise, Teller. Peace, starling."

"Peace, Sentry." SL'an hoped He spoke well, and L'al's expression told him He did.

Two Sentries volunteered to keep Watch for Hroo, and L'in and L'al were finally able to feed. The young starling had a hard time learning to break the shells to get the rich, oily seed inside, but after having the taste of one, He was motivated to practice. "Like this." L'al took a seed and moved it about his beak, crack-cracking it on each side until it finally released its splendid filling.

"You're right," SL'an said with His beak full. "I do like this food."

He tried to sound upbeat, but He couldn't help but think of Hroo grieving on her nest and the fact that Mother had let this happen. He noticed L'in ate very little and seemed to droop.

"Why don't you go to the tree and sleep?" L'al nibbled at his mate's neck.

"It's so early."

"It doesn't matter. You need rest, Love."

With a whoosh, she lifted away and returned gratefully to the nest tree, where she pulled herself in as tightly as she could and grieved for all the young she'd lost.

When SL'an asked, L'al explained the barrenness of the last years and why Hroo's grief was especially hard for his L'in.

"But you live by the Law," the starling shook His head. "How could bad things happen to you?"

"There aren't always obvious answers, SL'an, but there are always reasons."

SL'an blinked.

"Our nest has been barren, and we didn't know why. Still, we held faith. Then You came along, and only then was the reason clear. We were given time to become more involved in our professions as there were no young to brood. We were prepared for *You*, You see."

SL'an felt as though His mind was flying open.

"The wisdom doesn't speak particularly what I'm going to share now, but it does say that where there is great good, there is also great evil. I also believe that with no pain, there can be no joy."

"No?"

"I think not. Pain is like a bite on the wing that lets you know you are not dreaming, that you surely are alive – and life is the greatest joy of all."

Chapter Five

The Miracle

Everyone within the Sacred Space remained on alert, but five suns passed without a sighting of the Blooder or the loss of more nestlings.

L'al divided his time between meditating in the flowers and teaching starling SL'an the basics of the wisdom. The younger bird was a quick study and asked many challenging questions, telling the dove that the choice of Seeker was a good one. Since the young starling seemed prone to anger and strong feelings, as His response to the young redwing Sentry hinted, he took time to teach Him a skill usually reserved for Tellers much later in their training – the way to close the outside out and form a special space inside oneself. In this place a bird in need of calm and greater understanding could face a strong feeling or situation – spend time with it and let it show the truth it had come to show without causing the damage it would if it wasn't given voice. L'al was more than pleased at how quickly SL'an had grasped the idea and meditated this way easily.

L'al chose mornings for his own meditating. His favorite spot was a space of flowers planted within tiers of stone. He could meander through lilies and ferns, cranesbill and iris, placed and separated in an order only the Gods could create. Soft, warm pine bark shavings between plants made his walk perfectly silent, so he could focus on his questions and clear everything else away. Once, he had come face-to-face with God Flower here. So lost in thought as he was, he hadn't heard Her tending the area. As a God, She chose what plants should remain and which should leave, and She cleared away what didn't please Her. Piles gathered in the sun or rain until She placed them in a squeaky contraption and took them away.

The day he walked serenely, unknowingly, to where She crouched and removed unwanted plants was a crowning moment in his life. For an instant, he could see Her eyes, forward like most Blooders' but free of malice. There was only love in the eyes – love for Her birds. She stopped still, and so did L'al, with his heart in his beak. He wished he had the power to stay in the love of Her gaze – he could have died of happiness there – but the fear birds feel from being the presence of The Great Ones flooded him and sent him off in a flurry.

He held on to this memory as he walked there each sun since the slaughter of Hroo's nestlings. He began his walk each time asking silently for Her guidance.

On the fifth sun, he had a vision of announcing an Equal among them and great discord resulting. He saw dark skies, birds with claw against claw and beak against beak, and Blooders feasting on the carnage. *They are not ready,* a voice spoke in his mind. He saw the image of the starling Secret Keeper, called Bard, sitting on the top of God Flower's dwelling and singing to the sky.

"It's time He learned the depth of starling Lore as only Bard can share," he said to himself, and flew throughout the Sacred Space to find Bard and request his help. He found him trolling the short grass with his mate, Glee, and at least six others of his kind. L'al checked carefully to see if other birds were watching. Starling Bard was a Secret Keeper, a profession only known to the starling kind – not a scandalous thing in and of itself, but Bard was notorious for his belief in a specialized Lore – Lore some others resented. Most didn't know the details of it – its secrets usually whispered among starlings themselves and even then not all of them allowed to know it fully from what the dove understood. It should have been that L'al, as the Teller in this Sacred Space, would have worked with any starling flock's Secret Keeper to decide what, if any, bits of the Lore were shared with other kinds. But Bard had never acknowledged the dove, and released what seed bits of information he chose – just enough to let others know the Secret Keeper believed other kinds were somehow less, starlings holding some special right. It raised feathers on the backs of even normally understanding and patient birds.

L'al walked about the grassy area, pretending to look for something there until he saw the starling Secret Keeper and his mate wander just a bit from the others. "I have information you'll want," L'al said quietly, with his head down as if pecking a seed from the ground.

"You mean to speak to *me* Teller?" Thankfully Bard was savvy enough to behave like the dove. "It must be quite the seed-bit for you to risk sharing words." He stifled a laugh. Other birds were threatened by his beliefs, and it was right that they were. Bard knew if he hadn't been born starling, he would be ripped with envy too.

"It will take too long to share the information here, and we shouldn't be overheard," L'al said. They both searched for food in a long silence.

"Then meet me after all roost or settle in their nests," Bard finally replied. "There is a place just a mile's flight from here in a clearing in the woods."

L'al thought he knew it. "The one with the three ancient maple trees?"

"The very one," Bard said.

"I'll meet you." L'al knew the dangers of flying when it was black or even nearly black. Blooders often stalked under cover of dark, and owls ruled the skies, silent and deadly, with their eyes straight ahead like a fox or cat.

Myth said the ancestor of the owls had once been like fox but wished to be like bird, pining until the ancestors of the Gods heard. They granted the fox's wish, shrinking the legs into wings and feet, pulling the long nose into a beak, and exchanging the flame red fur for feathers brown like the bark of trees. However, the Gods were still young and Their powers weak. Before the transformation was complete, They became exhausted and stopped, leaving some owls with two tufts on the head where fox ears should have completely disappeared, and leaving all with a Blooder's lust and forward eyes. The owl, horrified by being half fox and half bird, hid in the shadows of the night so neither creature would lay eyes upon it. If a bird was unlucky enough to see an owl, it would try to tear the bird's flesh with sharp talons and a searing beak so the bird would keep silence forever.

L'al's heart seemed to swell in his breast, but he knew meeting by black was the only way. Fear could not stop him from the most important task of his life. He only hoped the black wouldn't force sleep over his mind so he couldn't fly at all, never mind think enough to share thoughts as he should.

He continued pecking at this and that on the ground until he'd wandered a distance from the starlings and felt it would be normal to lift from the ground and return to where his L'in tutored SL'an in etiquette, nest building, foraging and other necessities usually reserved for her own fledglings.

L'al found his mate preening her charge lovingly and teaching Him with all the patience of a true mother.

They had obviously just finished one successful lesson and were beginning another on reading the Watchers' signals and what to do if a Blooder was announced. "I thought Tellers decide what information should be shared. Shouldn't the Watchers inform their Teller before word goes out?" SL'an asked.

"When a Blooder is near, there's no time for such information to go from one beak to another. This kind of knowledge must be shared immediately. Seconds of delay could mean loss of life," L'in explained.

When He seemed to have no other question on that matter, she continued. "If Watchers alert to hawk in the sky at a distance, it isn't necessary to take cover right away, but it is imperative that You stop feeding, flying, loving – whatever You're doing – to locate the hawk in the sky and to be alert. If Watchers announce hawk directly overhead, all birds must take cover instantly. Remaining from curiosity or false bravado could be the last thing a bird ever does." She said it with a clap of her wings.

"The announcement of fox or cat requires birds to fly to the highest point. Fox do not climb trees, and birds are then safe in their limbs. Cats sometimes do climb, but most are too lazy to go far."

"Some are even *afraid* and become paralyzed with fear and unable to return to the ground," L'al added.

"They don't sound like much of an enemy," SL'an lifted his beak slightly.

"They aren't if they can be announced before they attack. Cats, however, are masters of shadow and can be lurking unseen until it is too late. Fox are bright as flame, but they blend into the yellow sunshine on golden grasses and often stay hidden there until they see a time to strike."

"The Watchers have a difficult profession." SL'an thought of the Sentry He nearly rubbed wings with just suns ago, and, while He still didn't agree with the lack of sensitivity for Hroo's pain, He understood his attitude better. Every life in the Sacred Space relied upon what these birds saw or missed. He was sobered by the thought of such responsibility. "If I see a Blooder before a Watcher does, what do I do?"

"You announce," L'in said with no hesitation. "If it is within or over the Sacred Space, there is no time to lose. If it is outside the Sacred Space or a distance away, try to find L'al and tell him what You've seen and where You saw it."

Mid-sun blazed over the trees and flowers of the Sacred Space. Even flies seemed slow and thick with moisture, and the air was becoming so hot it was almost difficult to breathe. Most birds conserved their energy and only flew when they needed to. Even the swallows did very little playing in the skies.

"Think on the things You've learned from L'in," the Teller said. "You and I will not have our lessons today; I must rest."

L'in's head shot up. "What are you preparing for, One?"

"When other birds are at roost, I need to meet starling Bard at the three ancient maples to arrange a special education for SL'an – one I can't give," L'al said gently.

"At roost! That is when the sky is nearly black. You can't *think* of flying out when the sun goes. There's too much danger!" She stood up as tall as she could.

"I don't want to go, but there isn't another option. I've sought guidance, and the answer I found was that it's too early to reveal

SL'an as an Equal and that it's time He learns starling Lore. I believe Flower's intention for Him could be revealed by His connection with the Secret Keeper.

"It's just like Bard to have you flying off in the black!" L'in ruffled her feathers. SL'an was surprised to see this side of the quiet bird. "He thinks he's invincible, L'al. He's narrowly escaped many deaths due to his sense of superiority!"

"But he does escape them," L'al pointed out. His mate clapped her wings and hooked her beak on the tree, working at the wood wildly. When she was through, it was as though she had been deflated.

"If anything happened to you, I couldn't live," she said quietly.

SL'an shifted His feet on the branch and turned His head away from His mentors embroiled in what should have been a private moment. Without a sound, He flew to the shade where the Sentries always gathered on break, eating from the feeder provided by Mother. He noticed there were different shifts of Watchers, one group or the other usually at this place. He searched for the Sentry He met suns ago, but the redwing was nowhere to be seen. SL'an was resolved to ask his name when they met again.

Even the Watchers seemed unable to move quickly in the haze, lounging gratefully in the shade before duty called again. The starling hoped one of them would be interested in conversation, but the tired Sentries seemed unwilling, moving away from Him if He fed too close. With nothing interesting happening at the feeding place, SL'an flew to one side of Mother's nest and found SLee and many other small birds flitting about like airborne jewels to and from another feeding place hung high with tiny green shoots coming from it, just the right size for finch feet. He saw many Seekers gathered there, remaining on the green shoots longer than other birds and taking a very long time to eat seeds so they could peer into the clear boxes on the side of Flower's nest and watch from a safe distance.

"May I see?" SL'an asked a bright yellow bird with snapping black marks and cap. "I'm becoming a Seeker as well."

"My name is Steep," the yellow Seeker piped.

"SL'an," the starling returned.

The goldfinch dropped the seed he'd just grabbed. "S…L'…an? Do you have parents like SLee?"

"Stop that!" A small, brown female fluttered in Steep's face, and he opened his beak at her in mock aggression. "SLee may hear you," she scolded.

"So!" The goldfinch grabbed another seed and cracked it quickly and expertly. "SLee knows his parents are a bit 'off the limb'."

"The Wisdom says it's right to respect parents and those with more seasons than you," SL'an interjected.

Steep laughed so hard he lost his balance, fluttering frantically to stay aboard. "Oh, *that's* where the L' comes from! Such an overachiever." Steep turned to the brown female, a purple finch called Swin. "Would you mind letting SL'an have your perch? He plans to be *both* a Seeker *and* a Teller, it seems."

"Why don't you leave *your* perch?" The feisty female snapped.

"It's just like a starling to want the nest *and* the tree," Steep said, but SL'an didn't feel any true malice in the words as the yellow bird hopped off and flew to a nearby bush so the starling could try His wing at landing on the Seeker's perch.

It was rather small for SL'an, and Steep laughed uproariously from the bush as his new friend slipped and flapped and grappled madly. "Rather loud laugh for such a small bird," SL'an quipped.

Steep laughed even louder, which the starling could hardly believe possible. "Oh! He'll never catch on! Try settling on the flat wood next to the clear box, O' Great Seeker and Teller. Are you brave enough to get so close? Perhaps you can keep position long enough to accomplish something *there*!"

SL'an laughed softly at Himself then eyed the flat surface. He flew to it before thinking too much could change His mind, and He landed well. "Great job!" Steep cheered from the bush. The heat didn't seem to bother this bird in the least – or his diminutive kind.

SL'an turned His head sideways to see through the clear box and felt a rush of emotion. There was the place Mother would perch, He in Her wings or sometimes on Her shoulder. There too was the tall wooden tree-that-was-not-a-tree where He would stay in His nest box until He cried for Mother and She would come to feed Him. He ached for Mother and wished, for the first time since the stormy night, to be inside with Her. "When I fulfill My destiny, will You take Me home again?" He whispered.

She appeared in the space, and SL'an would have startled and flown if not for what greeted His eyes. She held something in Her wings that looked strangely like a nestling – a robin – larger than any in Hroo's brood but not yet ready to fledge.

She moved out of sight, and He heard the sound of the moving wall Mother used when She took Him out to hunt insects or for trial flights. He raced from the flat wooden perch to follow. If He had been further away on the feeder with the green shoots, He would never have noticed.

"Hey great Seeker, where are you going?" Steep called, but SL'an didn't have time to be polite. He raced to the other side of Mother's nest and found Her walking across the short grass, today's purple plumage flowing behind Her, holding the babe in Her wing. SL'an landed on the fence and then on a low tree branch. Mother saw Him and sounds rang out, filling His heart. There was the word – His name! Then, She moved on until She was close to Hroo's nest. Only then did SL'an notice the strange contraption leaning against the tree there. Mother stepped upon it until She rose higher and higher and could reach wing up to place the young robin beside the two huddled nestlings, who were old enough now to understand one of the Gods was there, and to be paralyzed with the wonder.

The new addition piqued their curiosity, however, and they quickly popped their heads up to see this robin, nearly twice their size, looming awkwardly in their space.

SL'an watched Mother climb down, then carry the contraption away, back into the nest. Was this another Equal? Hroo wouldn't be far, so SL'an flew frantically to find her. She was just returning to her nestlings when He spotted her winging in. He was going to call to her when His new knowledge of the Law surfaced. He wanted desperately to tell her that Mother – God Flower – gave her the gift of this nestling, but it was the job of Seekers to share information with Tellers first. Dove L'al was still Teller of this Sacred Space. SL'an changed direction mid-air and rushed to His mentor.

L'al and L'in were sleeping lightly, L'al preparing for his night meeting and L'in for her sleepless worry. "What's afoot?" L'al blinked quickly to shed the mist of waking.

"Mother has left a nestling with Hroo's brood. He's larger than the others."

"An Equal?" L'al gasped.

"I don't know. Hroo is there and has discovered the event by now. I didn't know if you would want her to know what I witnessed."

"What did You see?"

"Mother inside the nest with a young robin in Her wings. She then placed it with Hroo's nestlings."

"You saw this?"

"I missed nothing."

"A true Seeker!" L'in cried out, perhaps more happily than expected, for SL'an's good work.

"Our Praise asking forgiveness from Flower has been heard," L'al said reverently. "You made a good decision coming to me first. Although I've no doubt You will become a Teller far beyond my skills someday, for now even a Starling God has many things to study."

"May we tell Hroo what I witnessed?"

"I will let You tell her – but be careful not to refer to God Flower as Mother or to say *Me* instead of *me*!"

The difference in Hroo was striking. "Teller!" She called out in the similar cheery tone of her sister. "See what miracle has happened here." She sat proudly at her nest, a strange mist in her eyes.

"I brought young SL'an to tell you what he witnessed here, but first, what do you already know?" L'al was surprised by Hroo's calm.

"I returned to my nestlings with food to find a third there who didn't belong. He is twice the size of my others – do you see? *Twice* the size. It's as though God Flower felt my pain and gave me back my two babes. He is only one, but the size of *two*."

"*God* Flower?" L'al gaped. "You know Her hand was responsible for this? You acknowledge Her?"

"The nestling says he comes from another Sacred Space. His mother died – he doesn't know how – but the message came to him that she was gone. His sisters and brother faded and died. He was determined to live, and leapt from the death in the nest well before his feathers were ready. A small one of the Gods found him and lifted him up. Somehow, he was brought to God Flower, who spent two suns providing a strange wet food. He said he felt much improved, and She carried him by Her wings and placed him with my babes. He's happy to be here!"

"I witnessed God Flower bringing this nestling to you," SL'an finally said.

"Teller, how blind I've been!" Hroo said 'Teller', but looked at all of them one at a time. "The Gods *do* have power. They *do* have the will to grant miracles even to someone as misled as I've been."

SL'an saw her whole being alight with euphoria. "I must gather more food," Hroo said briskly. "My gift still has strength to gain before he is ready for first Trial Flight."

"Gift shall be my name." The new nestling's head popped up. "I choose to be Praiser."

"Gift," Hroo said, and the group fell silent.

After some moments of nothing but a breeze starting to rustle the leaves, Hroo spoke again. "Though I missed my early chance to be in service of the Gods, Teller, I would ask to sing a song of my making for evening praise. I, too, would like to be a Praiser."

"It's not usual, Hroo, but nothing lately appears usual. I believe Flower would be pleased to hear from one who denied Her before – from a heart She has opened."

Chapter Six

Starry Night

Hroo's evening praise left all quiet in the Sacred Space. Watchers ceased their patrols, and trees and the strange taut limbs were full of groups who gathered to hear from the robin's beak what miracle occurred. Most had heard something already but came to be sure. Those who felt they were already sure came to be part of a truly historic moment. A Chosen One had been delivered to their own Sacred Space, and of all nests to receive such a rare gift, one resolved not to believe!

"I don't know many of these birds," L'al told SL'an and his L'in while the robin readied herself for singing and the groups continued to gather.

"It was wise to send messages to other Tellers in the area," his mate said. "This event will reach many who doubt the Gods." She turned to SL'an, who was sitting tucked and quiet beside his mentors. "Does it feel strange to You that someone only Chosen receives such a flock when here You sit, an Equal unrecognized?"

"I'm shamed to admit it," He bowed His head.

"Truth is never shameful, SL'an." Her eyes twinkled at him. "Feelings are neither bad nor good. They simply are. What You do with them is the important thing."

"Some birds may turn beak to other birds from strong feelings." L'al agreed with his mate. "Others seek to understand and create something good even with those same strong feelings. The choice, as L'in said, shows the finery of the feather."

"Would You tear the flesh of another bird, Dear One?" L'in asked the starling. He widened His eyes. "No!"

"Would You find ways to cause Gift other harm because of the interest he attracts?" She continued.

"I would never harm another bird but to save my life!" SL'an opened His beak in horror at the very thought.

"Then there's nothing wrong with Your feelings and good will come to You. Your time for greatness is ahead, young one, and the attention You attract will make this look small. Gift will fly in Your flock, and You will be leader." L'in breathed in deeply as she spoke. There was something different about her tonight, SL'an thought. There had been a difference since Gift was placed. When Hroo began to sing the evening praise, the difference was almost palpable. L'in was still, but radiated such energy and joy that SL'an could feel waves of it washing over Him and tickling His heart into beating faster. When the last strains of song had vanished into the air, birds remained thoughtful for a moment. It took time to digest such words, such emotion. "The Gods are good!" A voice suddenly called out, and was followed by a raucous chorus of the same from hundreds. The sound filled the air with power, and God Flower came out from within Her nest and stood among them, head raised to hear Her Praise.

As flocks filtered away to roost and nest for the night, L'in whispered quickly to the young starling. "Could You offer us the evening in privacy, SL'an?"

"Has L'al changed his mind about flying at black?" SL'an asked, surprised.

"No, Dear One. There is just...some *time* I wish to share with my One before he takes this risk."

SL'an nibbled at L'in's cheek and flew to a line of trees that bordered the Sacred Space. He quickly surveyed each and found the solid maple that weathered Him through the first storm, choosing a branch and clenching His feet around it. Nothing would shake Him from this place tonight. He cocked His head and looked through the branches. It looked so different now. He felt seasons older than when He'd flown from Mother's wings for that first flight.

He could see one of the clear boxes light up suddenly as Mother controlled the very sky inside Her nest. "Mother, protect Your Teller," He asked aloud. "Show him My purpose so I might make You proud."

As SL'an settled for the night, L'in turned soft eyes to her mate. "There have been great miracles here, One. Who can say there won't be more?" She spoke breathlessly, and crouched to present herself. There had never been another since they had chosen – there would never be another. "Perhaps a miracle will happen for us too! It is not too late to try another clutch. Fly with me!"

L'al felt the rush of love and passion for his beautiful mate, offering to join with him with all the hope and energy pulsing through her. Suddenly, he was not a Teller; there were no Gods or SL'an, or anything else in the world. There were only two of them, and then they were only One, Oh! Only One! His wings beat wildly until the joining was over, and they stayed together as long as they could after until the black began covering the mountains and the trees, and the moon was released from the mountains.

"I need to go," he whispered regretfully, "but you have filled me with strength. There's no fear in me now."

"It would be safer if you found a place to roost near the meeting place," L'in advised.

"I can't be seen coming from there in the early hours," L'al said after mulling the suggestion over.

"If you leave in the very early hours, even before Hralla begins morning praise, who would see?"

"I can't take the chance, Love. I'll return to you tonight, and I will be careful as I fly. There's a bright moon and stars; it won't be completely black. I must fly now. Bard will be waiting."

Without another word, L'al dove from the nest into the thick air. *Stay high. Stay awake,* the voice in his mind said, and he rose up above the trees and sailed toward the ancient maples as fast as he could. He pushed away thoughts of owls, who he was told hunted close to the earth where mice could be speared with their talons, and thoughts of fox, who could not fly. Before he knew it, he had arrived at the clearing unharmed, and landed on the one ancient maple toward the center of the space, on a limb high enough to keep him safe from ground Blooders, and open enough so Bard might see him arrive.

Shadows laced the ground and branches of the ancient maples. L'al sat in the full of the moonlight and felt strangely exposed in brightness while the dark patches kept their secrets. He felt his buff feathers glowing in reflection, making him a beacon to everything with eyes – not only Bard. There were crackles from the deeper forest. The Teller's throat tightened with fear until a voluminous moose picked its way from the deeper woods to the clearing and noisily pushed through the grasses and thorny raspberry bushes. The dove had been here with L'in many times before to eat the sweet seedful fruit when they were soft, red and fallen. However, he had certainly never seen the space at black. He couldn't believe what a different world came from the black and the light playing together over what used to appear as a bright, green space. Now the world was awash in silvers, the once color-drenched plants paled.

He didn't even know it when the veil of the black closed his waking thoughts. It was done in an instant, and then it was daytime, a lovely day bathed with sunlight. He and L'in were moving happily together between the raspberry bush stems, finding berries that had been knocked down and overlooked by the bears he knew had been there recently…

Wings fluttered near L'al's head and he opened his eyes and beak suddenly, flinging his wings wide in automatic defense as Bard settled on the branch beside him. "It is only a friend, Teller," Bard whispered. "I am glad to see you made the short flight here unharmed."

It took a moment for L'al to clear his mind and realize the daylight was a dream, and he really was here with the Secret Keeper in the black. "It was over quickly, but I must admit I'm relieved not to sit here alone."

"The danger of the black is overrated by most birds." Bard said this, but snapped his head to and fro, ever alert. "This is what makes the black the most opportune meeting time. I do much of my teaching in this place."

L'al was astounded. "Do many others ask you to reveal your secrets?"

"Not *many*, but more than you might think. The world is changing, Teller. Surely you see it. Many see it although it is only carefully spoken of – spoken of as a fledgling tale rather than a reality. There is a deepening divide between those who believe in the Gods and those who do not. There is a wasting away of the wisdom. Some are alarmed enough to seek answers, and they meet me here to see for themselves that I can provide some."

Another sharp *snap* cut the stillness, making L'al jump, but it was only the moose reentering the deeper woods. When he'd gathered his breath again, he asked, "You give your secrets to any who question?"

"Only those who are willing to come here in the black. If they are, they are serious in their quest, and worthy of trying."

"Trying?"

"Some hear my secrets and it isn't what they wish to hear. When it isn't what they wish to hear, they choose not to believe. Others, although the secrets may not be easy, do believe. They quietly teach their nestlings starling Lore. I cannot make any bird believe what they will not."

L'al knew the basics of starling Lore and understood why it was a difficult seed to crack. "I know some of your Lore, Bard, but there are deeper secrets you keep that I don't know. I may need to know them now, or I may not. When you hear what news I have for you, may knowledge and wisdom lead you in what to share."

"I am ready for your news, Teller."

"There is a fledgling named SL'an who has taken me as mentor."

"I have seen him with you," Bard said with an odd tone.

"He fledged from the wings of God Flower."

"Chosen? Why have you failed to announce this as you did the robin Gift?"

"Not Chosen. Equal." L'al shared the information with fear in his heart. Once it had been uttered, it couldn't be brought back, and whatever consequences would come had been unleashed. "He has no bird parentage. God Flower has created Him and fledged Him to us for Her greater purpose."

Bard was struck wordless, so L'al continued. "I have studied basics of starling Lore so I would have understanding. Still, in my heart, I never believed it possible. Now, with the fledging of SL'an, I see what seemed a myth is fact. I cannot teach Him all He needs to know. He needs a starling Secret Keeper to show him His way."

"Equal," Bard said at last. "I never thought this would happen in my lifetime."

"Nor I." L'al bobbed.

"Have SL'an join me in the morning. He needs to learn what the birthright is of starling at once. You have done a respectable job, Teller, with this accident of Him happening upon you before He came to my notice—"

"—Accident! The Gods make no mistakes, Bard. My L'in and I have been prepared for SL'an before His arrival. I know it is time to pass the teaching on to you, but His coming to me was part of the Gods' plan, I'm certain."

Bard preened a wing and then turned his head from the misguided dove. "SL'an is starling. We are the Gods' Chosen, as I am sure you know if you learned the basics of starling Lore, Teller. He is starling, and this is a starling matter. I admit you had good instincts not to share His identity with others at this time. It will be my place to do so."

L'al felt his breast fill with rage and had never felt so close to turning beak to another. "SL'an proves there is something special about the starlings." L'al had to stretch his beak repeatedly in a series of strange yawns to loosen the tension before he spoke. "However, I see God Flower providing for all bird kinds, not only for your kind. If you were the only ones, I don't see logic in Flower's attention to the rest. Perhaps some of your Lore is truth and some is not."

"There is nothing you can say that I haven't heard from other non-starlings," Bard said. "It is typical and understandable that others try to rationalize our Lore and make it meaningless. If I were born dove, finch, or any other, I would no doubt do the same. But think, Teller! You cannot say one part of the Lore is true and another is false because it does or doesn't suit you. If it were to be that way, every bird kind would take what they wished and toss what they wished. SL'an is proof of what our Lore has foretold. He is a Starling God who will come to live among us and show us how to be like His

Mother. The biggest secret I keep, Teller, is that the Gods themselves are changing to be more starling, and the starlings are changing to be more like the Gods. SL'an is the bridge. The time has come. Our kind will become Gods and it will be our world to oversee with Them."

"You feel your kind alone will rule with the Gods!" L'al's feathers fluffed to their fullest against his will.

"Peace, Teller. I will teach SL'an the rest, and He will soon teach you and all bird kinds. The transition will not be something to fear. It will be a great day for all of us. The wasting of the wisdom will cease, and starlings will make the world right again."

Chapter Seven
Mozart's Bird

"Gone!" L'in's eyes widened. "I understood Bard would teach Him, but what do you mean that SL'an is to be gone?"

"Peace, Love." L'al hung his head. He didn't know what words of comfort to give her. Bard had insisted that SL'an join his flock and have little contact with other kinds during His teaching. *He must not get the wrong messages. These lessons are crucial,* Bard said. He recounted the night meeting to L'in, and she was quiet.

"I believe in the wisdom, but I do not believe in Bard," she finally said in a hollow tone. "I hope we have done right. Still, every feather tells me we have not."

Her words cut L'al like a Blooder's tooth. She had never failed to trust his judgment before – but then why shouldn't she? He had doubts himself. He described his vision in Flower's garden of Bard on the roof singing to the tumultuous sky. "If it were not for this vision, I would also swear the direction is wrong. I asked for an answer from Flower, and this was the one She gave. I need to believe the Gods wouldn't lead us to harm."

"Bard is insufferable," L'in sniffed.

"I couldn't agree more. Perhaps that's why SL'an was sent to us first and not Bard himself!"

L'in chuckled. "SL'an will do great things. That I *do* believe. He is kind and good."

"If there is anything unsavory of Bard's words, also believe SL'an will not follow what His feathers tell Him is wrong. He is fledged from the Gods, after all. He knows in the very blood and bone what His destiny shall be. Bard and others will only awaken this knowledge. I don't believe they can lead him astray."

L'in sighed with some relief.

After morning praise, the dove found SL'an feeding in the short grass and told Him what He must do. The young starling didn't seem any more enthusiastic than L'in about His quarantine of sorts, and shared this with His mentor. "Can't I receive the lessons and then stay close to you?"

"Bard says no. Remember, while we don't always understand the reasons at first, they become clear later."

"May I say goodbye to L'in?"

"I think it may be best if You don't say goodbye to her. Instead, learn what You must and then come back to us. It needn't be goodbye that way."

SL'an didn't know if it was usual, but He reached with His beak and quickly nibbled His mentor's cheek as He had often done to L'in in the way of dove kind. He was a bit surprised when L'al returned the gesture. "Follow what Your feathers tell You is right," L'al said, and flew abruptly away.

The starling finished feeding, finding Himself particularly aware of the taste of each insect He found. He savored them as if every one was His last, and looked around at Hralla and her new fledglings, Hroo, SLee, Steep, and the groups of Watchers feeding, flying in and flying out from the Sacred Space. "I have to leave you for awhile," He said to Himself, "but I'll be back." He spotted a group of starlings in the back of Mother's nest, also foraging in short grasses, and saw one large male who watched him closely and then flapped his wings. "Are you Bard?" SL'an called as He flew to the male.

"I am your teacher, Starling God. Have you eaten your fill?"

"I have."

"This is my One, Glee." The larger male nodded his beak to a neighboring female.

"You have One like the doves!" SL'an cried out in excitement.

Perhaps His own kind would not be so different from His beloved mentors.

"We are like the Gods. We usually have One, but others may not choose that way. If a bad mating is made, it can be undone. It is the way of the Gods, and the way of their Chosen kind." Glee nodded in agreement with her mate's words.

"Dove L'al told Me starlings are special. Why?" SL'an finally had the chance to ask what his mentor had felt unfit to answer.

"Isn't it early to begin His lessons?" Glee asked lightly. SL'an was struck by her voice and the thrilling timbre of it. The tone was not unlike His own or Bard's, but there was a different lilt that stirred something distant inside. SL'an couldn't imagine what it was, but He wanted her to speak more. His wish was thwarted with Bard's terse reply.

"There's no time to waste, Glee. If He is ready to ask questions, then the time to answer is now. Come, SL'an. We will go to the most Sacred Space of all."

SL'an followed His new teacher up into the air and readied Himself for a longer flight away from all He knew and loved. He was shocked when Bard simply rose and alighted on the peaked top of Mother's nest.

"This is the most Sacred Space *within* the Sacred Space. It is where I also nest to be close to Your Mother. Below this peak, there is an opening that the God Flower left for Her Secret Keeper. I built my nest there when I was just a season older than You, and wooed Glee to join me. Together, Glee and I live as starlings should and will forevermore. We live within Their dwellings. What makes us special, Starling God –"

"—Please call Me SL'an," the young starling interrupted. Somehow, the title sounded uncomfortable to Him coming from Bard's beak.

"SL'an, then – is that we have been bonded to Them since the beginning, and we grow more and more like Them over time. Unlike the kinds that eat only seeds and fruit, or only insects, or even *mainly* one of those things or another, we eat of many things like the Gods. For example, robins must have insects and the like to live. One season, the robins returned to this Sacred Space when the snows should have gone, but they were not. Storms continued to strike and the winds lashed the barren trees. The snows covered the ground in all places for a great distance, and the robins gathered, starving, in the pathways of the Gods, hoping for salvation there."

"Why?"

"The Gods have the power to keep Their pathways free of snows."

"What happened?"

"Robins are not the Chosen kind, and the Gods saw fit to smite them for blocking Their paths. Many robins died struck down by the Gods. Many more starved because they are not like us – not like the Gods. Our kind flourished even against the challenge. When there are not insects, we can eat seeds. When there is not seed, we can eat insects. If either insects or seeds are hard to find, we have a special trick. Our beaks can open with force, not just close with force. We can drive our beaks into the ground and open them to uncover food where other kinds cannot."

"You said you live in Gods' dwellings because you are similar to Them. Many swallows live in the same fashion. Aren't they like the Gods, too, then?" SL'an looked at the swallows diving through the air, then coming to land in a huddled group on the taut limb.

Bard laughed. "Oh, I see Your fine mentor didn't feel You were ready to learn about swallows! Were You present for Hroo's evening praise after Gift came to her?"

"I was of course," SL'an said.

"Of all the birds who gathered that evening, it escaped You that there were no swallows except those who had to stay and tend nestlings?"

SL'an blinked. "I suppose I wasn't paying attention to that. There were so many other birds there, and that's what I noticed."

"Well, the swallows refused to be present. They have an entirely different belief from any other bird kind."

"They don't believe the Gods are higher than bird?"

Bard shook his head heartily. "Oh, much more than that. *Swallows* not only believe the Gods are not higher, but they see Them *a blight* to birds and all creatures that crawl or fly on the earth."

SL'an nearly lost His grip on the slippery peak. "Impossible! Can't they see all the good things Mother provides?" He flapped His wings angrily. "Can't they see how the flying insects they eat are drawn to the flowers placed by Her will? That Her own nest offers them shelter and protection from Blooders? Why, then, do they choose to build their nests so close to what they consider a blight?"

"Swallows believe that bird came before the Gods. Their version of the wisdom is that birds lived in harmony and plenty throughout the earth, and that the Gods, or "The Blight" as they call Them, rose up and overtook nesting places, changed sources of food, and that birds were forced out of their natural way of being. Swallows live with the Gods – The Blight – out of sheer defiance. They say they will not surrender the spaces of their ancestors." Bard squinted his eyes as if the story was all too horrible. "They are terribly misguided. You should never make the mistake of speaking with swallows, SL'an. They will only try to poison Your mind."

The young starling watched the huddled group of swallows swoop down from the taut metal limb, one at a time in a strategic formation, then rise into the air again, crisscrossing nimbly. He used to see them as joyful acrobats. Now they looked angry, militant. His breast hurt with the loss.

"But I suppose the answer to Your question, 'why are starlings special', has started at the end when it should really start at the beginning."

"I'm ready," SL'an said.

The morning sun was already licking them both with heat, and SL'an noticed for the first time how Bard's feathers gleamed with hints of many colors in the light, first one, then another, like constantly changing plumage. Bard raised his beak up toward the sky and began his tale.

"The Lore says that when the Gods were young, They had many powers that grew as They grew. The one gift They did not have was song. As the Gods were fruitful and multiplied and succeeded throughout the earth, They felt a great emptiness but had no power to fill it despite all else They could do. The Gods created birds at this time, and of course birds filled the air of the Gods with color and music. The Gods were wild with joy at the music, but soon felt empty again when They could not make music of Their own.

"All birds met to decide how to help the Gods end Their pain. They decided to teach Them how to make music. Kind after kind approached Them and tried to show Them the secret of making music, but kind after kind failed when they could not understand or speak sounds of the Gods. At last, starling alighted before Them and was able to make many of Their sounds. Only through this could the Gods learn the secret of music. So starling gave the gift of music, and Their hearts were filled.

"From that moment on, starlings were the Chosen Kind, and the Gods granted them partial powers that would set them apart from other birds and help them succeed where others would fail. In honor of this gift, starlings have lived in close proximity to the Gods everywhere on the earth. We have been like Them and have been fruitful and multiplied against all odds and have become more and more like the Gods. Where we have had difficulty, the Gods have helped us succeed with Their very wings. It is said that this place and all the many lands around it had no starlings at all until one of the Gods brought us here and set a small flock free to bring more music. In honor of that effort, the small flock multiplied and succeeded in a strange land with many challenges. Our success has been pleasing, and is proof that we are indeed Chosen!"

Bard drew in a full breath and held it for a moment with his eyes closed, head still raised to the sky. SL'an thought he was finished and was thinking of another question when the older bird continued.

"You are an Equal starling, SL'an. There has been one before You. Lore says there are different Gods that are great makers of music. There was One particular who was pleasing to His own, but still felt in His being the emptiness that the sounds were not equal to that of birds. He created a starling to teach Him more secrets of music, and this Equal lived His life beside the God Mozart and learned more of His own sounds, and taught Him more secrets of music. This Equal was so loved by God Mozart that when the starling died, the sounds of God Mozart's grief filled the air. That Equal starling was the first giant step to Gods and starling becoming one."

"Why couldn't I have had the joy of living out My life with Mother!" SL'an nearly wailed.

"You are the next giant step, SL'an. You are perhaps the *last* step. You will be the greatest. You will show us how living as Gods is to be done."

Chapter Eight
New Beginnings

SL'an shook His feathers and picked at them anxiously. He ran His beak from quill to tip over and over in rapid pulls, and with each motion it seemed to clear His worried brain. Bard looked about, waiting for the young starling to finish self-soothing. When He had, SL'an shook His feathers almost violently one last time and faced His new mentor. "I don't have anything to teach you about living as the Gods. There is so much I didn't know before Teller L'al took Me under his wing; if he had to teach Me, and he is bird, then perhaps I am not what you think I am?"

Bard turned his head, fixing his charge with one eye. "The Lore is not wrong. You have been formed by and lived alongside God Flower, and within You lies the spark of creation only She could bestow. I am sure You don't even know what truth You hold inside, but it will grow as You grow." Bard flew suddenly from the peak and landed on a patch of bare soil, loose and loamy, smelling of promise. After hesitating only for a moment, SL'an dove down to land beside him as the elder starling pushed his beak into the rich dark brown and came out with something that he dropped on the surface. "This is something the Gods create."

SL'an dipped His head to look closely. A small white shoot was pushing from a split in something brown, round and hard.

"This will grow into a plant that bears food for us and for the Gods Themselves," Bard nodded. "In the beginning of time, the Gods placed bits of Their knowledge in seeds like this – each seed with the exact knowledge it needs to become what it must be and to fulfill its purpose. This seed begins as hidden knowledge – even the seed doesn't realize itself, but it somehow does what it needs to do. It breaks from the shell and reaches for the sunshine it must have. It takes in what it must have from the soil, and as it grows, it unfolds each leaf. Each unfolding of a leaf is new knowledge that is awakening. Each inch it grows is a release of what the Gods have always intended it to share. When it is ready, it understands its destiny."

SL'an looked at the seed and widened His eyes. "And birds' eggs are the same!"

The elder starling breathed in deeply. "You are exactly right. See what You already understand? The Gods also placed bits of Their knowledge into the very form of eggs, and like this seed, the knowledge first grows without realizing itself. As the bird pushes its beak through to the light for the first time, there is little he knows, but as he grows, so the knowledge grows with him."

In the distance, birds were flying about, fewer than in the early morning because of the summer heat, but SL'an could see Dove L'al and his L'in bobbing along the short grass and eating seeds. He thought sadly of their eggless nest. "I see what you mean, but I don't understand how you can be sure I'll have knowledge that's any different from others,'" SL'an said, still watching His beloved mentors.

"The placing of the Gods' knowledge happened at the beginning of time. Since then, the information has always been basically the same, and is passed now from bird to egg instead of directly by the wings of the Gods. You were a new creation and a new beginning. God Flower would only create You directly if She had new knowledge to share. Also, You are starling, and together these facts agree with our Lore. There is no question in my mind You will hold the answers we need. But there is no purpose to worrying about this. You only need to learn to be starling now and let the answers come in time."

"You and Glee will teach me how to be starling?" SL'an turned His head to the doves once again, and He felt Bard's whole being tense.

"You have been unfortunately poisoned by the dove Tellers and how they live. They are misguided, and their ways are not what You should emulate," Bard said, strangely calm. "I can only blame myself for not being aware enough to find You first. Starlings have the correct way. Like the Gods, we send our young out together to learn. They will find unity in their own kind and learn from elders in groups once they are old enough to self-feed. You are at this stage, and will join the rest in their lessons. Follow me!"

Bard launched into the air, and, as he did, a dozen other starlings automatically rose from other trees, bushes, and from the grass not far away. The wing beats together made a mesmerizing sound, and without words at all, they followed Bard to a tall poplar just before the tree line of a nearby forest. It seemed stately – exceptionally straight and thick at the base, cascading with smallish leaves green on the top and silvery on the underneath. As the breezes came through, the leaves tinkled in a softer but similar way to some singing metal bits that Mother had hanging from the outside of the nest.

All of them landed, and SL'an saw there were many others already there. In a moment, another group flew in together, and then another. The sun moved in its sky a bit more, and still more groups arrived, usually just a small time between each arrival.

Finally, no more groups came, and Bard turned to the young Starling God. "This is where You will learn to be starling each day. You will usually start lessons here in the early sun, and You will return here together for our own evening praise before black. When the black does start to swallow the land, You will roost with all the other young males in the forest treetops. None here know who You are, and we will keep it that way for now – but they soon will."

"We need to find Your grouping." Bard raised his beak and barely lifted his wings, the strength of his voice cutting through the murmurings of hundreds of mainly young starlings. "Trill!"

Another elder seemed to suddenly appear on the branch, and he gave a quick bow to Bard. "Trill, this is young SL'an. He is new to the Sacred Space and will stay with us from now on. He needs to find his grouping if you could pitch him now."

Trill turned to face SL'an and tapped one foot against the wood. "Young one! Sing for me please!"

The young Starling God thought of the first song He heard when He fledged from Flower's nest – "Song of the Watch". He couldn't replicate the sweet-throated SLee, so He tried a few times until the song could be His own. Despite forgetting a few words in one place, He thought it a respectable job. Trill listened with his eyes closed, then opened them with a snap when the tune ended. "You pitch with the group halfway to the top."

"Is that good?" SL'an looked up at the crowd of birds there to see if they looked any better than others.

"There is no bad or good unless your beak will not open or your voice fails to sing at all!" Trill laughed. He seemed to nearly sing every phrase, and every phrase reached SL'an's own brain like a physical sensation.

SL'an said so. "I can't believe there isn't a difference at all from one group to another! Your voice has a special quality, and there is also something about Glee's."

Bard's head snapped toward his young charge. "I don't know what you are talking about. There is nothing in Glee's voice that is exceptional."

Trill clucked. "Now, Bard, I can't agree with you on that one." He squinted a bit at SL'an. "This one has a very good sense. In any case, we're already running late, and Diver is getting restless. He needs to begin his own teachings. You missed another mentor's lesson before the break, young SL'an, but I imagine you'll have no trouble catching up to the others. Now hurry and join your group! You will stay with them from now on."

Bard flew back to Flower's Sacred Space without a word, and Trill shook his head. "Good luck," he called, and also flew away, joined by a few others who winged until they disappeared from view.

SL'an felt almost more alone than the first night He was left by Mother for the first time. At least then He felt alone because He was alone. Now He sat with the sounds of a hundred or more others just like Him, but they were nothing to Him, and He was nothing to them. He closed His beak tightly and flew to the appointed group as He was told, the rattling of voices all around making him almost dizzy with fear. *Mother, what if I don't belong here? Can't I come home?* He thought. He longed for L'in's soft plumage and the way she would nibble His cheek in the way of dove kind. He wanted to sit on Mother's shoulder with His feet cushioned by the soft ground She could drape over Herself on that spot so He could nestle close to Her neck in comfort. He closed His eyes and remembered Her aura that seemed to flow from the long, downy feathers that crested from Her head and fluffed over those shoulders He loved so. He liked to bury His head in those feathers that He didn't realize at the time were so different from His own, and the sense of them had surrounded Him with love.

Another strong voice cut through the chattering, and SL'an was shocked by the instant silence. "Young starlings! I am Mentor Diver, and I am here to teach you the music as well…BUT," many of them jumped, "it will not be music as you know it. It will not be song as Mentor Trill teaches you. You will not need to ever open your beak for this music to be made. No! You will write music with your bodies and your very wings. The sky will receive you, and the power of Starling Union will be a beauty you never imagined."

He flapped his wings and a group of perhaps twenty adult starlings rose into the air with him. They ascended swiftly, then seemed to hover in the sky, dipping down a bit, then up again, moving straight as a tight group until they finally curled as if one being, slipping back toward the tree and landing in unison. When a minute passed and there was still a hush among the young starlings, Diver flapped quickly again, but with his feet firmly placed on the branch. "Observations, young ones?"

A female near SL'an called out, "You moved together perfectly – it was…*beautiful*."

A bird from a different Pitch Group said, "You moved as if you were one creature."

SL'an found His voice, although it seemed strange ringing out loud with so many listening. "You made music with the sound of your wings, and you also made music with your movements. It was like *seeing* music instead of hearing it." The young female who had spoken just earlier looked at SL'an curiously. He felt frozen, but Mentor Diver's words revived him. "Very good, young starlings! Instead of making music with our voices, we make music by the power of our union. There is power in the air-sound from our wings, and power in moving with the same wing beats. It is music for the eyes of the Gods, and it brings us closer to the Gods."

"How do you know where and when to move?" a male from the very top asked. "I don't know if I could remember so many steps."

"Yes!" Another voice rang out. "I'm afraid I will turn at the wrong time and be killed."

Diver preened his feathers. "I have been teaching Unified Flight for five years now. I have never seen a young starling killed by flying in the wrong direction, but there have been a few rare accidents. Once in a while there are birds who can't feel how to move, and they are invited to stay behind if they are not comfortable. There can be other jobs for starlings with such disabilities, but truthfully most do learn quickly. If you find you are having a serious problem, get yourself to the very edge of the movement and do your best to follow along. It's easier to get out of the way quickly there."

SL'an couldn't imagine being able to fly the way he had seen the group of adults do, but He didn't have time to wonder about it more because Diver was giving instructions. "You will practice first in your Pitch Groups. Each group will have one of my assistants leading it, and two advanced near-adults flying with you to help." The adult starlings left Diver's side and each joined a group. "Now off with you! I look forward to hearing about your experience when you return."

The air filled with starling groups following their Flight Leaders in various directions. A voice breathlessly called to SL'an as He lifted into the air as gracefully as He could. "That was a great observation earlier."

He turned His head to see the young female who had spoken first. Since flight was taking a good deal of his energy, His answer was a bit breathless too. "Thank you. Observation is one of my natural strengths. That's why I want to be a Seeker."

"Seeker? Starlings don't have Seekers."

"Well, I have chosen the professions of Seeker and Teller."

SL'an thought the young female was going to fall out of the sky when her wings missed some beats and she dropped a bit, flapping faster to recover. "No! There are no Tellers or Seekers! That is for other bird kinds, not starlings!"

"Well, it's the choice I've made. I am SL'an."

"The elders will make you change your name once you have had some learning."

SL'an would have ruffled His feathers if He weren't airborne. "I have another name but—" He broke off suddenly.

"But what? Is it a more sensible name?"

"The name SL'an is the one I want. I chose it when in the care of dove Tellers."

"In the care of dove Tellers? How horrid! Where were your parents? Were they killed? Why didn't other starlings foster you?"

SL'an's head was reeling for a way to answer her when their Flight Leaders landed in the branches of a large, dead tree. "Space out, young ones! Space out well so you can take flight when the time comes and have room to learn how we move safely. As you improve, we will tighten the group, but for now, we will stay loose."

The young female sidled close to SL'an before putting the distance between them. "By the way, I am named Flora." Then she winked before hurrying away. "A much more sensible name, don't you think?"

The Flight Leader assured they were all far enough apart, and then told them to close their eyes. "I want you to breathe the Gods' air deeply into your breast. Let it fill you, and then let it out slowly. Now focus on the birds closest to you. NO! Don't open your eyes; just *feel* them. Feel the heat from their feathers and get the sense of them. Hear the air as it moves across their bodies. Do this until you can see them in your mind without ever opening your eyes. Imagine where they are. See them sitting on their branches. Now open your eyes and see if your visions were correct."

There were chirps of astonishment when many found their neighbors were in the exact places, or close, as they had imagined.

SL'an could see some looking disappointed, but the Leaders assured everyone they would catch on.

"This is a good part of staying safe in the sky when we fly as one. You cannot be distracted by anything else. You lose yourself in the moment – in being part of the Gods' greater whole. Instead of feeling separate, we become part of the everything. By feeling how the wind moves around each of us and is moved by us, we know our place, and know where to go. Let us practice! I will take flight and you will follow." When he saw a number of the young starlings closing their eyes, he laughed. "I know I had you close your eyes for the practice, but you need to have them open for this even though your eyes will be the least of what will guide you."

The first flights were messy at best, but as SL'an felt the force of the wing beats moving fairly close together and the rush of the air as the group moved first this way and then that, He began to lose himself. A thrill filled His heart as He heard the wing beats rise in a strong drumming, then change in timbre as they hovered and then dropped, the sounds filling His mind until His eyes seemed closed while they were open; all else faded away except the sounds and sense of wings together, of the body of starling moving as one unit through the sky.

They practiced over and over, moving a bit closer together each time until they were almost as close as the adults had been in their demonstration. There was not a word spoken as they were all swept up in the oneness, and for the first time He could remember since fledging Mother's nest, He didn't feel even a bit alone.

Chapter Nine

The Great Teacher

The Unified Flight practices lasted until later mid-sun; then the young ones were allowed to disperse into their smaller Pitch Groups to rest and feed. They landed on the short grass of the Sacred Space and began trolling – some digging for grubs as they had been taught while others satisfied themselves with winged snacks that presented themselves. SL'an could see some of the elder birds and near-adults sticking close to the redwing Watchers, although the Watchers seemed to pay them little heed. He remembered trying to talk to some of them just suns ago, and the way they had moved away from Him coolly.

"Why do they stay so close to the Watchers when the redwings don't seem to want them there?" SL'an mused aloud.

"Oh, don't you know all of the rest of us are jealous of you starlings," a familiar voice chimed. Steep darted by in a flash of bright yellow and black, and SL'an laughed. The little bird swooped by again and landed on a bush not too far from where the young Starling God fed. "According to Bard, the Watchers *owe* the starlings special protection when they want it, so some of them who are more fearful travel close to the Watchers, even moving with their flocks!" Steep threw his head back and chirruped a string of jubilance. "I suppose even you can see why the Watchers might be annoyed."

Steep darted away, grabbed a seed, and darted back in what seemed less than an instant. SL'an's own laughter ebbed away, and a bit of tightness filled His breast. "How would you know so much about it?"

"I'm a SSSssseeeker, remember, SSSsssL'an? It's my duty to seek information, and I've learned more than a little bit about Bard's starlings."

"Bard's starlings?"

"I hear it's pretty common for starlings to believe in the Lore, and I don't know the whole story of it – but I do have the feeling not all starling Lore is as... *specialized* as Bard's." An elder starling noticed Steep and SL'an together and started to strut over. "My-my! You've been spotted actually talking to one of us lesser beings! I'd better go before you get into trouble." Steep's tiny wings propelled him off in blinding speed just as the elder arrived.

"What was that about?" The elder female barked. "Young one, you are in lessons, and while in lessons you are to have little if any interaction with other bird kinds. Has that not been made clear to you?"

SL'an lowered His head. "It has."

"Then you would do well to remember it. It isn't safe to be listening to the others. They are jealous and keen to spread their lies. Become firm in your understanding of what it is to be starling and then you'll be stronger and ready against them." She wandered away again without bothering to introduce herself, blending in with the Watchers as best she could although they tried as they might to keep some distance.

Flora was feeding nearby, choosing to dig for grubs. After devouring an especially juicy morsel, she made a low flight over and landed neatly next to her new acquaintance. "Break will be over soon, so we'd better talk fast. You never told me what happened to your parents and how it happened that you were taken in by dove Tellers."

"It's a long story, and we don't have a long time right now." SL'an pretended to be searching for grubs so His beak would be too busy to speak further. "Does Bard know the long story?" she persisted. When He shoved his beak further into the soil, she provided her own answer. "Of course he does. He wouldn't have you join us without knowing the important things about you – so I guess I can just ask him and he'll have the time to tell me."

SL'an pulled his beak quickly out, grub-less. "Why would he tell you my story?"

"Father would tell me anything I want to know."

"Bard is your father?"

Flora glanced smugly at Him before winging away as the young ones were called back for the last lesson of the day.

When all the groups returned to the Meeting Tree, Bard was there to offer his own lessons. "I will meet with you every few suns to show you how the Gods love us enough to teach us things with Their very wings. They want so much to have us learn to be like Them that They take Their time to challenge us – for only through such challenges can we be as strong and successful as the Gods have been.

"This late sun, we will fly to a Sacred Space not far from here where one of the Gods has been training His starlings for years. Alight on the short grass where I land, but do not interfere. You are there to watch, and we will discuss what you see afterward."

When everyone had assembled, Bard spoke. "You will see a starling pair has built their nest as they should along the nest of the God that oversees here. Now we must busy ourselves and wait. Soon you will see what I brought you here to learn."

Two young male starlings from the Pitch Group had landed close to SL'an. They were nestling brothers, Risk and Song. SL'an got to know them a bit in between practicing Unified Flights. Risk strolled closer. "What do you think we're going to see?"

SL'an looked up and saw a starling pair traveling to and fro with bits to build their nest, which was close to finished. There was a tall, silver item leaning against the wall of the God's nest, reaching toward where the starlings worked feverishly. "Well, I've seen something similar to what is leaning there. M – God Flower – used it to climb to Hroo's nest when She placed Gift there."

"Could He be bringing them a Gift of their own?" Song wondered.

"I see why you'd think that, but the nest isn't even finished and it certainly isn't ready for nestlings. They'd fall out of that unfinished end over there."

A pair of swallows was also building a nest a bit further over.

They swooped and danced so gracefully, but all SL'an could ever see now was the defiance in it. They brought bits of mud and added to each layer, letting the sun dry what they made to a solid. As He watched both bird pairs work, something seemed strange to the young Starling God. "But why are they building nests now? All nests should have been built long ago, shouldn't they?"

The God came out of His own nest carrying something in one wing. He climbed what He had leaned against His sacred nest until He got within wing's reach of where the starlings were building. The swallows swooped and screamed, diving at the God's head, which carried dark, short plumage unlike the long down of SL'an's Mother. The starling pair retreated in love-fear and watched as the God raised His wing and whatever He held in it. SL'an cried out as the thing slashed through the half-built home, sending bits of it flying through the air and landing on the ground in sad pieces. The wing lifted over and over and pulled away every bit of what had been a hopeful nest until the spot in the eaves was as bare and clean as if the nest had never been. The God then climbed down and moved the tall thing to where the swallows' nest was also nearly complete. They never stopped swooping at the God's head and screaming in their anger at Him. "Vile! Putrid, Vile beast! You will *not beat us*. You will *not win*! We hate you with our blood! We hate you with our breath! Beast!" They screamed over and over, but the God climbed the thing and raised His wing to their effort as well, sending bits of hardened mud and mud still soft enough to land with a small plop on the earth. Other swallows joined in the frenzy and they all swooped through the air, diving and almost crashing into the God as He finally climbed down to reach the grass again. The starling pair huddled in a nearby tree and never complained, although within a moment they vanished into bushes far off.

SL'an started to rise and rush after them, His stomach churning with horror at what the God had just done to His own birds, but Bard swept in and batted his wings in His face, forcing Him down. "I said to not intervene but only watch."

The young starling could only stare at Bard while breathing heavily, heart racing. He looked at the others and saw similar looks of shock and dismay; Flora looked the most sick of all. She had flattened her body into the grass, staring wide-eyed at the God who lifted the tall, silver thing and carried it away. *So your father doesn't tell you everything,* SL'an thought sadly.

Bard looked around at his young charges with what SL'an thought was obscene joy. "Follow me back to the Meeting Tree and you will learn how great the Gods are to their Chosen!"

Not one Pitch Group practiced Unified Flight in the short distance back. In fact, rather than powerful, the wing beats sounded muted and resigned. When they all landed, Bard laughed. It was an almost unnatural sound coming from him, but it came anyway, forced out of his beak and into the air that was so ripe with disbelief. "I know how you are feeling. A travesty, you say? Perhaps the swallows are right? The Gods couldn't possibly love us if They would commit such a horror?" He laughed again, and SL'an could feel the tension mount as more than one young starling ruffled feathers in anger.

"Would you take me on, young ones? Would you attack me for laughing at what we just saw? Your numbers are great and I am only one. I don't have my assistants by my side this late sun, and certainly even a leader couldn't defend against you! But would you dare to never have the answer? Look in your hearts and search yourselves. Search past the anger and disgust that is boiling on the surface. Look deeply and ask yourself what you *feel* about the Gods in your very breasts. Are you sure the God of that Sacred Space had no good intentions for what He did? I am the starling Secret Keeper, and I know what you do not and *will* not unless I share the things you must know to be starling."

The tension in the air melted into confusion, and Bard raised his head again to the sky. "It is more simple than you can imagine, young ones. When there are great storms, or fires or floods, the nests of the Gods can be destroyed, sometimes in part and sometimes in whole. When this happens, they are strong and resilient! They build again, and if something else or more of the same sweeps through to destroy Their creation, They build yet again. This God is testing His Chosen! He is also teaching us to be like the Gods and unlike the robins or many others who will fly away, beaten by a situation; starlings must keep building again. It is a harsh lesson, but a very important one. One of the things that has grown us closer to the Gods is our ability to learn how to stand against all that would try to beat us down. And in the end? We succeed! It is pleasing to the Gods that it is so, and this God is a Great Teacher."

There was a long pause as the confused starlings tried to understand, but Flora broke the silence. "I don't believe it."

Bard tightened his feathers to his body. "My own nestling doubts my words?"

"If it is a great lesson as you say, then why would He also teach the swallows who despise Him?"

SL'an admired her pluck, but wasn't sure if her status as Bard's nestling was enough to keep her safe.

"You are not the first to notice this, Flora. Of course it does seem to be the same, but it is not when you feel deeper for the answer. The same action is not for the same reason. The Gods choose to mould us closer to Themselves, but there are birds They must punish as well. The swallows do not believe, and in fact hate, so the Gods punish them. Still, the Gods are not truly cruel. It is a punishment because the swallows make it so. They rebuild not out of understanding and love and a willingness to learn, but out of defiance. A God could give two birds seed. It could be the same seed, but one could eat it and be nourished by it, and another could reject it and waste away."

"So the swallows could take the punishment and turn it into a lesson if they choose!" A voice cried out.

Bard seemed to grow larger with pleasure. "Yes! Any bird could if he could see, but others cannot see as we can. The swallows, nor the others, will ever see as we can."

Trill arrived at the tree just as the energy in the air was moving from confused to euphoric. "The Gods are great," Bard shouted, "and we are the Chosen!" He lowered his voice to the other elder. "They are ready for you, Trill. Tonight their praise will shake the earth."

Trill assigned each Pitch Group a phrase to sing at precisely the right times in a round:

"The Gods are great
We are Their Chosen Ones

As one we will be."

The wild singing began, and like the drumbeat of wings in the sky of Unified Flight, SL'an felt raised up as if on a powerful tide, carried away and filled to the top until, for those dizzying moments, there was not a bit of Himself left. Over a hundred starlings chorused as the sun dropped in the sky, then Trill gave them the signal to stop and move as one in the first complete Unified Flight to another tall tree near the edge of Flower's Sacred Space. They chorused there again as the sun sank even lower, moved once more until black threatened to take over the Space, then finally stopped, thrilled and spent, for the night. SL'an followed the other young males to the edge of the forest where they found places to roost on high together.

Chapter Ten

The Circle of Promise

Rain pelted the leafy canopy through the night and into the dawn, but the young male starlings kept fairly dry together under the branches. The spattering finally ended as the sky was just becoming grey enough for birds to see – the time before the rolling mountains would release another sun. The other starlings were still sleeping when SL'an found Himself wide awake. He still felt a strange vibration inside from the day before, and for some reason a panic jabbed as if a Blooder's jaws were about to close on His back. He jerked His head from one side to the other, looking all about Him, but saw nothing but complete peace.

Mother.

He thought of the Sacred Space so close, and the jab of panic squeezed into a longing. *If I leave now, I could go just long enough to hear the morning praise. I could be back before anyone missed Me,* He thought. SL'an dropped silently from the branch where He had slept, not flapping, but allowing the air to help him glide until He dared to use His wings just long enough to keep Him aloft and barely above the ground. With His young, dun-brown feathers, He blended into the grey light just starting to show the grasses and trees. Mother's nest was in view in a moment, as Hralla began to sing her morning praise.

The first song was always the same. SL'an let the singular sound, unburdened by any other voice, touch His very being. It was a very different feeling from when the chorus of starlings had filled Him to euphoria, but it still filled Him. *How one voice can do so much…* The light gently brightened as her song continued, repeated over and over in joy, then the others began to raise their voices too – just a few at first – then more. Instead of singing along or doing rounds as the starling group did, they were the individual bubblings of morning news. SL'an happily listened to the progress of nestlings, and where a new batch of berries would be ripening soon, and, among them, SL'an thought He heard the gentle voice of L'al. He focused hard on it, and yes!

"My L'in has laid eggs. We try again!"

He knew He should leave, and probably should have already been gone, but He couldn't stop Himself from winging quickly to where the dove sat on the wooden fence rail, breast puffed and proud, calling his news. He pulled his head back quickly when he saw the Starling God coming to land beside him.

"You should be with the other starlings now!"

"I know, but I won't be here long. I have to wish you luck with the eggs, and I would very much love to see L'in too if only for this moment."

The dove left the rail immediately with SL'an to go the short distance to the simple ramshackle nest where L'in settled protectively on their greatest hope. "SL'an!" She cried out. There was a mother's softness and light in her eyes, and settled there, she seemed fuller and more rounded than the young starling remembered.

"How many?"

She laughed. "Only two. Dove kind always has two."

He hesitated a moment, not sure if He should ask, but L'in sensed His question. "We won't know if life is there for some time, but after just fourteen suns we will have babes if the Gods are willing! And You? Are You well? Are You where You belong?"

"I have so much I wish I could tell you already!" SL'an leaned forward to nibble her cheek as best He could.

L'al nudged Him. "And as Teller, I wish You could stay and share, but You mustn't now. Bard has his rules, and I'm sure that doesn't include You being here before he feels You're ready!"

"I'll go, but don't be surprised if you see Me again when the hatchlings arrive!" SL'an swooped from the small tree and felt a bit sick when He realized how much the sun had released. He flew low to the ground again, flapping only when He had to gain enough height, using any bushes and trees available as cover while He made His way back to where the other young males were clearly awake and getting ready to leave the trees to browse for breakfast.

Risk saw Him first. "Where have you been?"

"Just taking a few moments to stretch my wings before we start." *It's not completely untrue*, He thought.

One of the elders came to land among them, and waited until the young males noticed her and were silenced. "Starlings, I have already told the females that you will not be on your own for morning meal, but will all meet briefly first at the Meeting Tree. Please arrive in your Pitch groups."

When she flew off, the first group followed, then shortly after, the next, until all convened in the Meeting Tree. SL'an saw Flora already there with the other females from His Pitch, so He landed beside her. "Good sun!"

She looked at him with a tilt of her head. "Good sun…Seeker."

Her feathers stayed unruffled, nor did they tighten, and He saw no change of expression in her eyes when she gazed at Him briefly, then turned her attention to the large elder female who had gathered them.

"I am Mentor Beckon. I hear your rumbling stomachs, and I assure you they will be filled in just a moment, but today, and from each day forward, at least one of the group meals will be in special service to the Gods. While it is true that They provide birds with the fruit, seed and grounds to find insects we all need to survive, we can also do service as we find the pleasure in eating."

"I already know what this is about," Flora whispered, but once again SL'an couldn't tell if she was stating the fact or trying to point out she knew something He didn't.

Mentor Beckon hopped on her branch, turning to face the distance toward the short grass kept by Flower. "The love between Gods and starlings shows itself in circles, young ones. Not long after the beginning of time, when the sun was young and had only released a very few times, the Gods began creating all of the shelter and food for

Their birds and all other life. They raised the grasses, trees and flowers, and plants of every kind. They also placed many kinds of insects so we would have every choice of good things to eat. The plants were happy to be loved by the Gods, and in return for life, they willingly gave theirs when it was needed and shared their children and their bounty with all other life. The insects, however, talked amongst themselves while the Gods slept. They felt they had the right to be created and did not feel that being sometimes used as food was fair. They tried many things, but their fate could not be changed. In response, they decided to spend their lives creating misery for the Gods when they could."

She took a breath and bowed her head. "They began to breed in great numbers, and they and their young would often ravage what the Gods sought to create. They made sure grubs would destroy roots and bulbs, while other kinds' young and adults would overwhelm leaves and fruits so that little would be left, or the Gods would find what was left unacceptable. The Gods grieved as They saw one of Their own creations turned against Them. Although the Gods are powerful, They could not undo what had been done and worried that all They had created, both plant and breathing, would die despite what They tried to offer them."

"Starling had just given the Gods the gift of music. With it, They sang to the sky, calling Their Chosen One down to Them again. Starling promised the Gods that he would tell birds to wage war on the insects. Those that could eat them would fly in flocks and troll the grounds to clear as many away as they could. The Gods were so pleased with starling's willingness, They gave he and his kind the gift of a powerful beak that can thrust into the earth, even when it is frozen, and force open to find and then eat those insects and their grubs hiding beneath the soil.

"Young ones, it is in celebration of this ancient promise that we eat with the very purpose of service in our breasts. We do our Creators' bidding when we take our very meals, and in return, we are nourished. It is the Circle of Promise."

Mentor Beckon dove from the branch and the groups followed in order, covering the short grasses of Flower's Sacred Space and moving gingerly through on foot, heads down in deep concentration.

"Be thorough!" The elder called out.

SL'an found His first grub and made sure to really feel it in His beak. He tasted what Mother provided Him and felt glad that He was doing Her work as He lived. *Mother, you gave Me life.* With each grub or insect He found, He was newly aware. It was no longer an act of making the ache in the belly stop. It was something deep in the blood – the blood that ran between the Gods and Their Chosen Ones. The food was no longer only food, but something to vanquish.

"Move in lines, young ones, then change direction when you reach the end of the short grasses. I need a group to go into the flowers," Beckon directed. SL'an saw a number of elder females and males in the large area where Mother grew plants for Herself. Glee was among them. She flew from the spot and alighted so close to Him, He could feel her heat. "How go Your lessons, Starling God?"

"Please, call me SL'an…All goes well!" There was that timbre in her voice again that did things to His brain He couldn't understand.

"I don't want to keep You from Your service, SL'an, but I wanted to make sure there isn't anything You need. You are *special*. Although so few realize it right now, I realize it."

"Thank you, Glee." He automatically bobbed His head as He'd seen L'al do so many times.

The elder female laughed. "That is not the starling way! But no matter – there is no one You should bow your head to. Instead, all others will bow theirs to You someday." She flew back to her post, looked back at Him briefly, then began her insect hunting in Flower's honor once again.

Flora walked close to where the young Starling God was eating. "Why would my mother come to you?"

SL'an looked around furtively, hoping all the interruptions of service wouldn't be a problem. Mentor Beckon seemed busy advising another group, so He relaxed. "She wanted to see how my lessons are going."

"Why?"

SL'an blinked.

"Why would my mother want to know about your progress? You aren't fledged from her, and she doesn't ask the others."

"Your parents helped me when I needed it."

She nodded enthusiastically. "That's right. You are the mystery starling taken in by doves. I suppose that means you *would* need extra help." She moved away from Him a bit and continued looking for insects. SL'an felt suddenly very full and hoped He would be able to fly.

"When you feel you can eat no more, you may leave and rest. Until the sun reaches the top of the Meeting Tree, the time is your own." *Mentor Beckon read My mind!* He thought with a chuckle.

Everywhere He looked, SL'an could see the other bird kinds flitting about, gathering food for their nestlings or brooding mates, visiting on the taut metal limb, and a few actively trying to see what was going on inside Mother's nest. He was afraid He wouldn't resist the urge to go visit with all those who were off limits, so He chose to rest at the edge of the forest where He and the other young males had spent the night. Risk and Song tried to entice Him to stay in the Sacred Space, but He thanked them and went His own way. When He winged between the branches of the first line of trees, He caught the aura of something that made His neck feathers rise, but then the feeling was gone. He landed, searching the air but not finding anything but the warm, green sense of leaves and musky bark. *Maybe the same sense we use for Unified Flight would help here*, He thought. He closed His eyes and breathed calmly, pulling in the air all around Him and not letting sight confuse His other senses. He heard the angry chatters of a squirrel telling another to go collect his *own* seeds. He heard the gentle rustle of leaves in the wind, and His mind could envision each leaf in its place, moving against the others, and the sunshine dappling in between them. A forest bird sang a lonely hymn deep in the woods – a kind and voice He didn't recognize –

I wish I could shut off my hearing too for just a moment!

Maybe He could! He tried breathing again and imagined having no hearing. The only sense He had was for aura. The sounds seemed to ebb away and dull to almost nothing, and He began to feel the heat of the sun. Through aura, His mind could see the leaves rotting on the forest floor, and the sap oozing from small breaks in the trees. He sensed mice under logs tending to young, and just as He nearly forgot what He was trying to find to begin with, lost in admiration of life around Him, His heart seized and His mind was covered in nothing but blood red. It was the same aura at Hroo's nest after her babes were taken and killed!

The aura was old now, but He felt it wasn't so old that the Blooder had left the area. *Mother, what do I do?*

If He alerted the Watchers, He would break the rules again in broad sun. He had no idea where Bard could be, and by the time He found him, the Blooder may be too far to be discovered. *Every Blooder has a way of hunting, and if we know what it is and how it is trying to catch us, we can be safe,* He thought quickly. SL'an flew from tree to tree, stopping to close His eyes and reach His senses out. The aura did grow stronger in places, but there didn't seem to be a clear trail He could follow. The more intense the aura got, the harder it was for Him to close His eyes and keep them closed long enough to relax. Almost against His will, His eyes popped open over and over, and His breath refused to be deep and slow, pumping in and out rapidly instead in time with His throbbing heart. Soon He couldn't tell where the aura was coming from, and He had to give up and fly back to the Meeting Tree.

It wasn't time for the next lesson yet, but starlings were starting to return slowly. SL'an looked everywhere for an elder, but there was none to be found. "Where are all the elders? They must be somewhere nearby," He asked a young male He'd seen, but had never spoken to before.

The bird regarded Him quizzically. "Hey, be glad we have a little time on our own!"

SL'an shook His feathers and winged as fast as He could back to His Mother's Sacred Space. Starlings were scattered in their Pitch Groups, and a few were actually straying to visit with other starlings as the Pitch Groups were already dissolving, becoming more of a secondary function. He searched for Glee, but she and the other elders were no longer feeding in service. In the distance, a group was moving neatly toward the Meeting Tree – so neatly they must have been elders! He shot toward them faster than He ever thought He could have flown, and intercepted before they reached their destination. "Stop!" SL'an beat His wings forward, hovering in the air in front of Bard, heading up the group.

An assistant came forward. "You'd better back off, young one! Do you know whom you're speaking to? Respect!" SL'an saw the male lunge and tried to shift His flight too late. The larger male's beak knocked His head. Quick, searing pain made His vision change, the colors whirling together as He tumbled to the ground. He landed, panting with shock, and could vaguely see a form land beside him.

SL'an willed the word out, although for a moment it was almost as if He had forgotten how. "Blooder!"

The blurred form stopped. Another joined, and Bard's voice bellowed, "Peace!" For a moment, SL'an thought the starling Secret Keeper was using the same mediation as L'al had when He'd nearly brushed feathers with the young Watcher, but the assistant answered to it as a name instead.

"Bard?"

"Leave this one. I thank you for defending me, but I will see what nonsense this young one is about. Go and begin the lesson without me. You know what to do, and I need to have a talk with this young male."

SL'an still couldn't see clearly, but He heard the force of air as the group of elders lifted and disappeared toward His peers. Even in His haze, He tried stretching out His mind. Focusing on the sound, He could see them all, each in the right spot, flying closely and correctly, the assistant now leading the way.

When they were gone, Bard poked at SL'an with his beak. "Are You fit?"

"I can't see clearly."

"You have taken an unfortunate blow to Your head, Starling God. It would be good to remember that even though You are created by and of the Gods, You have starling form. I imagine Your life can end."

This didn't help SL'an's reeling head. He had certainly thought about death, and felt the potential in His breast when He sensed the Blooder, but He never truly thought of His own life *ending*.

"I can't imagine God Flower would allow You to die, but You still shouldn't take foolish chances. What is this about?"

SL'an tried to focus on the dark form in front of Him. He blinked hard. After a strange swimming sensation, His vision seemed to clear, but the ache reminded Him of the assistant's beak. "The unknown Blooder – I went to the roosting place during free time to rest, and I sensed the aura of it. It was the same that was there when Hroo's nestlings were taken." He shook His head, but was sorry when the ache pounded into something He nearly couldn't stand. He squinted His eyes shut against it. "I tried to find it. I thought if I could see what it was and see how it lived, I could tell the rest how to stay safe."

Bard's voice softened. "Very brave, Starling God. You truly do have the best interest of Your Chosen Ones at heart. But You couldn't find it?"

"No."

"Put it out of Your mind."

For a moment, the pain almost paled next to SL'an's relief. "Will you share this with the Watchers and the Tellers? Perhaps a party of Seekers can go to the woods and try to find the trail I lost?"

"No, that isn't necessary. I know You were badly swayed by living with other bird kind when You fledged from Flower's nest, but You need to understand something now and forever. We are the Chosen Ones. Have You seen in the sky how many of us there are? This training flock seems large to you, but when it is almost time for the sun to spend as much time resting as it does waking, You will see there are not a hundred or more, but thousands at once! We are great in numbers because we are becoming more like the Gods themselves. There is little that harms us, and when it does, there is good reason. Let the Blooder prey on whom the Gods want. You of all must feel this is the truth and the way."

SL'an almost crumpled under the thought of it. "You're saying the same thing the Watchers say, then? Hroo *deserved* to lose her nestlings?"

"Look at the wonder of Your Mother God Flower, SL'an! She did punish Hroo by taking the lives of two nestlings, but it wasn't for waste!" Bard's eyes were wide with passion. "When God Flower replaced them, She created a believer out of one who never believed before. What if we had interfered and thwarted the Blooder? Flower's will would not be done. Let this be and keep it to Yourself. It is unlikely that the Gods will strike at Her Chosen Ones, but only She and Her kind know the plan." Bard inspected SL'an with a critical eye. "Are You able to fly? Peace has a strong beak, but he usually doesn't strike hard enough to cause serious harm."

"I think I can fly."

"Then we will join the rest at the Meeting Tree. They should have completed their morning praise and will be preparing to take off for the next level in Unified Flight. The others will have had instruction, but Your senses are keen. I think You will be able to follow well. If You find yourself lost, though, what will You do?"

SL'an stretched His wings to see how it felt. "I will fly to the outside of the group where I have more room to make mistakes."

Bard pulled his head up and lifted his breast with satisfaction. "Very good!"

SL'an joined the group just before takeoff.

"All is settled with this one, and he knows his place." Bard dropped the slight note that announced SL'an as '*He*', and for a moment the Starling God wished that dropping the sound and the title would make it so.

As Bard predicted, the young starling's senses served Him well. Despite a lingering ache, He allowed the drumming of the wings to carry His mind away, and blissfully lost Himself once again.

Chapter Eleven
Life

L'al brought food to L'in as she kept hope and eggs warm. She was awash with love as he tirelessly came and went, not only filling his crop but hers as well. He gladly took his turns on the eggs mornings so she could stretch her wings, drink and bathe, but she always finished as quickly as she could to get back to her nest and her beloved.

Those who had known her as "Lin" when she fledged and grew into a young adult were surprised but pleased when she settled at last. Although she was gentle and fine with a good mind and many suitors, the young males' dances and songs of passion did nothing to stir her heart. She would fly away with soft apologies, but they would follow her over and over, certain that if they persisted she would want them. It only made her feel more lonely and different – and less apt to ever offer her life. Some of them became angry and turned beak to her, but when they did they quickly found that the soft-eyed beauty had fire and steel underneath, and those males retreated in shame.

She had seen two springs and still chose to be alone when L'al came to Flower's Sacred Space. Hatched a half sun's wing away, he was moved to be a Teller and had to leave home to find his place since an established dove already did the work well there. He had visited several other Sacred Spaces, but there was no room for a new Teller in those places either.

L'in sighed as she sat on the nest, remembering the first time she watched him winging in. Something had clutched around her heart like a bird's toes tightly to a branch, and she wasn't sure if what she felt was excitement or dread. She almost heard the words in her mind, *you are meeting HIM.* The power of it frightened her, and she didn't want it to be so. She didn't want to lose herself as she had seen happen to others; who would she be then?

So she spent much of her energy being where L'al was not.

Despite her effort, curiosity got the better of her sometimes, and she would pretend to look for feed while watching his quest for the position of Teller unfold. Flower's Sacred Space had been without a Teller for longer than it should have after Teller L'une died peacefully as he had lived. The kind, old dove would be difficult to replace, as much loved as he had been.

The break for L'al came when a group of blue jays ventured through in early spring, as they always did, and demanded first-sun place at the seed. The ground had only just started showing green, and the trees barely hinted at the color they would hold in a few suns. When the smaller birds who wintered over in the Sacred Space complained loudly, L'al bobbed forward to everyone's surprise. Some of the redwing Watchers had returned, and a then-young Rem flared against the blue jay leader.

"You are only passing through, jay! Wait until those who serve this Sacred Space feed!" Rem puffed to show his already bright red spots, and the jay raised his crest in response.

"What kind of Sacred Space doesn't offer first hospitality to travelers? We need shelter and feed. Would you deny us the Gods' wings?"

That was when L'al spoke, and his words captivated Lin where she stood. "Every bird is worthy of God Flower's seed and shelter for different reasons. Jay, you have traveled and are always welcome here, but redwings have traveled farther than that and protect this space throughout the warm season when we raise our families. Sparrows and chickadees and the nuthatches have wintered here like others of us, and truly this is our home. So, as you all can see, there is not one that is undeserving or that doesn't have need."

The jay scoffed. "Are you suggesting that we try to all fit on the feeder at once? Ridiculous! A decision must be made and someone must go first."

L'al's small head craned to one side and then bobbed to the other as he looked the seed space over. "It seems to me that we don't all need to be at the feed top. What I do suggest is that either redwings or blue jays feed, but rake their beaks through often to spill seeds to the ground where all others may partake. Every bird kind using the feed top should do so, except the small ones since their beaks are not large enough to handle such work."

Lin found herself moving closer and closer to the group almost against her will. Soon, she was standing close to L'al. "And how will these fine birds now decide who will feed at the top and who won't?"

L'al looked at her with surprise. "Both redwing and blue jay are the Gods' birds. I'm sure they will know what to do now."

Watcher Rem bowed his head to L'al and stepped back. "Teller, this traveler has certainly made a good point about hospitality, and I'm happy to ask our kind to ground feed if the jays are willing to share as you suggest."

The blue jay's crest relaxed. "We are. We didn't come to fight, Watcher. My hunger spoke for me, I'm afraid."

L'al was the accepted Teller from that point on, and after the jays left to raise their young a short distance away, young Watcher Rem remembered the lesson and made very certain his kind at the Sacred Space learned it as well.

Just suns later, Teller L'al landed beside Lin where she was picking gravel for her gullet, in from the path of the Gods. She felt a mingling of terror and joy and hoped it wouldn't show.

"Lin, I have something I would like to share with you if you would be willing to follow." Without another word, the Teller flew to one edge of Flower's Space, where a tree that was really more of a bush grew. When she was safely beside him, he faced her and bobbed his offer. "This tree will be covered with red berries, almost as sweet and beautiful as you are. I see you have not taken a One, and I would be honored to build a nest here with you and be One with you for as long as we live."

Lin dipped her head and squinted her eyes. "How do you know we should be One?"

"How could I not know? Don't you know it too?"

L'in shifted on the nest, feeling the eggs beneath her and loving them even more for the memories. *How foolish I was to fear losing myself to my One! I am still myself but only more so.* When L'al came winging in again to bring food and this time to stay with her a bit, she rested her head over his back. "I have good news. You are not working so hard for nothing. Our eggs – there is *life*."

That evening, Teller L'al almost glowed from joy, almost more for his L'in, who would finally be a mother, than for himself. The emptiness in her would be ended. Truly it must have been the right thing for SL'an to learn from Bard's flock if the years of barrenness had been lifted.

He kept the news to himself until the sun started to sink toward the mountains, pulled back to where it rested during the black. SLee was the first to hear when the Teller asked him to give the evening praise, making a special song request. The purple finch flapped his wings with quick joy when he heard the news he would share. "Dove L'al, I wouldn't be worthy of sharing this news! You have done great service here, and of all birds to deserve a full nest, it's you and your L'in. I'd like to invite a special singer if I might."

Dove L'al agreed, but he couldn't get SLee to say more.

When evening finally fell, a yellow warbler L'al had seen passing through but did not know landed at the very top of the tallest apple tree in Flower's Space. He knew instantly why the warbler chose that place to praise rather than the taut metal limb. When the snows left and the suns started truly feeling longer at last, the tree was full of white flowers that conceived by the Gods' perfect design. Now there were small apples forming with all the promise of full fruit soon. The fruits would drop to the ground as fledglings leaving the nest, and the cycle would begin again.

The warbler first announced the news, then he raised his head and let his song ring through the coloring sky with clarity and strength that only SLee could come close to. L'al and L'in watched the tiny bird's throat muscles work, his beak opening wide to let the strains out more at times and less at others, as he delivered 'The Song of Life' flawlessly. This was a song with no words, but just music – the notes speaking more than any word could, a song older than time itself.

L'in was breathless, and the entire Space was quiet but somehow still humming with the spirit of the song long after the warbler finished.

At last she whispered, "I wonder if SL'an could hear?"

L'al shook his head. "The young males are roosting at the forest edge. I don't see how He could have, One."

"But I think the beautiful warbler's song was so clear it could be heard in every Sacred Space in the world!" She laughed with joy, and L'al found himself laughing with her.

"It could well be, but Bard has them sing their own evening praise just before ours and as ours begins. I don't think it's possible for any of them to hear when their senses are so full of words of their own."

"Which is *exactly* the way Bard wants it!" L'in shook quickly, but couldn't stay angry, even with Bard. "Perhaps I could fly to let SL'an know! If you stay with the eggs, I could leave now – I'd be there and back before the sun rests."

L'al shifted uncomfortably. "Why not wait until tomorrow when there's more light?"

"He's like one of my own, L'al. I can hardly wait to tell Him the news of how His Mother has rewarded us after so long. I can't help but think He couldn't hear it in evening praise because He was meant to be told from my own beak." She sighed deeply. "Also, He said He would come to see if there are hatchlings. You know He can't keep leaving the starling flock to visit without being caught at some point. It would be easier for me to explain my flying through than His leaving."

The Teller looked into his mate's eyes, so full of a wish he couldn't deny. "Then go quickly and be careful. I don't know what Bard or the other adults will do if they see you trying to talk to one of their own. Please, One – if they notice you, make as if you are just passing through to come home."

She fluffed with pleasure, stepping carefully out of the nest to reveal their two white eggs. She was hardly off them when L'al settled quickly in her place. She preened his neck feathers, and he ducked his head to let her reach a difficult spot. "I'll miss you even for this time."

L'in was gone with a rush of air, and she made good to her promise and moved as quickly as she could. Although dove kind was peaceful, she, as all of them, was a strong and fast flier. She carefully avoided the most open spaces, and used trees and brush for cover, just as SL'an had done days before. She reached the Meeting Tree and saw over a hundred young starlings lacing the branches, some coming and going after the evening praise, but many still lost in it.

The different voices rattled through almost like leaves rustling in a chaotic wind, and she strained to hear SL'an's among them but could only hear the one strange sound created by the many. Her heart quickened – she had to find Him soon or she would be in danger of being taken by the black. She knew L'al found the power somehow to stay alert enough to fly the night he met Bard in the clearing, but she also knew there would be no such strength within her. When the black came, she would be overcome with sleep, her brain taken by whatever fog the black brought with it. There would be no flight for her then.

Some starlings were leaving the tree in a small group, and she glimpsed SL'an among them. The twelve or so young birds dipped down from high in their meeting place and moved in a loose, unified movement into the forest. By the sound, L'in thought they landed not too far in. "It's a good thing," she whispered to herself. As always, it felt like her L'al was beside her, listening and experiencing everything with her although he was at the Sacred Space tending the nest. It was this way since they had first joined. No matter what one did, each felt the presence of the other in the breast and brain.

L'in had never ventured into the forest before. Although it was still somewhat light, the leaf-laden branches blocked out much of what was left from the late evening sun, and she caught her breath as if she had plunged into deep water. Thankfully, she found the group of starlings only a few trees in, starting to settle in what looked to be established places. SL'an was there among them, she knew, but the lack of light made her almost as good as blind. "Young one," she cooed softly. Several starlings heard and left their branches to investigate. One was Song.

He landed next to the dove and peered at her curiously. "Late for you to be out, lady dove. What is your business here?"

Risk joined them, but the few others who heard something saw the dove was being attended to and went back to their places.

"I am here to give a message to one among you named SL'an."

Risk stomped his foot as he had seen the elders do. "None of us should really be speaking with you, dove."

"My name, young starling, is L'in, One of Teller L'al. I have a message only for SL'an. I am aware of the rule, but the message is important to me and will be to SL'an, so I choose to risk breaking rules this once. There will only be trouble if you choose to share with the elders that you have seen me here."

Song poked his brother. "It's going to be black soon – just let her tell him what she came to tell him. Who cares?"

Risk eyed his brother, then L'in. "I'll get him, but you should go further out – under those lower limbs there where the two of you won't be seen. If you fly there now, I'll send him down to you and no one will know. I'll tell the others who saw you that we've driven you off."

L'in bobbed her gratitude and winged away, pretending to go out of the woods, then circling back behind the trees to the lower branches of the large pine as they suggested. She was settled in for a brief wait when a horrible aura suddenly consumed her.

Chapter Twelve

By the Wings of the Gods

SL'an flew to where He was told L'in waited, but when the breeze shifted from North to South in a quick twist, His senses reeled with horror. He snapped His body back, flapping to stop His motion toward the dreaded feeling.

The Blooder's aura reeked from the low tree branches, and as He clumsily hovered, He searched there for any sign of the dove. *The light is dim – she may just be out of my sight!* "L'in!" He called out. "Fly quickly! Fly! The Blooder is close!"

There was no rush of a dove's wings, and SL'an felt the web of Himself torn in two. Every sense told Him not to go toward danger, but His affection for L'in told Him to discover her.

He pressed His eyes shut and reached for the aura since His eyes would be hindered from the quickly lowering sun and the shadows in the forest. When He felt His courage fail and the urge to wing away clawed at Him, He imagined L'in looking at Him. Her light plumage seemed soft and glowing; her eyes were full of peace. He could not let such a one die.

He plunged into the forest, fixed on the Blooder and racing toward the thick of it. He already knew there was nothing to be gained by stopping at the branches where they were to meet. If L'in had still been there, she would have flown at His warning. At last, He opened His eyes to get the vague sense of the trees, His body dipping and swerving to avoid them and low-lying branches. This part of the forest was still more open. *Mother, help Me! If I don't reach the Blooder soon, it will*

take Our L'in where I can't follow! The breath of the breeze was
different here, and the sense of the forest was quickly changing to
mushrooms, mud and cedar. He somehow knew there would be many
fallen trees and branches closely knit together like walls up ahead.
Mice and squirrels would find this excellent cover – and rabbits too –
but passage would be impossible for a bird on the wing.

Just then He saw it. The dark form moved long against the
ground, and the quills of SL'an's feathers prickled in his skin. There
was the horrid reek of the Blooder, but there was also death in the air
– fresh blood and torn feathers mingled with fading terror, like an
echo of song drifting away. SL'an lost all fear and dove madly toward
the Blooder, passing it and turning in mid-flight to face the enemy.
"You will STOP!" He pounded His wings toward the Blooder's furred
face, and He could see through His rage that L'in's light form hung
limply from the jaws, her wing splayed in an impossible position.
Mother, her wing is broken, but You can fix it, He thought even as His
head thrust forward to peck at the Blooder's eyes. It made a strange
gurgling growl and did stop, hunching its back and dropping L'in to
the ground.

"I have enough to eat tonight and you're safe, bird. Leave me to
my meal."

SL'an dropped to the ground, stunned that it could speak. He
never thought of the Blooders as having words or anything similar to
birds. They were just mindless creatures that killed. The voice was
strange, but subtly female.

The young Starling God looked at L'in's still form on the forest
floor, the splayed wing, the blood covering her breast and neck, and
He searched the eye He could see for the soft awareness that had
always been there. Her eye was partially open, but there was no
sparkle. No fear. No love. No life.

The shock at hearing the Blooder's words swept away in a wave
of fury. "You had no right to kill her!"

"I have the same right to eat as you, bird. I told you I have enough
for now and you're safe, but if you make my dinner get cold, it will
not taste the way it should and I could change my mind." The
Blooder's eyes caught some of the lingering light that shone through a

branch moved by the evening breeze, and they twinkled strangely. SL'an was taken by a ripple of fear.

"I smell your fear. It's a wise thing to fear me. Now go on your way."

The Blooder reached down and grasped L'in's body in her mouth. SL'an flew at the face again, trying to claw and peck out the glittering eyes. He wanted to kill this thing – this thing –

She dropped L'in again and hunched up higher this time, swatting at the furious starling. "You can't hurt me badly, bird, but you *are* different than the others, aren't you? You dare to be in reach of my claws and teeth?"

"Dare?" SL'an's voice sounded more like the crow cleaners He heard only in the distance. "I am not any bird, Blooder. I am Equal to the Gods, created and placed by God Flower here, and She will see to it you hurt no other! I will see to it!"

The Blooder bared her teeth and panted in what must have been a laugh. "Equal to the Gods? What Gods do you ramble about?"

"Those like My Mother, God Flower, who built the nest near the taut metal limbs and placed the flowers and short grasses and seed so Her birds will have all they need. This bird you have taken is the One of our Teller, L'al. He is the Teller of the Sacred Space. You have taken the One of another! Many suns ago, you took nestlings from their mother!"

The Blooder never took her eyes off of SL'an, who had settled back again to the forest floor, but she pushed L'in's body a bit with her nose. "You're lucky that this meal is still edible…I know the creatures that you call Gods, but they're no Gods of mine."

"They are Gods of everything!" SL'an's breath came hard.

"So they are Gods to you. Have it as you will."

"I am not only 'bird'. I am starling." SL'an puffed His breast feathers.

"Well, starling, I am fisher. I warn you again that if you don't leave soon, learning of my kind will be the last thing you do."

"I will not let you leave with the dove. This Teller's One, and My friend and mentor, will return with me to the Sacred Space. She will not be your meal tonight. My Mother will heal her."

"Foolish. There is death, starling. She is only good as food now, so leave it be."

"I will ask Mother to give life back to L'in and She will do it. Mother is the greatest of all the Gods, and I am her Starling God. If She could create Me, She can bring life back."

The fisher female seemed to lose interest in food for the first time, settling back slightly and tilting her head to regard SL'an carefully. "Why is it, starling, that you think you were created by these Gods of yours?"

"All My life, Mother is all I've known. She raised Me in Her nest as I grew feathers. She fed Me and loved Me, and taught Me what I needed to know to fly and feed on My own. I fledged from Her wings, and She placed Me among Her birds in Her Sacred Space to learn to be bird, and to be Her Equal among them."

"And you believe birds are special to these Gods of yours because they create you and offer you places to live and eat?"

"And Mother protects us from most of you Blooders," SL'an nearly spat the words.

"So that is what I am? A Blooder?" The fisher female looked to the sky between the branches. "It is nearly black, special bird, or are you so special you can see when it's black? There will be no moon tonight."

SL'an realized it was true that the figure of the fisher female was becoming more and more vague, and it was only His mind's inner eye that could see her clearly, focused on the aura and sound of her voice. SL'an couldn't give up. "Leave the dove to Me."

"Well, as special as you are, I am special too and need my food. When you eat the grub or the worm, aren't you eating something else alive? So you eat the grub, and I eat you. But imagine this, special starling! There is nothing that eats me. I think that makes me as special as you. Maybe more so, because if these Gods protect you, then see how they protect me more."

SL'an couldn't speak, confused for a moment and unable to move. The fisher started to pick L'in's body up in her mouth, then hesitated. "Another thing, special starling – the Gods you speak of, though they are no Gods of mine, brought me here with their own 'wings'.

The young starling could barely get words out of His beak. "You lie."

"No. What I tell you is the truth. I was captured by these creatures and brought here and released with a male I didn't know. The nestlings you remember were my first meal here; we don't like to leave the forest, but the smell of all that food so close together was very tempting, and I was so hungry and afraid. Yes! Even 'Blooders' can be afraid, special starling." She looked to a nearby tree. "The male, Brontoo, and I joined. It made sense since we smell no other of our own kind here. This dove will feed me, and more. She will feed the young waiting to grow in my belly. Your Gods didn't only place us here close to you, special starling. They made sure there will be more of us. Hmmmm…." The sound came like a growling purr from her throat. "Maybe these creatures are our Gods too, after all."

She lifted L'in and scampered to the base of the tree she had just gazed at, climbing the thick trunk and disappearing from SL'an's dissipating vision, the sounds of the Blooder's claws against bark scraping in His brain long after the real sound had ended.

SL'an felt empty, but not like the way He was emptied of Himself during Unified Flight or during starling evening praise. At those times He was vacant and yet more full than He'd ever been – one with all. Now He was so much Himself that there was nothing else. Nothing else could touch Him or be inside Him but Himself, and it was a horrible pain that entered His bones and muscles and pulsed with His blood. There was no place without pain, but at the same time no place with feeling. There was only Himself that He felt He would never get away from.

This crushing sensation kept Him glued to the forest floor, although something about the forest didn't seem real. He reached for some kind of grounding in His mind desperately – anything to squelch the consuming pain and nothingness. *Mother. Mother. How could You let this happen?*

He suddenly thought of L'al, and although the painful nothing was all too there, it weakened a bit when He thought of His mentor. If L'in had come, and there were eggs in the nest, L'al must be tending them while she had come to…to see Him. *She died coming to see Me. To tell Me something. Mother, why?*

He had to find a way to fly out of here despite what gripped Him. He had to get to L'al's nest…L'al and L'in's nest. His mentor would be worried by now, He was certain. It was nearly black. An image came to SL'an's mind of the dove Teller settled on the two eggs in the nest, feathers full to keep their future warm, anxious but knowing he could not leave them or they would become cold and there would be no life in them for certain. *What news I have to bring you, My mentor. Forgive Me.*

SL'an stood on wobbly legs and spread His wings a bit to see if they would do as He wished. When He felt they would, He lifted just over the ground and used His senses as best He could to find the way back to where the young males roosted, already drifting to sleep now and hardly aware of one of their own winging past, toward the Meeting Tree, and further on still until He reached the Sacred Space.

He saw L'al and L'in's small tree like a shadow and winged toward it with the painful nothing still threatening to pull Him under. He alighted next to the nest, and L'al's thin neck and small head stretched out longer than seemingly possible, eyes wide with alarm. "Where is my L'in?"

SL'an tried to form the words, but the painful nothing filled His lungs and made Him mute. He could only pull His own head in tightly against dun feathers.

"She went to see You but now You're here without her! Where is L'in?"

When SL'an opened His beak but still nothing came out, L'al stood up from his place on the eggs. "The black has fallen, SL'an! It isn't safe for her. Where is my One?"

Only one word sliced through the darkness. "Gone."

Chapter Thirteen
Dance of the Swallows

The dove's legs collapsed beneath him, landing him squarely on the eggs again. As the last of the sun's light crept away and left black, the young starling watched His mentor's unblinking eyes until He couldn't see him at all anymore. He settled in as close to the nest as possible and slept there, although visions of L'in's lifeless body dangling from the fisher's jaws woke Him over and over again. He half expected to find the Blooder climbing the delicate branches of the berry tree in the black; part of Him hoped she would…

…But Hralla's morning praise woke Him as the hills released the sun again.

He looked over at L'al, still in the same position in the nest, eyes still open. "Did you sleep at all?"

The dove never blinked or moved.

The morning news began at the last strains of Hralla's praise. It sounded so different now; such normal things and mostly happy announcements. Life was going on as if nothing had happened, and SL'an felt suddenly that none of their news mattered. He couldn't imagine it ever mattering again: They didn't know beautiful L'in was taken by a Blooder's jaws. Surely all else would stop when they knew.

There was other news He had that all of bird kind at the Sacred Space would have to know, though – so important, SL'an stirred to action. "I have news that we should share with the others, Teller." When there was no response, He continued, "For the safety of the Sacred Space."

SL'an tried to wait, preening His feathers nervously. *If I am the way I am from L'in's going, then it must be unimaginably harder for L'al,* He thought, dropping a small feather to the ground that had pulled loose. *But there are many lives at stake.*

"L'in must not be gone for nothing, L'al. She was taken by the Blooder last night – the same that took Hroo's nestlings."

Dove L'al pulled his head into his body as if he hoped to bury it there.

"I know what it is. I know a bit of how it lives…and I know more that, as a Seeker, I need to share with My Teller. You need to know and decide what should be shared and what should not. L'al! I don't know what to do!"

L'al squinted his eyes shut tightly. "Could You not save her? Could YOU not save her? You're Equal. You're one of the Gods."

"I tried, but by the time I flew to her, she was already gone. I hoped to bring her here to Mother so She could bring the life back in her, but I failed at that too." The painful nothing hadn't let SL'an think much about the horrible night, but now it raised the black from His mind quickly and He realized it all. First, L'in had flown into the forest when it was so close to black to see Him. Then, He was unable to know she was in danger, or help her once she was taken. Now He had no idea what to do. *What kind of a Starling God could I be when I cannot save the life of one bird I love? Mother, were You testing My strength? If You were, then I've failed. I have failed.*

"Are You sure she was dead? Perhaps she was only shocked or playing so the Blooder would leave her?" L'al's eyes opened suddenly.

SL'an sighed. "No. There was no life in her. I may be sure of nothing else, but I am sure of that." He had to fight being swallowed by the unbearable, painful nothing.

The morning news continued – news about fledglings and weather and the sighting of Cleaners circling the sky some distance away, but close enough to be seen by the bird's eye. Seeker Steep announced he would fly to where they were and bring back news. This kind of information was simple curiosity and gossip, SL'an knew. L'in taught Him that when Cleaners circled, there was often something lying dead in the path of the Gods. *"There are often groundhogs, deer and sometimes even one of the Blooders,"* L'in's voice came into His head from what she had taught Him not long ago. He felt a pang in His breast and wished with all of Himself that she was there to tell Him more.

"Teller, should I ask SLee or one of the others to announce what has happened? That L'in has been taken from us?"

L'al stood up for the first time and pushed the two eggs sorrowfully with his beak, turning them a bit so they warmed evenly. "There is life here. That's what she flew to tell You. There is life and now she will never know the fulfillment of her own babes." He settled on them again. "I've spent my life giving all I could give to the Gods."

"The Blooder, L'al. I must tell you about it, and you must tell Me what to do."

"You've all abandoned me." L'al's eyes stared off again.

"I won't abandon you, but I must know what to share."

L'al remained unmoving and almost unblinking.

SL'an dropped down to where Mother set the rich sunflower seeds for Her birds. He gathered what He could fit in his beak from the ground and returned to his mentor's nest, leaving them on the edge. "I will not abandon you. I will take care that you are fed so you may stay and so there will be nestlings." *Now I must do what you can't, mentor,* He thought, and dropped down to where birds were feeding, some redwings among them.

"Please tell Rem I have discovered the new Blooder that killed in the Sacred Space. Tell him that the Blooder's jaws closed around the life of L'in, and there is more." The redwing He spoke to lifted his head from the seed tray; SL'an saw it was the one He had almost rubbed beaks with. There was nothing but duty in the youngish redwing's eyes now, and he flew immediately down to a valley where waters pooled and the redwings preferred to nest. SL'an vaguely thought He still didn't ask the sentry's name. But did it matter?

The wait was only brief, but SL'an felt it stretched forever. At last Rem approached and landed on the ground beside the sagging starling, his red spots flaring. SL'an shared parts that He knew about the Blooder called a fisher – especially where she seemed to live, and the fact that there would be more soon. *I'm sorry I'm not telling you everything,* He thought. Something inside told Him not to share that the new Blooders were delivered by the wings of the Gods. "L'al is not fit," He told the Watcher. "We'll have to do whatever will be done."

Rem twitched, trying to contain his rage. "L'al has true reason not to be fit, and the Blooder shall pay. There are few birds of any kind the likes of L'in. She'll be missed." The redwing shook out his feathers, but they refused to lay sleek again. "Young one, we should announce L'in gone, but I don't know what to do with the rest. You have the wish to be a Teller someday, and have spent time with the doves. What do you suggest?"

"I know the fear this has made me feel. I worry that bird kind here will panic if they think they're not safe."

"Truth." Rem looked about him. "Perhaps we could tell them we know what the Blooder is, that it is this creature called 'fisher', and to be safe, they need only stay out of the forest near black."

"She did say that she came to the Sacred Space because she was afraid and starving," SL'an nodded.

"She?"

"The fisher female."

"Blooders may bear young, but they are not to be spoken of as 'she' or 'he'. They are only Blooders!" Rem's eyes widened, and SL'an lowered His head to keep the peace. Rem didn't relax. "They feel no fear. They're not like us."

The Watcher's fury wasn't against Him, but it was fury born of pain. *"This is the most dangerous anger of all,"* He remembered L'in saying. *"Nothing alive thinks clearly when great pain has caused great anger."*

SLee was called in to make the announcement that L'in had been taken outside of the Sacred Space. The news made birds solemn, and SLee himself had trouble sharing it. "Why would L'in have flown there so close to black?" SL'an heard many birds asking each other in low tones. Sometimes the words were a bit different, but the meaning was the same. His wings felt weighted.

Birds were flying down to eat and leaving their nests to find food for themselves and for young. The movements were slower – the air quieter – but still things went on. SL'an brought L'al more seeds, but He saw the ones He'd already placed there hadn't been touched. He crouched down on a branch near the nest and felt His eyes drawn to the sky. He saw four Cleaners circling where the morning news had said, and then, even higher, His eyes caught moving specks in the air. The specks glided dreamily up then dropped suddenly down, like the swallows when they danced. Just then two swallows left a nest packed under the eaves of Flower's own and flew upward until they joined the troupe, and He then realized the specks *were* the swallows.

They were impossibly high! SL'an had never seen any bird spend time so close to the sun. They were moving as if feeding, but instinctively He knew there could be no insects flying as high as the swallows were then.

"They honor my L'in." L'al's voice jolted the starling so He nearly fell off the branch.

"Even the swallows? I didn't know they would do such a thing."

There was no answer from L'al. SL'an nudged a few of the seeds closer to the dove, but he only turned his head away a bit and closed his eyes just as Bard came swiftly winging in. "Come with me," the elder starling barked.

SL'an obediently followed. He expected to be in trouble, but it didn't seem to matter any more. They landed together behind Flower's nest in the short grass, and Bard drew himself up to be above the Starling God. "You have broken our rules. I am told You did not roost with the other young males last night, and You were not present for morning praise or for the first lesson."

"Haven't you heard of L'in?"

"I have. She also broke the rules coming to see You, and the Gods dealt with her well. You are Equal and one of the Gods' Chosen – You have been spared and must return now to Your own and continue lessons!"

SL'an's blood felt as though it stopped in His veins. He stared back at Bard. "I can't believe L'in's taking was what Mother wanted."

"I told You, You have been poisoned by accidentally being fostered by the doves and living with other kinds when first fledged. All the more reason to keep You away from the rest, and to keep them away from You until You see."

"What I see is I have a duty here to L'al." SL'an dared raise Himself to match Bard's posture.

"You have duty to Your own kind!" Bard's head shot forward, then stopped. SL'an knew he was exercising all the self-control he could not to peck Him into submission as he would any other young rebel.

"There is much I don't know, but I am sure of this today – all bird kinds are My own."

SL'an was ready when Bard's wings cracked hard, hoping to smack each side of His head. He pulled back and watched the elder slap air instead. "You will ruin everything! The Lore does not lie, and You are to show us how living is to be done. You *must* do what You were created to do!"

"I won't go back with you. If you believe I'm Equal to Mother, then you have no right to tell Me how to live. Mother placed My purpose inside Me, as you said yourself. I will follow what messages open inside, and this is the message I have now. I will stay with L'al and not abandon him as he fears the Gods have."

Bard trembled. "I cannot force You to do what You should know is right. But think carefully on what You are choosing. You are choosing to help one who would even doubt the will of the Gods. This is what happens to a 'great Teller' when he is faced with an action of the Gods that he doesn't like! *This* kind is who You are choosing over Your own."

Bard flapped his wings hard and flew toward the Meeting Tree.

SL'an lowered His body at last and felt the cool, short grass blades surround Him, sinking into their comfort. He realized then that He hadn't eaten either, and although He wasn't sure if there was hunger, He dug his beak into the soil and found a worm. The fisher's words echoed in His mind and He choked. Yes, He was eating a living thing. He wondered for a moment if there would be anyone to miss the worm that had just been part of His breakfast. He wished He could be more like the doves and some of the others who were happy eating only seeds. Were birds no different from Blooders, then?

There were no more redwings at the seed tray now. SL'an watched many other kinds come and go in their place – chickadees, sparrows, blue jays and even a rose-breasted grosbeak with a female close by. Rem perched a distance away with Glee, close together and clearly having an animated discussion. The Sacred Space was teeming with life – but it never felt so empty.

All birds at the seed tray suddenly took to the air, and SL'an saw Mother moving toward it, carrying something with one of Her featherless wings in a way only the Gods could do. She poured more seed into the seed tray space then rested on a large, round stone almost completely surrounded by flowers and humming bees. She stayed as Her birds tentatively returned to partake of what She offered. SL'an felt a pang of rage, then gasped at His own feelings. For a moment, He had hated Her. In the Teller way that L'al had described, He closed His eyes and created a space in the center of His body. He breathed it open, and created strong walls to contain the rage there so He could safely face those feelings and understand them better. He built it like a nest of air, not sure how much time was passing as He worked – it could not be rushed. His mind kept perfecting and poking at the imagined walls inside until it felt ready and good, then He allowed the rage to slip down within that space as His mind followed to face it.

With eyes closed, His inner vision saw the place He had created and the rage waiting there – looking like a swimming mass of algae. It moved about until it coalesced into the image of His Mother. *Mother! How could You provide all You do and then take the life of such a one dedicated to You?*

The form of God Flower only smiled at Him and pushed back the long feathers that draped from Her head, motioning for Him to perch on Her shoulder as He did when only a nestling. He remained rooted to His spot. *I'm angry. I'm lost. I need to know what reason You could have for this! The Gods placed a Blooder among Their own? With male and female so there will be more to come after innocent nestlings and birds who make such small mistakes? L'in's mistake was no worse than any I have made, and she made the mistake because she loved Me as she loved You."*

The feeling of rage swelled suddenly inside SL'an, and the growth of it forced God Flower's form to stretch grotesquely. It expanded and grimaced strangely until the misshapen God pushed against the inner walls SL'an had painstakingly created. The thing that now only resembled His Mother in colors stayed there for a moment, pushing and pulling like waves on the shore. He breathed more air into His inner space and opened it, and Himself, a bit more. Instead of giving the Mother Rage more room to grow, it began to pull back into form again. When it looked whole and almost real once again, She pushed back the long feathers and reached a wing down to SL'an. This time, He hopped onto the wing tip as She pointed to one of the walls that seemed now to be a clear view to the outside of Himself. He could see the swallows dancing for L'in in the sky. Her head tossed back and Her beakless mouth opened, burbling strange, musical sounds before looking back at Him with those Blooder-like eyes and smiling again. There were so many things SL'an never noticed about Mother before, and it was startling. Before, He only knew Her as His beautiful Mother; all about Her was as it should be. And now, He saw only how She was different from Him and how strange She seemed to be.

The wall where Her wing tip pointed seemed to glow with light and dissolve, leaving a gaping hole that She suddenly flew up through, although He knew the Gods could not fly. At first SL'an still held tightly to Her other wing tip with His feet, but the force of the wind against Him – so strong and real even though it could not be – made Him instinctively open His own wings and release the grip. They shot together almost straight into the air – His eyes widened as the specks of swallows grew larger and closer until They were among them. They hovered and Mother's beakless mouth opened and spoke so He could understand for the first time. "We will fly with the swallows for beautiful L'in."

SL'an was about to say He didn't know how, but He saw L'in's gentle face for a moment as clearly as if she was there, and He simply began to swoop, first high up, then dropping down. It was not the oneness of Unified Flight. He didn't lose Himself and feel blissfully emptied, but it was everything He needed.

The rage was understood, faced and gone. With no more use for the space in the center of His body, He released the air that had formed it slowly, and He opened His eyes at last to find Himself truly with the swallows, the only starling and other kind among them, higher in the sky than He could imagine and dancing in celebration of a life that had made a difference, in its quiet way, to so many.

Chapter Fourteen
The Seeker

On the third sun after L'in had gone, SL'an finally convinced L'al to leave the nest. He had eaten nothing the first day, and then a bit the second. Although he still wouldn't look at the young starling and hardly spoke, he did eat some seeds piled there when Hralla's sister Hroo came and reminded him of what he and his L'in had told her not long ago – that the babes still needed care and that there was duty above grief.

"Raising babes is what L'in always wanted, and this is your chance to do something for love of her. She is still in our hearts, and through these babes, she will still live – but only if you live to tend them."

So L'al flew from the nest and SL'an settled on the eggs, feeling the strange roundness below His own under-feathers. They vibrated subtly, and He knew that must have told L'in there was life there. *I am your brother,* He thought to them, hoping somehow they would hear. *I don't look like you, but I am no less your own tail and feather.*

He hoped L'al would go to the seed tray where he might be drawn out by the many birds who cared for him there, but instead the dove flew to the fence rail where he and L'in had spent so much time together looking over the Sacred Space and sharing their thoughts. First he paced slowly back and forth, then a bit faster, then he bobbed his head up and then down low as he sang in his haunting voice, "L'in, my love!" Over and over, "L'in, my love!" He finally exhausted himself and sat there as still as if he was on the nest. SL'an remained on the gently vibrating eggs that seemed to tell Him there would be crying for food soon. In just suns, the eggs would become bird, and then He would need to help L'al feed and care for the new nestlings.

His thoughts were interrupted by the incoming whoo-whoo-whoo of three sets of dove wings as those landed neatly on branches near the nest. "What," the largest bird, clearly an elder, cried out, "are you doing on a dove's nest, starling? Have you commandeered this place? Isn't this Teller L'al's home?"

"I'm only helping," SL'an quickly explained. He had learned from His mentors that as peaceful as dove kind could be, they could also be strong defenders if they must. "L'in has been taken by a Blooder —"

"—Goodness, of course I *know* that. Why else would we be here?" The elder male dove shook his feathers. "Why, by The Featherless Gods, would L'al have a *starling* Helper? This isn't the way things are done. Where is L'al?"

"He is there on the fence rail. He is not feeling fit to raise nestlings alone or to function as Teller—"

"—Clearly not! Why else would there be a *starling* on a dove's eggs? We've come just in time."

The other two doves took SL'an in by stretching their long necks and turning their small heads, first one way, then another. They were much like the elder, but there was something smaller and fresh about them, telling SL'an these were young apprentices of some sort. "Shall we encourage him off the nest, father?" one said, his round, blue-outlined eye staring wide and disbelieving at where SL'an held His post.

"I will not easily be 'encouraged' away, with respect to all of you." SL'an did His best to bob peace in a brooding position, causing the elder to pull his head back and puff his chest out. "Yes, dove. I know some of your ways. L'al and L'in were my first mentors at this place. I owe them much, and helping L'al with the eggs and nestlings to come is my choice."

The elder bobbed tentatively and cocked his head a bit. "Interesting, starling, although a starling mentoring under a dove is unheard of. Why not mentor with your own? What starling parents would allow their nestling to be mentored by another kind? It is unlikely for any of the bird kinds, but especially so for starlings!"

"I'm choosing to be a Teller and a Seeker. While I have mentored with starling elders, I decided there is more I need to learn, and I cannot learn these things from my own flock." *This is the truth now,* SL'an thought.

"But the starling Lore has no Seekers – no Tellers—"

"—I don't have to be what starlings have always been."

"Most unusual!" The dove elder turned his head one way and then another to carefully take in everything, and the two young apprentices enthusiastically did more of the same.

SL'an stood abruptly in the nest to turn the eggs with His beak as He had seen L'al do. "My name is SL'an; may I learn your names?"

"I am Dove Leed. L'al and I were fledged from the same parents, but from different broods."

"L'al's brother!" Suddenly SL'an could see the likeness, and it seemed to soften Dove Leed's abrupt manner.

"These are two of my young who have not yet chosen a One, Libn and Lorn. They are here to be Helpers to L'al when the eggs hatch, which I understand they should in just suns. This will teach them about caring for nestlings and show them the ways of fledging out young ones, and it will be a great help to L'al during this time."

SL'an could see that the female, Libn, was shifting constantly on her branch, looking expectantly at the nest He now occupied.

Leed chuckled. "Soon, young one!" Then he turned again to SL'an. "What you're doing here is deeply admirable, but it's the dove way to have family attend in times of need. In any case, there are things you can't provide that we can once the nestlings arrive." When SL'an opened his beak to protest, Leed fixed him with one eye. "Can you make dove's milk, young starling? We feed our kind with dove's milk – it is not like your kind carrying insects to the nest. You're well-meaning, but that form of helping from you isn't possible. You're not our kind, and you're not family."

SL'an wanted with all of the power in His breast to tell Leed He was as much family to L'al as they were; did He feel even closer to the dove now than His own Mother? He was struck in the breast with sharp regret that actually hurt. He snapped His beak with the pain.

"Is something wrong?"

He made as if to snatch a passing fly. "Nothing."

"I'll fly down to speak with L'al about this arrangement privately."

With that, the elder dove made the short flight to where L'al sat unmoving, not even having noticed the arrival of other doves or activity at his own nest. The two young Helpers stood on their branches, continuing to look at SL'an with great interest, and for awhile all the Starling God could do was stare back at them. *I can't abandon L'al. Even if he has these Helpers, if I leave, it will be as if the Gods have truly abandoned him as he believes.* Like the flick of a wing, He had an idea.

"As I said, I'm trying to learn more about other bird kinds. Certainly it's usual for family to be the Helpers, but perhaps I could assist as well. It really would make no difference if there were two helping or three."

"But you cannot make dove's milk." Libn preened one wing.

"I can do other things. I'm sure feeding isn't the only important part of raising nestlings."

Libn and Lorn looked at each other, and Libn delicately hopped closer to the nest. "May I see the eggs?"

SL'an stood up and aside so she could peer in at the two white eggs. "Would you like to take your turn keeping them warm?"

Libn was nearly settled before the sound of SL'an's words dissolved into air.

"Lorn, why don't you and I take a break then? Let me show you where God Flower sets seed for those who serve Her."

When they approached the ground, the feed tray was vacant. SL'an took the opportunity to rake His beak back and forth to knock seeds to the ground where Lorn automatically landed. "Please eat! I'll be down to join you," the young starling called, raking His beak again to make sure there'd be plenty.

"What I've heard about this Sacred Space is true." Lorn dipped his head reverently and closed his eyes with pleasure at the oily flavor. "This is a place where bird kind has done right and the Gods here reward the faithful."

SL'an felt another pang of pain as L'in's gentle face entered His mind. *Where the Gods reward the faithful...* He forced the thought away and ate some seed by the young dove's side. "L'al is not of the mind to care for nestlings alone right now. It's good that there's help," SL'an ventured.

"We're glad to be here, and although I have not had a One, I know in my breast that it would be a terrible thing to lose that love. The Oneness of L'al and L'in is something even Father and Mother have talked about." Lorn nodded at the memory of stories. "It must be all he can do to live."

"Truth," SL'an said. "This is another good reason for me to stay and help you as well. L'al is not able to do the Telling he should so you know your way around this new Sacred Space. Although most is good here, there are usual dangers, and of course the new Blooder called fisher that took L'in. It would be safest for me to teach you about these things since L'al can't."

"But the fisher took L'in outside the Sacred Space!" Lorn shuddered and widened his eyes so SL'an thought they might pop out of his head.

"Yes, but there are things I know about fisher that will help you and Libn be safe." He walked about in the grass, pretending to look for certain seeds. "I can show you some very good places to find other feed too. I think you'll need me to stay."

"Well, it does make some sense," Lorn said slowly. "I suppose it wouldn't do harm."

"Of course there would be no harm to it at all, Lorn. The life of every bird in the Sacred Space is important, but the Teller gives so much of himself that we need to do all we can to restore L'al's wounds..." His voice trailed off. "Is it possible for a dove who has lost his One to become whole again?"

Lorn finished the seed he was eating and sighed. "I don't know if L'al will ever be the same, but he could heal. I think what we'll find is that he becomes different. Whole? Part? I'm not sure, but most who go through this are deeply changed. Many do pair again, although it's hardly ever with the same intensity of the first One. Some stay alone. Some have died. Father believes if it wasn't for the miracle of nestlings to come, L'al would die." The young apprentice dove looked to where L'al and his own father were still perched closely beside each other on the fence rail. "I think you're right that the most important thing is that these nestlings live. On behalf of Libn and myself, I gratefully accept your help."

SL'an breathed out, not even realizing He had been holding the breath inside for too long.

Finally, it was arranged. Though L'al said very little to the two Helpers, he did seem somehow grateful, and returned to the nest after getting some gravel for his gullet and at least some seeds, although not nearly as much as he would normally take. The two young doves went together to do more of their own feeding while L'al settled in again, SL'an beside him as soon as Leed was gone.

"You have good help from a loving family," SL'an said, "but I'll stay to help as well. I won't abandon you."

During the next few suns, the groups of starlings came through the short grass regularly to feed in service; SL'an watched them move methodically and with the energy of great purpose. He saw Flora looking toward Him at times, but she stayed within the confines of the flock. The hardest was to see the Unified Flight groups coming through the Sacred Space or sometimes appearing like a living cloud in the distance. SL'an closed His eyes and imagined moving among them and losing Himself to the invisible rhythm.

"Do you wish to go back?" Steep appeared beside Him as He wistfully looked after His kind one day.

"Yes, but not now. There's something amiss with the way things work in Bard's flock."

"So the Seeker is coming out in you now," Steep piped with unmasked delight. "You're different from the other starlings somehow – I mean, other than your obvious illusions of grandeur wanting to be both Seeker *and* Teller. But finish what you're also noticing or wondering, SsssL'llllan!"

"How do you think the Blooders came to be?"

"Like everything, they were placed by the wings of the Gods."

"But why?"

"You know as well as I do – we're not given the answers to everything, but certainly the weak of spirit or the faithless have been punished by Blooder teeth."

"Do you think L'in was weak of spirit or deserved to be punished?"

Steep's usually jubilant façade faded. "Not for any reason I can think, although I have heard through listening carefully to the starlings passing through that they feel she broke their rules by going to see you."

"Then it would follow if L'in was punished by the Gods for breaking a starling rule; starlings are favored by the Gods as the Lore says."

Steep pulled his head back and didn't answer for a long while. When he opened his beak to try, SL'an spat, "I do *not* believe it can be true. I'm no better than any of you, and L'in certainly was a truer bird to the Gods than any. There's something wrong."

For the first time, SL'an heard Steep's voice soften. "Then, Seeker, I suppose you have to get to it. This is dangerous territory you place your wings in, friend, but I feel something strange in the air too ever since you came here. You aren't usual, and there is an energy growing in the air we breathe – like a berry on the vine. It's ripening, and when it is ready, there will be either a wonderful feast or poison on the inside."

"Have I brought this thing?" SL'an opened His beak and panted.

"Perhaps *You* have."

SL'an was struck still by the '*You*' that no birds other than L'in, L'al, Bard and Glee had ever spoken.

"Is it true, what Bard whispers to Glee? Are you Equal?"

"Mother is God Flower," SL'an said, feeling half relieved and a bit defeated that this information might become free to everyone in the Sacred Space.

"By the Gods!" Steep's voice squeaked. "I knew it was true!"

"Neither L'al nor Bard feel others are ready to hear this. It's the one thing they *do* agree on," SL'an said.

Steep softened his voice as much as possible again. "I honor my Teller, and I'll honor You. I'm a Seeker, but it's not my duty to share what shouldn't be shared. When You and L'al tell me it's time, that's the only time. For You, Your time to be Seeker has arrived, and what will You find? What will You discover for us?"

"I want answers more than you know, but I can't leave L'al now."

"Perhaps Your Seeking can be done within and just outside the Sacred Space?"

"But what will I learn here that I don't already know?"

"There are some to speak to and learn from that none of us speak to and learn from…" Steep looked to the sky where a small group of swallows were resting together on the taut metal limb, the creaks of their voices carrying enough for SL'an to know they were speaking to each other, but not clearly enough to know what they were saying.

SL'an lowered His own voice. He hoped Steep could understand. "But they think the Gods are Blight!"

"Yes. I told You – You are winging in on dangerous territory, but I think there is no bird kind You should ignore if the truth is to be understood, don't You?"

"I need to think of a way to speak with them where I won't be seen. Is there a leader like Bard or a Teller like L'al that you know of?"

"I know very little of swallow ways, although they live among us. It seems that they discuss and decide things by groups instead of by one. I would recommend You go to that wooden space over there where God Flower – Your Mother – keeps the things She uses to work the soil and keep the grasses short for us. If You can visit there just as the sun is beginning to release, and just as Hralla *begins* the morning praise, it will be light enough to see where You're going, but grey enough so others will be less likely to notice. All others are just stirring in their nests then."

SL'an nodded. "And then if I'm lucky, the morning news will still be in full chorus when I leave. There'll be too much activity for most to pay any attention to Me." SL'an puffed a bit, but then His feathers tightened again. "But will they speak to Me at all?"

Steep's laughter peeled out, making a number of nearby finches stop to stare. "Starling God, they may not accept everything about You, but they already know You're special and have tolerated You before. I think Your chances are good." When SL'an looked confused, Steep continued, "For Love of Flower, You *danced* with them. No bird I know has ever joined the swallows when they've paid honor to a fallen one. I know little about them, but I know if they hadn't seen something interesting about You, they would have driven You down with beak and nail."

Chapter Fifteen

Blight and Rebirth

During the night, SL'an roosted in His usual spot not far from L'al's nest. Libn and Lorn chose a tree close by, huddled together like the nestlings they had just recently been. The young starling envied it; He had always been the only one. *Where do I belong?* The group of starling males would be roosting together now, but He didn't feel He belonged there. Other birds nestled with their brothers and sisters, their Ones or their nestlings.

Of course L'al was alone too.

What's worse, Mother – always having been alone and different, or having what L'al had and losing it? The thought of Mother made Him feel heavy again. He almost couldn't remember what it was like inside the nest, and wished to go back to the way things were then – when He didn't know He was different, when there was no death, no Gods, just things seeming right.

Now nothing was right. *If I hadn't come here, L'in would live.*

If He was Equal to the Gods and like one of Them, He didn't know what the purpose of it was or what He was to do. It was His last thought before the black forced sleep into His mind, and along with it, dreams.

He found Himself surrounded by moist soil. It was warm and rousing, filling Him with a pulsing energy that built gradually until He felt He surely had to stretch his wings to release some of it. When He did, He found He had to break through something hard, but it did crack at last and He pushed up through the soil. He was surrounded by young plants and realized He was one of them. Some of the seeds, like He realized He had just been, were on the top of the ground instead of blanketed by earth, and a sparrow He had seen but didn't know came to grab one and then another, eating happily. SL'an felt a movement as if He was being pulled back down. He was a worm, pushing through with others close by. Curious what the world would look like to a worm, He worked back to the top and saw Hralla moving toward Him with her usual bouncing gait. The initial joy He felt froze with the realization that He was now the perfect meal for His one-time friend, and He retreated quickly back to the soil only to sense the fisher female; the tingling of His feather quills made it clear He was bird again.

He tried to fly but couldn't seem to move. The soil that was protection from Hralla now was a prison! He frantically tried to flap His wings, but there was no chance. The aura was getting stronger – SL'an worked and worked with His wings until the strain was nearly unbearable, but the soil finally began to loosen and move. His head and shoulders fought to the air that He pulled gratefully into His starved lungs, but not without the taste of fisher so thick He could it feel it cling to His tongue. She loomed over Him, grinning and hungry. *I have as much right to eat as you,* she somehow said. Although her mouth didn't move, He recognized the strange voice that was now more clearly female since He heard it again. SL'an had not yet pulled His wings free, and with paralyzing fear, He waited for the Blooder's jaws to end all of His loneliness and confusion.

He shut His eyes tightly, but when nothing happened, He opened them again. The fisher female had turned away and was running in her humping motion toward Mother, who had Her body close to the ground and wings spread forward with L'in sitting calmly before Her. SL'an tried to find His voice, but there was none when He opened His beak. He could only watch as Mother seemed to offer L'in to the fisher, who swallowed the gift whole and gamboled around Her joyfully. Fisher sang in a strange guttural tone, *They are my Gods too! See how They protect me even more!* SL'an saw His Mother reach down to fisher, who climbed Her wings like a tree branch and settled as they folded around her. Smiling, the God others called Flower leaned Her head forward, long feathers falling down around fisher, and bared Her teeth, plunging them into the female's spine.

SL'an jolted awake, heart racing as if He was in a flight for His life, shaking, taking moments to look about and realize He was still in the red-berry tree close to L'al. The sky was not black, yet the new sun had not released. Hralla would begin morning praise soon; it was time to begin seeking the knowledge He must have, although the images from the dream were difficult to ignore.

Without thinking more, the young starling pushed Himself from His roosting place and mostly glided to where some of the swallows made their nests. There was something on one side like the clear boxes on Mother's nest, but one section of where the clear-but-solid material should have been was missing, leaving an even hole. This was how swallows came and went from the structure, and so they could make their own nests inside a space of the Gods.

SL'an flew carefully through and found Himself in a darker area that reminded Him uncomfortably of being in the forest at near black. He shut down His sense of sight and pulled to His aura-sense and hearing. There was the aura of nestlings and droppings, mud warmed by feathered bodies, some kind of acrid bite in the air always known with the things Mother used to keep the grasses short, and even a tinge of earth. What struck SL'an was the lack of moisture in the space – little rain could fall here no matter how strong the storm – the two nests in the space had privileged protection.

"This space was placed by the wings of the Gods and offers your nestlings the best of protection. Still, you think They are a Blight?" SL'an heard a quick stirring after His voice cut the silence.

"Who goes there?"

"The Starling SL'an. Peace. I'm here as a Seeker."

There were more muffled sounds of the nestlings moving fitfully and the parents whispering comforts. "The Dancer? We have no need for Seekers, starling. What need could you possibly have for us? We know what most of bird kinds think of us."

"I'm not here to judge the beliefs of others. I'm here to learn."

"Your dancing was impressive, and we allowed it, but don't think we owe you more."

"Are you bird or aren't you?" SL'an held strong but kept one eye on the open space in the clear box.

"We are swallows."

"But you're also bird. I am bird. The division here is unfortunate and wrong."

The swallow's crackling voice creaked in laughter. "Fine words coming from a starling! How can you speak of unfortunate divisions – of all bird kinds you are the *last* to question our separation from others! *Chosen Ones!*"

In the distance, Hralla's cheery song began its first strains in the gradually lightening sky. SL'an could see the form of the adult swallows in the nest, still covering their young. The male was speaking, leaning over the edge and looking down where the young starling had landed on the dry, hard earth.

SL'an persevered. "Speak with me. I'm not like the others. I am SL'an. I'm not only starling. Something is wrong. Something doesn't make sense, and I'm going to seek the answers to see if things can be made right."

The two adults conferred quietly, and the adults from the other nest flew over to also be part. Finally the original male looked down to SL'an again. "I am Creal. We've decided I'll speak to you. We agree that something is wrong. Something has been wrong for more generations than can be counted. It's been wrong since The Blight came."

"The stories I've heard say that the Gods created bird, and that bird gave the Gods the gift of music in return," SL'an spoke carefully.

"This is not correct, but something The Blight would have birds believe."

SL'an fought the desire to argue. "I'm open to learning. Tell me what you believe."

"What do you suspect already, Dancer?" Creal dropped down from the nest to where SL'an waited. "If you feel there's something wrong, then you've thought about it already."

The young starling felt a little ill, but knew that sharing truth had to go both ways. He remembered how Mother's eyes looked forward, and the dream where She drove Her teeth into the fisher's spine. "Are the Gods Blooders?"

"They are not."

SL'an's entire body relaxed, but tensed again when Creal continued.

"At least Blooders are honest and do what they do for a reason. We're their food and they know this. We know this. It's clear although unpleasant for us. When we see a Blooder, we know what it means. It kills us because it must eat. It needs to provide for its kind. When it doesn't need food, it's no threat."

"As we eat the worm, the insects, or even the seeds," SL'an murmured, thinking how strange it was that a Blooder had explained this very thing to him not long ago.

"Yes. The Blight, however, work nothing like Blooders. They're great evil and great betrayers." Creal's eyes flashed in the quickly rising light.

"But see God Flower! See all She provides even for you!" SL'an's right foot started lifting off the ground to stomp, but He caught it and forced it to return gently against the solid brown soil.

"Dancer, this is the infection of The Blight; they provide with one side and kill with the other. There's no rhyme or reason, and no way to understand it. They are ill, and they spread their illness as they themselves spread." Creal closed his eyes and raised his head, much like Bard had on the peak of the most Sacred Space of the Sacred Space, and began the tale of The Blight.

"Longer ago than the generations can be counted, bird and all other creatures lived here in the water, on the soil and in the air. Some were Blooders and some were not, but there was a harmony and an understanding. The Blight lived in the sky beyond our vision, but they could see below them. They longed for the ground beneath their feet and felt that if only they had the ground and lived with the other creatures, they would be filled. The world is a world of plenty, so all the creatures agreed this new kind could come and live among them.

"Still, these newcomers were not filled. They loved the peaceful ways of the non-Blooders, and so tried to eat berries and seeds and plants like they did. Somehow, living on the ground and foraging with other creatures wasn't enough, so they broke the ground and forced it to grow what and how much they wanted. Still they were not filled. They looked at the ways of the Blooders, eating the flesh of others. They began finding others and consuming their flesh, but somehow hunting like the Blooders wasn't enough, so they clutched certain kinds to them in bondage so they could kill and eat whatever and how much they wanted. Still they were not filled. They thought that the power to take life would be the answer, so they began killing for many reasons that had little to do with living. The more they killed, the more powerful they felt, and they began to imagine it was their right to kill anything they wanted for any reason at any time. Still, this didn't fill them."

Creal sighed and continued. "They looked about at the many kinds of dens and nests different creatures had, and they thought if they had bigger and better nests, and more nests, they would be filled. They began building their nests over every bit of territory – and still do until other creatures are without places to live and food to eat."

"But Gods like Flower provide both food and shelter for us, so this can't be true," SL'an burst out.

"Now she provides. A time will come when she will not. Others provide to some kinds and then kill other kinds for reasons known only to them. They are ill in the mind and cannot be trusted to do what's rational and good."

SL'an fought the lump in His throat. "I'm sorry. Please continue."

"Because they don't belong here, they will never live as we live. They will never fit in, and they will never be filled. They will consume us and this space, and all the spaces around them, until there is no more space to be had, and it will be the end of all things."

There was silence. The cheery notes of Hralla's morning praise repeated, hollow now in SL'an's ears. *"Joy of morning, Come and see! What dear Gods bring you and me!"*

At last, Creal spoke again. "I can see this has upset you, Dancing One. It goes against all you've been told and it's understandable that you will question what I say. If you are a true Seeker, as you say you want to be, fly – leave this place – and see what you will see of these "Gods" out there. Sun by sun you must make up your own mind."

Birds were starting to share morning news. SL'an thanked Creal and left as quickly as He could. At first He was going to return to the red-berry tree and L'al, but a deep, primal fear stirred inside and pushed Him on a racing wing to where the young starlings were joined in the Meeting Tree and finishing their own morning praise. He stayed hidden in deep grass until Diver arrived with Bard to begin practice of Unified Flight. "Bard!" SL'an heard His own call cry out like an injured nestling, and Bard quickly swerved in mid-air toward the sound.

The elder landed and fluffed his feathers. "I'm glad You've come to Your senses and returned."

"I can't stay, but I would like to fly with the others this morning if you will let Me be part."

Bard turned his head and fixed the younger starling with a glare. "Do You think You can come and go as You please?"

SL'an felt as if His legs wouldn't hold Him, and He willed them to stay strong. "My purpose is unfolding, just as you said it would. If I am to lead My kind, then you need to let the path be Mine. I'll fly it the way I must. I need this today."

Bard nodded and joined Diver just as the Pitch Groups were getting ready to launch with the assistants; SL'an joined His. Flora immediately winged in beside Him and whispered fiercely, "What's going on? Why haven't you been with us?"

"I can't tell you now, Flora. I'm sorry."

"I know it has to do with the dove L'in – I know that much, and I know it hurt you to lose her to the Blooder. Mother has told me so."

"I don't want – I can't – talk about it right now."

"Then I will fly close to you, SL'an. You won't give me your words or listen to mine, but we will feel each other in the wind."

They were the last words He heard before the rush of wings as they left the tree in unison, all of the Pitch Groups letting go of everything but the oneness. At first He thought He wouldn't be able to be free, but thoughts and time quickly vanished until there was nothing else once again but starlings moving as a single being. Nothing ever felt so welcome. The only thing He was gently aware of was the heat and sense of Flora as she flew to one side, the rush of air from her wings helping to guide Him.

When the Unified Flight came to an end, the starlings were granted some free time to feed and rest. SL'an felt most of His unease return, but somehow He was able to step back and look at it in the same way as He had the terrible anger at Mother after L'in had been taken. Once He was able to look at it inside Himself, it appeared as something that could be moved and formed – at least, to some degree. He was considering what to do with it when Flora's voice broke through the walls of the little inner room He had formed in His core.

"Are you sleeping?"

The young starling's eyes popped open quickly, but before they did, He was struck by a familiar timbre in her tone. It was like Glee's voice, although still undeveloped in some way. "I'm only resting," SL'an said.

"I think you managed admirably during Unified Flight even though you haven't been with us lately to practice." She dipped her head and caught an insect crawling foolishly close on the branch where they perched.

"Thank you. I could feel you beside me. It helped me stay where I needed to be."

Flora dipped her head again, but this time there was nothing to catch. "Why did you leave? Will you stay now?"

SL'an looked toward Mother's nest and the tree where L'al, Libn and Lorn were taking care of eggs that would become hatchlings any day – perhaps even today. "There are nestlings soon to hatch that will never know the love of the best mother, and it's because of me. I belong by L'al's side to help him."

Flora spoke slowly. "But although this L'in was special to you, she made her own mistake, and what became of her isn't any doing of yours. It was a foolhardy decision to fly so close to the black."

"Flora, is it foolhardy to love others as much as she did? She came to try and see me because of love, and to share news of love. Now there's no more of her beauty. It's been struck away."

"I still say it is not you who is to blame, SL'an. Mother says it is the Blooder who should pay. It is the Blooder's jaws that ended her life."

"She was doing what she needs to do to live," SL'an said, and was filled with a strange sense of peace. When Flora stared at Him strangely, He continued, "The fisher is female... Every part of me wishes L'in would still be alive, but I don't blame the fisher for needing to eat. Because of me, L'in was an easy meal like the worms that come to the air after a rain."

Flora looked at SL'an, never blinking. "You speak as if it was not the Gods' will."

"I don't believe one such as L'in would be punished for an act of love. Other than that, I don't know what to believe anymore."

"If Father hears that he will kill you!" Flora whispered fiercely and pecked at His wing. He drew away quickly, although there wasn't enough force to cause pain.

"Can you tell me you believe that the Great Teacher smashes the nests of the starlings and swallows from His own because He's teaching them how to be strong against all things?" SL'an well remembered how she had flattened into the grass when Bard brought them to watch.

"I didn't, but Father and Mother say this is the way of the Gods and we must be thankful for what they teach us. They are trying to make us more like them so we will be as one kind someday."

"I know." The Starling God looked out to the Sacred Space where groups of starlings and other ground feeders were moving about finishing their meals. They were starting to fly to and fro in even smaller groups than the usual Pitch Groups – sisters and brothers or groups of friends that developed within the greater flock. Suddenly, the knowledge that He could not be part of it all made Him appreciate Flora in a warm rush like the vibration of the taut metal limbs that ran through the air. "Flora, I can't stay, but the moments with you make me feel like I belong somewhere. Thank you."

Before she could answer, He launched from the branch and flew toward the red-berry tree and L'al's nest.

He was shocked at the transformation in His mentor.

Chapter Sixteen
Like the Gods

For a moment, SL'an thought He'd dreamed all of the horrible things – they couldn't be true when L'al stood with his head so high and posture familiar again; there was another dove there with him too that was smaller and finer – L'in? The young starling heard the murmuring of a voice in the back of His mind saying it couldn't be possible, but He shoved it aside and grasped for that moment to the wild hope. He forced His wings to beat with all their strength. She was alive! He would give anything if she were alive!

Everything crumbled when He saw the smaller, finer dove was Libn. "Nestlings!" She cried out as SL'an landed nearby. "Two perfect little ones have hatched this morning. L'al has given them their first meal and all is well!"

SL'an hopped to a lower branch, close enough to peer in at the nestlings mostly covered by Libn's soft feathers. He tried to look cheerful, but the disappointment gripped His heart with the clutch of talons. "Male or female?" His voice creaked a bit like the swallows', causing L'al to tilt his own head knowingly.

"One of each. I have hopes that my little female will take the name of Lin when she fledges." The Teller's eyes were still pained, but there was the light of purpose there too.

SL'an had never seen nestlings fresh from the egg, and as if reading His mind, Libn stood quickly to let Him have a better look. They were featherless, squirming with the discomfort from the rush of air, eyes still sealed closed and unknowing to all except the subtle hum Lorn made when he winged in at almost the same time. The two clumsy, small heads craned upward with open beaks while Lorn took his own turn providing dove's milk for the hatchlings. SL'an reached out and nibbled His mentor's cheek. "I'm glad this has brought light into you again."

"I wouldn't have believed it," L'al pulled his head back and squinted his eyes, "yet in the nest is my reason for living. I don't know how I will feel tomorrow because L'in is not here with me to have what she always wanted for so long. I don't know how I will feel tonight when the black falls and everything's still – but I know that I feel love now. I will take it for what it is and when it is."

"Thanks to the Gods," Lorn cooed softly.

L'al tapped one foot quickly. "I don't know if I am ready to say thanks to the Gods. I still accept this moment for what it is."

Libn was loath to leave the nestlings, but L'al moved with the obvious intention of taking over. "Thanks to you," L'al bobbed before fluffing and settling on the naked ones.

Hroo asked that she be allowed to make the announcement, and because there was a renewed light so much like when she received Gift, it seemed a logical choice. Her voice wasn't as practiced and sweet as her sister's, but there was true joy in the tones that was infectious throughout the Sacred Space. There was an almost palpable relief that the Gods, although they had taken something precious, had done something else to make up for the loss once again. While Hroo sang, the swallows lined up along one of the taut metal limbs. SL'an couldn't help but notice that Creal seemed to watch Him. Although every other bird quieted for the announcement, SL'an could hear the distant creakings of the swallows' voices as they shared thoughts He couldn't quite make out. *Are you thinking we are so easily fooled? So easily satisfied by such trades?* He glanced quickly up at the line of them there and admitted He was thinking the same thing.

When the black began to fall, L'al was back on the nest; with the sun's leaving, the light in the dove's eyes also faded as he had foreseen. He looked slumped and defeated once again, losing his voice and his interest. SL'an nudged him before going to His own nearby spot for the night. "Tomorrow, the hunger cries of your nestlings will stir you again." L'al didn't answer, but squeezed his eyes shut tightly.

The young starling was preparing for His own slumber when He saw Flora land nearby, flicking her wings to catch His attention. So close to black! He flew to her without another thought.

"SL'an, my mother has sent me with a message. She said I am to meet you here and lead you to a place tomorrow – where the Gods make Their travels. There is a place where the path of the Gods turns sharply, marked by a very large stone and a dead tree on the side. I am to meet you just as the mountains are releasing the sun and take you there. Mother has shown me the way so I may guide you."

"Why?" SL'an looked around quickly at the ever-darkening sky. "Never mind telling me why. Fly back to safety. The last bird who tried to bring me a message so close to black died for it."

Flora seemed to fluff larger, but not with anger. "I will not die tonight! And I couldn't answer your question anyway. What I told you is all I know."

The rush of her wings carrying her away blew across SL'an's own feathers. He was certain that questioning would keep Him awake, but once settled near L'al, it was only a moment before He closed His eyes and opened them to find morning praise had already begun.

He blinked with disbelief, but was glad there would be no waiting and worrying. He would know what Glee wanted to show Him soon.

Flora was already nearby, clearly awake longer than SL'an had been. "Follow me," she called, and flew immediately, straight and true, toward the forest where L'in had lost her life. Her movements were energetic and full of purpose. SL'an closed His eyes and thought He could feel the strong energy pouring from her.

They flew above the treetops in the crisp morning air that had breathed moistness over everything. When the sun was released completely, it would take the cool moisture away, but for now it freshened them both. The world around them was still grey, but there was a golden promise beneath it that would spread soon.

The tree canopy was shadowy green and continuous below them, flooding by quickly until SL'an thought He could see a darker line twisting through. Was that the path of the Gods? Flora's wing beats were less frequent, and the Starling God followed her lead, drifting lower until they came to rest on a tree that was dying, the bare limb they chose giving a complete view of what surely was of the Gods. SL'an breathed in with wonder as He saw it. There was a path that led to His Mother's nest, but it was gravel, and while the grass and scattered trees and shrubs didn't grow on it, it couldn't rival what He witnessed now. SL'an knew a growing tree could split a great rock, sending roots within tiny cracks and forcing them further apart. L'al had shown Him this. Birds chose to sleep among the trees because of their great power. Despite this great power, the forest here of both old and young trees grew obediently to the edge of the Gods' path, then stopped completely. Nothing grew within the path – not a sapling tried to conquer it. The trees began to grow again on the other side as if they had always been there, knowing they couldn't trespass further. The forest's thickness spread everywhere His eyes could see except on that path.

He turned with wide eyes to Flora. "The trees obey and don't grow there."

She turned her head to the left. "There are some that try to reach over the paths. The Gods tolerate it in some places, I'm told, but look to those near us that have been so foolish."

When SL'an followed her gaze, He saw broken branches on the path's side, the trees above with white flesh showing where the limbs had been severed. He felt a strange twinge inside His own wings looking at the exposed wounds, the trees seeming frozen in pain of some kind. He looked up at the tree where they alighted. "Is that what happened to this one? Do you suppose it tried to go where the Gods didn't want it to be?"

"I don't know," Flora mused. "This one has been dying for a very long time, it seems."

They perched together for some moments while both pondered the dying tree. "This isn't far from where L'in was lost," SL'an said quietly.

"I know."

"Do you know anything more about why Glee wanted me here?"

"I don't, but she was very excited about whatever it is. There was a bright light in her eyes! I think it must be important that I bring you here." She seemed fluffed up again, with a gentle light in her own eyes.

SL'an saw a robin fly in the air across the Gods' path and thought of something Bard had told Him. "Your father said that one spring the snows stayed longer than usual, and that when robins returned from their Winter Stay, they had to gather in places like these, hoping for salvation. He said the Gods killed them for being in Their paths – because they aren't the Chosen Ones."

Flora shuddered. "I am no older than you, of course, but I've heard the story as part of the teachings. The paths of the Gods are dangerous places." As if on cue, a strange, metal creature roared along, the wind from its speed making the closest leaves wave. A few moments later, another followed. "Sometimes the Gods move rapidly with these things, and if one of Their birds is in the path, They will spare them. Most of the time, though, They will not."

They had a similar choking sense as from what Mother used to keep the grasses short. SL'an had seen a thing like this large, fast roaring beast next to Mother's nest, and sometimes She did disappear inside it and it moved away. Still, He'd never seen Hers move so fast or growl so angrily. "Flora, do you think God Flower would strike down those in Her path?"

He never heard Flora's answer because Cleaners began circling the sky just above them. The largest one landed, shiny and black, on one of the wounded limbs. "Strange!" Flora quickly scratched her beak and shook her head. "There is nothing here for them to clean."

Before SL'an could comment, Flora took off and landed near the much larger Cleaner. His crow's feathers were nearly gleaming – the young starling could imagine the luster they would have when the sun released. He heard Flora's clear tones with the beginning of her mother's engaging timbre: "There's nothing here to clean now. You must be mistaken."

The Cleaner gave Flora a sidelong look. "Young one, there's no mistake. I am here on agreement."

"What does she want, Jal?" Another Cleaner rasped from nearby. Jal gave his large, black feathers a hefty shrug and turned to Flora. "There'll be answers to your questions soon enough. What I do need you to know is that you and your friend should only watch, and trust that everything that will happen here is in agreement. It's no mistake."

Flora flew back to the dying tree, eyes narrowed. "I am so tired of being told to do things without being told why!"

"I heard what Cleaner Jal said," SL'an sighed.

A loud rumble came from the distance, causing Jal and the other Cleaners to rasp excitedly. "Right on time! Right on time!"

"Brothers and Sisters, the agreement has been kept on our end." Jal gave a throaty laugh.

It was that moment when Glee came fluttering from between the trees as if trying to stay aloft. Her wings flailed and she fell to the smooth ground of the Gods' path, screeching in fear. "Mother!" Flora cried, but Glee didn't respond. Her eyes were wide with terror, and she hopped and furiously flapped as if trying to rise again, but something seemed to hold her down. "SL'an! She is injured! Mother! You must move out of the path!"

The rumbling noise quickly grew louder. SL'an saw the fisher female moving to the edge of the path, close to where Glee struggled. Glee saw her too, and wailed. "It is over! I cannot fly and it is over!"

"Mother, you *must* move now! SL'an, we have to help her." Flora's eyes were wild.

I am the Starling God, He thought quickly. *You couldn't help L'in but now is Your chance to do things differently.* He rushed down to where the fisher was stepping onto the path and beat His wings into her face. She lunged for Him, but He darted out of the way only to bludgeon her once again.

"You again," she huffed. "This one will die no matter what you do. Let me put a quick end to this. If it's not mine, it will be another's stomach she fills." SL'an slapped His wings at her again, trying to block her advance. "I'm quite hungry and have room today for two," she growled, and lunged upward, catching His wing with her teeth.

He felt a pinprick as the grasp of her fangs slid off – she hadn't had a complete grip that time.

"SL'an, *let it be!*" Glee's voice was strained. "Let the Blooder come!"

The fisher eyed her definite prey and decided to grab at the sure thing first. She ran with the strange humping motion of her kind fully into the path, pushing past SL'an's violent attacks toward Glee, who flopped toward the other path side. As she nearly reached her goal, Glee suddenly flew up and into the air to the safety of a nearby limb. Stunned, the fisher stopped only in time to get a glimpse of the roaring thing that was upon her. She knew nothing but bright light, and then nothing at all.

The roar of the enormous thing lessened as it continued out of sight down the twisting path. When it was only a hum in the distance, the near silence remained unbroken for what seemed a very long time. Glee sat on her branch, breathing heavily, SL'an and Flora unable to move as they looked at the fisher female with parts of her inner body exposed and not recognizable anymore. The Cleaners were preening, then broke the stillness by swooping down one at a time around what had once been alive.

"Stay sharp!" Jal landed and looked up and down the path of the Gods with a practiced calm. As they began picking at the fresh kill, SL'an felt sick. He had almost shared the fisher's fate, but became aware of the thing bearing down on them at the last moment, winging to the left just in time. He didn't see the fisher's end, but heard the thud. It was a sound He knew would stay in His brain like the lifeless image of L'in. Together, the two would share a special and strange place in His memory.

Glee finally joined Flora and SL'an on the greying branch, seeming to have no injury at all. "It is done." She ruffled her feathers and smoothed them quickly again. "The Blooder that caused you pain has paid."

The idea of what might have happened started to form in His mind, but He rejected it quickly. "Your wing isn't broken?"

Flora broke in. "What happened here? You couldn't fly and I was certain the Blooder would have you; now I am so happy you are here alive – but I don't understand."

"I am fine, Daughter. I worked very hard to be sure the Blooder would believe I was an easy meal, and led it here where the Cleaners told me one of the large metal things always comes at this same time each sun."

Jal and his Cleaners winged away, slowly and unconcerned, when another small metal thing moved along the path. They balanced shakily on some small branches and dropped down again as soon as the way was clear once again. Glee looked to SL'an where He watched what was the fisher female get picked apart, bit by bit, by the Cleaners' practiced work. Flora followed her mother's gaze. "This was a great risk. Why did you do it? How could Father agree to have your life in danger this way?"

Glee preened. "Bard knows nothing of this. It was a decision I made alone, and one he will never know about."

"But Father is our Secret Keeper. He said it was the Gods' will that L'in be taken for breaking our rules. Why would you betray your own One?"

A strange calm seemed to possess Glee; her eyes fixed on SL'an. "I did this for you. The thing that caused you pain is gone."

Flora's voice dropped. "Why would you do such a thing for him?"

"I have my reasons, and they are good ones. You did well for me and for SL'an too, Flora. You trusted me and did as I asked you. You need to leave now so I may speak with SL'an alone." When Glee saw her daughter draw herself up, she dropped her voice as well. "Flora, do not question me. I am your mother, and I am telling you to go – and speak nothing of this to anyone. Prove to me you deserve the trust I have given you today."

Flora cast a bewildered look at SL'an, but flew quickly back toward the Sacred Space and the Meeting Tree.

Glee's body nearly melted into a puddle against the branch, like a fledgling begging for food, the moment Flora was gone. "I hope You are pleased!"

When SL'an couldn't find His voice, Glee crouched down even further, vibrating her wings quickly in a humming flutter. He could feel her desperation and wild need, but what did she want from Him? He finally found some halting words. "I'm sorry – I don't know what to be. I don't know what to think of this – I don't understand why you would do this for Me."

"This Blooder caused You such pain and it caused You to leave us. I have shown You and the rest of the Gods I will do anything for You. Now things have been made even and You can return to us and to Your purpose!"

The sense of blood and death was rising clearly from the path, nearly choking SL'an although He tried to ignore it. "We're not Blooders, and still you have killed like a Blooder – but not for the need to eat."

"But it was for good reason. There is no better reason than love! I am Bard's One now, but it is my destiny to be the One of the greatest of starlings. Until You came, Bard was the great Secret Keeper of our kind, but now You are here."

Everything around SL'an seemed to slow down in time, and He could hear every sound exposed and drawn out. The leaves roared from the wind forced between them each time a metal thing passed; the wings of the Cleaners beat rhythmically to carry them out of harm's way; the nauseating wet thump of the fisher's body being pressed once again against the dark path assaulted him over and over again. He began to shiver from the pressure of so many sounds entering so vividly at once.

"SL'an?" The rich timbre in Glee's voice was lost as her throat became so tight she nearly squeaked. "I know You will not be ready for a One until You have reached another spring, but when that time comes, I will offer myself to You and help bring the Gods and Their Chosen Ones together at last! Soon they will all know who You are, and I want to make my feelings known now—"

"—But you're the One of another!"

"But we are like the Gods this way. We can make a better match if we are moved to do so. It would be the greatest honor of my life if I would be Your One – then there will never need be another. You will teach me how to be like the Gods, and I will in turn help You teach the others."

SL'an shot a quick look at the fisher's devastated remains once more, and thought of the swallows' tale. *I think you have already proven yourself more like the Gods than you know.*

Chapter Seventeen

Purpose

SL'an chose to fly back to the Sacred Space alone since thankfully Glee said it would be wise to keep others from wondering where they had been together and why. Flora had already returned, morning news was over, and birds were scattered about in a wide range of business. Although starlings did stay mainly in their groupings, it wasn't completely uncommon for a stray bird or few to take a brief sojourn at times. Bard and the elders only worried about it if there seemed to be a mixing of the young ones with other kinds.

"You are the closest to the dove Teller. Would You share with him that the Blooder that took the life of his One has been killed in the path of the Gods?" Glee had asked SL'an before He flew desperately away. *"Say only that I watched it happen and told You about it. He will surely want the news shared as soon as possible, and will take great pleasure in it! I know the Gods inspired me to this plan – imagine how much more birds will praise Them for punishing such a vile creature."*

SL'an couldn't explain what had changed inside. He was certain He would have agreed that the fisher female was a vile creature the night L'in was taken, or even in the first suns that followed. Now there was fear in the memory of her hunger and strength, but besides that there was only another aching sadness. He thought of the unborn waiting in her belly, and of the male that would now be alone out there with no other of his kind. They didn't seem to spend time together after joining as many of the birds, but still, the male would be completely alone. SL'an could, on some level, understand how that felt. *You should still be glad for the lives of the others that she is gone and there will be no more to grow and take her place,* SL'an thought, but it was banished by what He knew. He knew that once settled in the forest, she and her kind would not venture often, if at all, to kill around the Sacred Space. She would have only come if no food could be found within her trees. If any ventured in her territory, as L'in had unwittingly done and Glee did with forethought and menace, she would hunt accordingly. He couldn't hate her and wished the morning could be undone.

Since it couldn't be undone, He returned to L'al's nest where the three doves were busy attending to the nestlings. They already looked stronger than the day before, and clamored for the dove's milk that each adult brought. With three taking shifts, there was plenty of time for each adult to feed as well and take breaks, so SL'an found His mentor sitting among the flowers where he often went to be alone and to let his mind accept inspiration from the Gods.

"Young one!" L'al cocked his head and ruffled his feathers a bit.

"I'm sorry to bother you here – I know this is a place where you wish to be alone, but I have news you'll want first, and if you're feeling fit to be Teller, I would like to know what we should do next."

L'al raised his head at alert. "Share."

"The fisher female was taken in the path of the Gods." SL'an halted the words poised to come next. He was going to only say that Glee had witnessed the death, and that the Cleaners were taking care of things as they spoke, but even though it was the truth, it was missing so much it seemed like a lie the young starling couldn't bring Himself to offer.

L'al's eyes seemed to churn first with delight, then pain, then doubt. "How do You know this?"

"I was there, and I saw it happen, but Glee and her daughter Flora were also there. Glee wishes the others to think she was alone and the only one to see."

There must have been something in SL'an's tone, or maybe the shaking He felt inside was somehow making its way to the outside. L'al walked wordlessly deeper into the lily fronds with the young

136

starling close behind. They were cupped in green from above and on all sides, with warm bark chips under their feet. L'al lowered his voice. "What would be the purpose of hiding the truth?"

It seemed the place did clear a bird's mind and give up answers, because SL'an suddenly felt very sure telling L'al everything was important. He shared each detail, hearing all of it out loud for the first time as if it was something that didn't happen to Him, but was instead one of the bits of Lore. There was so much more He could see about it this way, when it didn't belong to Him. It was clear that it was a killing that should not have happened. When He finished the story, He was emptied and exhausted. "I went one morning to talk to the swallows; they said the Gods aren't right in Their thinking, and that They kill for reasons other than needing to eat. Are the swallows telling the truth? Do you know?"

"Others don't talk to swallows because they only have poison to share. That is what I've always been told and all I can know." L'al paced as much as he could in the tiny space between lily fronds. "After what happened to my L'in, though, I have to admit I've questioned...I have questioned. Why would the Gods take her when we've done everything we could see as right? We have worshipped and listened and tried our best. But could this be the Gods' way of making things better? Did They not realize how badly I would suffer without my One, and is taking the Blooder the way to make things right? Do the Gods make mistakes? Is it possible They don't know everything? After all, You are here, and there is much that You don't know yet."

"From all you've learned as a Teller, do you think the Gods would allow a life to be taken for a reason other than for food?"

L'al stopped walking abruptly. "The Blooder is now food for the Cleaners. The killing was for food."

"But it only happened that way because they were the ones who could tell Glee when the large metal thing comes. They were only there because they know the Gods' paths better than any other kind. The intent was to kill for – for—" SL'an searched, but there was no word to describe what had been done and why. "—Glee made sure the fisher would die because she thought it would please Me. She thought taking that life in return for L'in's would make My pain leave, and that I might remember that and take her someday as My One."

SL'an looked wide-eyed at the dove. "Has knowing the fisher is gone made *your* pain go away?"

"No. My L'in is not here with me raising the babes."

"It's done nothing for My pain either – except to make something heavier in My feathers and breast. Do you think the Gods would kill in such a way that would feel so wrong?"

SL'an waited for His mentor to answer. Bees flew by and the familiar vibration of a hummingbird massaged the air briefly, and then zipped away. L'al settled close to the brown, warm bits below him and closed his eyes. "I don't know."

"I think there has never been anything more important for a Seeker than to try and discover this answer. Are the Gods what the swallows say? If so, is it something starlings or any bird kind want to become?" SL'an thought of Mother's bubbling sounds, so light and happy and beautiful, Her long feathers falling around Him as He would sit on Her shoulder, the feathers fresh and feeling softer than any bird feather He had since known. *I hope You don't feel I am betraying You, Mother*, He thought sadly.

As if reading His mind, L'al brightened a bit. "Flower has never harmed a one that I've seen. Even when Blooders come here rarely, if She sees, She frightens them, but has never hurt or killed any. I think the swallows must be wrong, and I think Glee is the one thinking and acting wrongly on her own."

"I want you to be right," the young starling sighed, "but I have to take wing outside of this Sacred Space to see what other Gods are doing. We want the truth to be what we want it to be, and it may end up being so. Until I've followed what is pushing inside Me and found answers, I won't feel things are certain."

When the dove looked deflated, SL'an bobbed. "I know I said I would stay with you, but I promise I am not abandoning you, L'al! I will be the Seeker I am meant to be and come back to you with the answers. Family is taking good care of you and the nestlings now. I know you're safe. Continue to live for them and find what joy you can in their lives."

"If L'in heard You speaking of leaving, young one, she would be furious. It's dangerous for a bird to travel alone. The suns are still long, but they're starting to be pulled back behind the mountains to the black sooner already. You are starling. You'll be getting Your white speckles and will be easier for Blooders to see."

"There must be other starling flocks elsewhere?" SL'an had always thought only of Bard's flock, but then again, the Secret Keeper had mentioned that the smaller flock would group with still others, and become huge in the air of Unified Flight. So this must mean others!

"There are of course others, but You don't belong to their flocks, and also have to be careful with this. You're starling, but You are one of Bard's starlings. Some may have heard of him and some may not, but the fact will remain that You will be a young male from the outside. Elders of unknown flocks may not welcome You." L'al was sounding so much like the advisor He had known before that SL'an had to hide His rush of happiness.

"I'll be as careful as I can be, but I know this must be done."

The two of them nestled together for a while, letting the peace of the flowers flow over them while they were still together. After a time, there was one more bit that SL'an knew He had to share. "There's something about the fisher female I knew but felt it wasn't time yet to tell you before."

L'al's eyes widened again.

"On the night she took L'in, she said that the Gods placed her there along with a male she didn't know."

"It must be a lie!" L'al snapped his beak.

"I believe in My breast it isn't. She came to the Sacred Space and took Hroo's nestlings because she didn't know the area here and was afraid and hungry."

L'al's voice broke. *"Why would the Gods do such a thing?"*

"I don't know, but I hope wherever I go, I'll find the answer to that too."

SL'an knew He had to share the details of the fisher then, but the facts set L'al back to despair. He flew to the nest and looked over the two young ones from a nearby branch. For the rest of the day, he only sat and stared at the gaping-mouthed babes between shutting his eyes and sleeping, while, thankfully, Libn and Lorn continued to feed and warm them.

Since the Teller was unable to function again, at least for a while, SL'an had to call SLee over and ask him to announce the ending of the fisher's life in the path of the Gods. Not a bird questioned how it happened, but the skies within the Sacred Space rang with rejoicing.

Chapter Eighteen
Another Beginning

The next sun came, and as soon as it had, SL'an saw Steep's bright yellow body snapped with black darting toward Him, almost like a minute sun himself. The starling had just left L'al's tree and was probing for breakfast in the short grasses. A rocky structure was nearby with lilies at the base, nodding their heads gracefully in the breeze. L'in had told her young charge that God Flower, Mother, created this thing and made the flowers grow around it, as was fitting for Her namesake. Her own wings had placed this here and brought life forth around it.

Steep landed spritely on one of the lily stems, hanging on tight and swaying his body along with the motion of the plant to keep his balance. "I understand You'll be Seeking farther out!"

SL'an looked at the little goldfinch and shook His head, bemused. "How do you know everyone's business?"

"It's a Seeker's job to know everyone's business, as You have to realize if You're going to do this right."

SL'an found an excellent grub and savored it.

"So where will You go?" A stronger breeze blew through and wagged the lily stem so hard that Steep was forced to let go and land on the ground. He stayed for a moment, hopped a bit, flew in a rush to the top of the stones, then returned to the ground again, almost without giving his feet time to have touched the stones, still cool from evening.

"Can't you decide where to be?" SL'an laughed, cocking His head to one side and studying the Seeker before lowering it to search for more food.

"Oh, You think it's all fine to spend so much time on the ground, but not my kind! I might grab a seed or two that's fallen somewhere, but the ground is no safe place as far as I'm concerned. Most of the Blooders seem to find us easy pickings there."

The starling sighed. "Would it make you feel safer if we went to a tree to talk?"

"Only if You've had enough to eat!" Steep chirped it so loudly that there was no question it was the right answer.

Well, you have clearly eaten enough already, but I really could eat more! SL'an thought grudgingly, then realized He didn't know when He would see His spunky friend again – and He could use another's thoughts. Where was He going to go? He had no idea.

Steep led the way to a poplar tree growing within a line of others along the back edge of the Sacred Space. Instead of grass or ground, they seemed lodged in a row of stones much larger than the ones Mother used to create Her lily-circled structure. A few other trees grew among them, one of them the same that SL'an spent His first stormy night roosting in. He never noticed how the trees were growing out of the lined piles of rocks before, but it seemed obvious now after witnessing the path of the Gods and seeing how the trees there came to a sudden stop, edged on both sides only by grasses. "This is like the reverse of the Gods' path where the fisher lost her life," SL'an observed. "Instead of a line where the trees must not be, this is a line where they must be."

Steep settled, as much as the bird could settle, next to the Starling God. "Good eye! I don't know what that means, but we often don't know what's important until later. As a Seeker, You'll notice things that others may not, keep those things tucked like some birds keep pebbles and seed in their crops, and sometimes the pieces mean more when the bits have had the chance to grind around together."

"Steep, I think you've been Seeking much longer than I have."

"For the turning of five warm seasons to cold seasons!"

SL'an was shocked. *But he looks so young!* He decided to share this with the goldfinch, who flapped his wings and chirruped loudly with merriment. "And why don't you have a One or nestlings?" It burst from the starling's beak at the same time He realized there could be a painful past similar to L'al's.

"A fair question I don't mind answering to a Seeker and an Equal! When a bird chooses to be Seeker, there isn't time to take a One or to join and raise nestlings together. It must be one way or the other. There are a few who try doing it all, but they really aren't Seekers in the true sense of the word. They are nosy, yes, but not really Seekers. If I'm Seeking, I must observe everything around me and not be worried about helping to build a nest or running back and forth to feed nestlings."

"Aren't you lonely?" SL'an felt a bit of terror. He never thought about what being a Seeker meant or what He would give up. He hadn't thought of it because He hadn't known. Why hadn't L'al and L'in told Him when He made the choice of vocation?

"I'm too busy to be lonely. Anyway, we can't *all* join and raise young! Imagine how many of us there would be! If I had not chosen Seeker, I wouldn't be here now to help You. I would be at this moment busy with a One, bringing her bits so she could build a nest for eggs. Then there would be the endless rushing back and forth to bring her food, and then rushing back and forth to bring them all food – ugh!" The small bird shuddered. "I know, I know, a miracle and all of that! Not for me!"

SL'an laughed with surprise. He never knew what Steep was going to say, and whatever he did say was usually a way of looking at things that the Starling God had never heard before.

"You make it sound like you only begin a brood this late in the Turn," SL'an suddenly realized aloud.

"First of all, let me say it again! No brooding for me! Not now and not ever! But yes, I meant what I said; our kind begins now when the suns are past their longest."

This wasn't even touching on what SL'an had hoped to discuss, but curiosity kept bubbling like stream waters over rocks. "But I've seen others of your kind since I came here early on – singing songs to each other and flirting."

"Young Seeker-Equal…SeEqual." Steep playfully bounced about

with the discovery of a new nickname. "I wouldn't want what they do, but I do respect the unique joy of love others of my kind have. Think of it. There isn't a rush of meeting and joining and getting on with the work of nesting. No! There are suns after suns of knowing each other and loving each other and playing before the drudgery! Then there is only one brood each Turn. As I said, if we didn't do things thoughtfully like this, how many of us would there be!"

Suddenly Steep stopped very still and looked sharply at the starling. "SeEqual, You have managed to distract me completely from my original topic. I heard You are planning to Seek farther out and I want to know where You plan to go."

SL'an said, "I have no idea where to go. I suppose I could just fly in any direction and I'd see and learn wherever I land."

"That You would." The goldfinch jumped quickly from the branch they were on to another just above, and leaned his body forward to peer down at his friend. "But I feel You should travel first toward the cooler lands – just for a sun or two – and then wing toward where the sun releases. I have never been there, but others who migrate from those spaces speak of a Great Undrinkable Water that goes on further than a bird can see and further than most can fly."

SL'an felt a prickling in His skin, and for a moment saw a vision of strange, roaring blue waters. In it, there were shapes that curled out of them and melted back again; He thought they were odd, large bubbles rising up, but as they lifted up again in the vision, they seemed to be alive. If only He could look closer! He closed off everything around Him for a moment to focus, and it was as if He was drifting just above the water. His heart leaped when something broke the water like an enormous bullet, hovered for a moment, and then fell back toward the blue with an almost deafening splash. As it fell, the young starling saw a giant eye regarding Him. Familiar. Yes! It was the eye He had seen before that seemed like a dream! There was something wise and playful in the gaze that wrapped Him in confidence. "Whale."

"Yes!" Steep squealed. "They speak of creatures that live in this Undrinkable Water called whales. There are unimaginable others living there too, although I don't know how they can survive in something others can't even drink – but the whales are special somehow."

"They are *very* big." SL'an breathed in deeply with the memory.

"I've never seen one, but I've been told this," Steep piped. "Have You spoken with one who has seen the whales?"

"No."

"How would You know about their size then, or what they are called?"

"I don't know. You were talking about the water, and it was as if I could see it. Then I saw them curling and jumping out of the water. It was as if I was really there for a moment."

The goldfinch became still and softened his voice again. "I forget sometimes, even when I think I never will, that You are different. And the kind? How did You know what to call the kind?"

SL'an didn't know how to answer that at first, but then He remembered the giant, gentle, almost laughing eye staring into His own. "I don't know how, but I think he told Me."

"He?"

"Yes. The whale. He never spoke a word in My vision, but I understood just the same." The two birds preened for a long time, absorbing what had happened, until SL'an finally broke the silence. "I'm not so different from you. I only had the vision because you somehow knew where I should travel first. That instinct of yours must be no different than My own."

"Perhaps not, SeEqual… When will You leave?"

"Now."

"That's the way! Is there anyone You want me to tell? You'll be missed, especially by Bard and his elders. They've been letting You be, but they've been watching You closely, make no mistake about it."

"Tell no one," SL'an spoke slowly. "Everyone who should know already knows."

"I'll honor it!"

He thought of saying goodbye to His mentor, but then thought better of it. L'al already knew what He planned, and another goodbye was probably something the dove Teller couldn't take.

"I'm not certain how long I'll be gone." SL'an looked around at the Sacred Space and felt the weight of His feathers.

"If You go all the way to the Undrinkable Water and stop to do proper Seeking, I don't think I'll see You again until the snows leave and the flowers start to bloom again."

"So long!"

"It won't seem as bad if You keep busy, and You won't have much choice but to do that," Steep reasoned. "I wish You cover, good food, and freedom from Blooders, bold SeEqual!"

"I appreciate that." SL'an lifted His head and squinted His eyes. "And please watch over L'al as you can."

"I will." With that, Steep took wing and his own post at the seed area for smaller birds, taking some food in his beak and looking into the clear box on Flower's nest's side as he did.

SL'an took one more look around at everything familiar – birds He knew by song or by sight, and some He had grown to know more than that. They flew in and out of the Sacred Space. Nothing would change for them, and they had no idea things would be so different for Him. The starlings flew in with a wing-rush and began trolling the short grass. Bard and Glee weren't there yet, but Flora was among them. He saw her look His way just as He made the leap from the branch and into the air.

The only times He had left the greater Sacred Space were when He followed the fisher to try and save L'in, and when He had gone with Flora to unknowingly watch a killing that should not have happened. *Nothing good came of the times I left here before. This must be different*, He thought fiercely. He winged past the boundary and was suddenly in new territory; although He had seen it before from a distance, even the air around His feathers felt strange. It was stranger still when all He had ever seen by eye faded away.

Chapter Nineteen

No Place Like Here

For a time, everything looked similar to the Sacred Space He just left. The Gods' nests were scattered about with ample room between them, separated by short grasses closest to where They lived, and then mostly taller grasses and trees beyond. However, the nests varied in style as they did with bird kinds. Some were ramshackle and loose like a dove's nest, while others seemed tightly woven. There were variations of colors and sizes. *Few have the true beauty of Mother's nest and Sacred Space,* SL'an thought proudly. Many of the Spaces He passed by had very few, if any, flowers. Some had feeding places for the Gods' own birds and some had none He could see. He took it all in as He winged in the direction of the cooler lands, although He didn't stop long. At most, He rested in a tree at the edge of a given Space and watched from a distance.

When His stomach rumbled, He longed to go to short grasses to look for insects and grubs, but He didn't know if it would be wise. Birds of other Sacred Spaces wouldn't know Him, and He had no flock to claim and protect Him if something went wrong. Instead, He made do by snatching insects climbing on the trees that offered Him safe places to rest and watch.

One such tree rested quite close to one of the Gods' paths. After SL'an ate what He could find, He settled in and watched as loud things roared by in one direction or another with shadowy images of one or more of the Gods inside. *They must use these paths to get to places that are important to Them,* SL'an mused silently. *If I fly along one of the paths that moves toward the cooler lands, I might see more of what the Gods are really about.*

When He traveled once more, He followed the path nearest His resting tree; it didn't lead to the cooler lands directly, but wound this way and that, breaking off into other, smaller paths at times, but all of those leading in the wrong direction. Finally, just as He was questioning His idea, the path abruptly sprouted in two. *These paths are like tree branches, except instead of the next shoots being smaller than the parent branch, the smaller branch leads to the larger one,* He marveled. This had to be a good sign. From what He had been told, bodies of water did the same thing – which would perhaps lead to the largest water of all – the endless, Undrinkable Water. SL'an wasn't certain of the exact line of water travel, but He felt fairly sure that smaller did lead to larger. This was the way to go!

One of the new, larger paths led almost directly toward the cooler lands, so the starling pumped His wings in that direction with renewed excitement. Before long, the Gods' nests were placed closer and closer together. More small paths joined into this larger one, and more loud things moved along, although slower now. Just a bit further and the nests became clustered one against another, with Gods walking along the large path's edges.

Since He'd flown into this area, the air had felt strangely stifling – SL'an didn't know if it was the nostril-biting auras or the fact that it seemed so much warmer here, but it nearly knocked the breath out of Him. *This isn't like the other Sacred Spaces I've seen! Where are the birds?* He winged about the increasingly large God nests that seemed to radiate reek and heat, looking for robins or redwings or any other kinds He knew. There were none at all until His eyes caught flight near one large, loud God's nest. On the nest's top, where Bard told Him was the most Sacred Space of all within a Sacred Space, was a large line of some bird kind SL'an had never seen before. They flew and moved rather like His dove mentors, but were much larger, and feathered with many different colors and patterns. *Yet they seem to be the same kind – the same kind but not the same,* He thought.

Since they were the only birds He could see at the moment, He fought fear and drew closer. One with almost rainbow colors shimmering over grey cocked his head and saw the starling. "A visitor!" He announced. A quick, excited babbling of many voices echoed, "A visitor!" SL'an felt His tension ease with the somehow familiar tones, also similar in some way to L'al's. SL'an watched the news of a visitor move almost physically down the line of these birds, each standing a bit at attention, bobbing their heads and shifting to and fro in their small roosting spaces to show they had received the message. Like the Gods' nests here, these birds were nearly one against another.

"Come and join us!" The rainbow bird called.

SL'an landed close to him. "Thank you. My name is SL'an. I'm a Seeker from the Sacred Space of God Flower."

"Well you've come to the right place if you're seeking! There's everything here a bird could want. Seek no further."

The starling looked around but saw only stunted lines of small trees growing out of the flat, stone-like ground on either side of the main path and on one side of another, adjoining path. The trees were not branched enough or private enough for nesting, and there was no grass except for a few small spaces. He wondered what kind of 'everything' there could be here, but thought better of saying it. Instead, He focused on the thing He had noticed about this kind from the beginning. "I have friends who are doves," SL'an ventured, "and you seem like them in some way."

"We should." The rainbow bird drew up his breast proudly. "We are cousin kind. We are pigeons. The doves you speak of are usually dwellers Out There, and although some of us do live Out There, most of us prefer places that are Here."

The Starling God shook His head, trying to follow. Wasn't wherever a bird was 'here'?

"We live where the Gods are at Their most. Places that are Here, as this place is, are where there is room for everyone. There is not a one border defining a Sacred Space, but the majesty of Here is everywhere it is."

When SL'an looked bewildered, the pigeon sighed. "We now roost on the top of a giant feeder. The sound you hear is a great thing that provides a seedlike food. The Gods take some away, but They leave plenty for us. We spend a good deal of our time here, but if we want, we can fly to any God's nest around to look for different food or places to raise our young. No one God nest is a specific Sacred Space. Instead, it is a great Here of plenty."

Another pigeon was sitting butted up against the rainbow bird. She had similar greys, but instead of being rainbow colored, some of her feathers were spattered with black and white, striking and quite different from all the others. The female nudged SL'an's new acquaintance gently. "Love, you're being rude. The starling SL'an has introduced his name, but you still have not."

"Oh!" The rainbow pigeon ruffled his feathers and smoothed them again quickly. "My deepest regrets! I am Coor, and beside me is my One, Claire."

SL'an bobbed a bit in greeting to the female before continuing. "I see you have plenty Here, but if this is such a place, why don't more bird kinds call this home?"

Coor looked out over the many nest tops and moving loud things. "It seems to invite certain kinds, and I admit there aren't many. Those of us who choose this place live truly beside the Gods. There are pigeons, of course, and some sparrows, and starlings can be found in some spots, although you are the first I've seen Here in a long time."

"Then of course there are the gulls," Claire added.

"Yes! The gulls, like we pigeons, love it Here. Wherever there is a Here with water nearby, gulls call it home."

"Is there water nearby? Large water?" SL'an perked up. "Is it drinkable water?"

Coor laughed softly. "Well of course it is! What other water would there be but a drinkable kind? And yes, it is large, I'd say."

Claire shifted her feet and turned direction several times where she roosted. "Coor, the time."

"Yes! It's time for us to fly, visitor SL'an. We have a very important appointment to keep."

"Since I'm a Seeker, may I ask what kinds of things pigeons and others must do Here? It does seem very different from the Sacred Space where I come from."

Claire answered. "There's a God that roosts on the same perch each day if the weather is clear. He eats and shares food with His pigeons. There are others like Him, but this God is especially true to this part of the sun. When the sun is in this position, then so is He. We mustn't disappoint Him!"

With that, about twenty of the pigeons launched from their roost on the top of the enormous nest-like feeder and flew. Without questioning, SL'an followed. It was a bit hard to keep up because the pigeons, like their dove cousins, were strong, fast fliers. He thought His lungs might burst from the effort just as they all slowed, changed wing beats and landed on the stone-like surface where one of the Gods roosted. He took a first bite of something and then tossed a handful of something else to the ground, as pigeons ran as fast as they could on foot to where food landed, grabbed it up quickly and gobbled hungrily before others could steal it away. Although they were very close to the God, they showed no fear.

"We make a fine game of it, though sometimes a bird or two will lose his sense of humor," Coor blurted before racing to grab a bit. "If you want to get the sense of how things are Here, visitor, why don't you try your beak at things?"

The milling about and grabbing for food was different than anything SL'an had experienced. If it was a game, then He admitted sourly to Himself He wasn't very good at it. He would see a bit of food land on the ground and just begin to move toward it when the seasoned pigeons would already be there, triumphant. After too many failed attempts, He moved back and chose to watch this particular God instead. The God stretched His wing into a space in His body plumage and drew out seeds to toss into the milling group of pigeons. Unlike Mother, with long, soft feathers on Her head, this God had feathers that were a dirty white and stuck up all over like a kind of crest. Instead of being smooth around the eyes like Mother, there were folds that reminded the Starling God of tree bark. The God's eyes, like all of the Gods' eyes, were forward like a Blooder's, but were the color of a dull sky in the somehow dingy body. *If I saw a bird at home that looked like this, I would think it was very sick or injured,* He mused.

As SL'an studied this God, the sky eyes fixed Him directly. SL'an froze, and the God bared His teeth in the motion L'in taught Him was not aggressive like a Blooder, but the look of a God that is pleased. Mother often bared Her teeth, but somehow the way She did it didn't look as strange as this. The God made sounds that creaked, reminiscent of the swallows, pulled something off the edge of what He was eating, and extended His wing in SL'an's direction, still making the creaking noises.

Pigeons gathered around the God's feet, almost touching Him, but He kept His sky eyes on the starling. When the young bird didn't move forward, the God tossed the bit so it landed beside SL'an on the ground. He grabbed it before the pigeons could claim it while Coor hurried to His side.

"Visitor! Well done. There's something about you that gained favor with the God! And surely now you can see what's so plentiful Here?"

A sparrow pair fluttered in and grabbed at seeds that bounced out of pigeon reach. So these pigeons and sparrows were two of the main kinds that preferred to live Here, but there was one other SL'an knew He must meet – the gulls. If they lived wherever there was water, then perhaps they knew something about the Great Undrinkable Water and the whales.

The Starling God asked Coor if he could tell Him where to find the water and the gulls, but Coor stomped his foot. "It isn't far, but the sun will be going away before long. You may find them, but I think it's more important that you find somewhere to rest for the night."

One of the sparrows hopped forward, overhearing the conversation. It reminded SL'an so much of Steep that He had to repress a chuckle. "I see we have a visitor in our midst," the sparrow chirped. "I would be pleased to have you come visit with us for the night."

Coor made an exasperated coo. "They think their roosting and nesting area is the best Here."

The starling dipped gratefully. "I'm certain that all places Here are differently pleasing, but Coor, since I've spent some time with you and have not had the opportunity to spend time yet with the sparrows,

I would be no Seeker at all if I didn't experience a bit of their lives Here as well."

"Seeker? I've heard of such things but haven't met one myself before now." The sparrow looked curiously at his future guest.

SL'an stepped back in shock. "Don't you have Seekers? Tellers? Watchers?"

The pigeon was scanning the ground for any missed bits of food. "Those are things for birds who live Out There. We live Here. There is no need for it."

"Don't you want to learn about the Gods? Don't you need protection?" The starling stammered.

Coor cooed again. "Everything we need is Here. What else is there to know or question? There is little Here that will harm us. We walk with the Gods and live with Them and eat with Them."

"Aren't there Blooders Here?" SL'an looked from Coor to the sparrow, but it was Coor who continued to speak.

"There are cats at times, and raccoons, but we're too busy – there's far too much to do – to worry about Watching for others. A smart bird will Watch for himself. If he fails to Watch, well, then he is eaten."

With His head rattled a bit from what He'd just learned, SL'an thanked Coor and Claire and also gave thanks to all the pigeons who had shared their meal and their game with Him – if sharing is what the activity in the game could be called.

The sparrows, Chip and Sweet, led Him to another strange and magnificent sight. They winged in to an enormous Gods' nest that had uncovered spaces close to the top. It was through one of these spaces the sparrows darted, and SL'an carefully followed. His wings stopped beating for a moment when He got His first glimpse of the inside. It was wide and open, the nest's cover also very high so there was more room to fly within the space inside than He had ever imagined possible. The ground appeared to be stone-like as most grounds Here seemed to be, but on top of it or growing from it was lush garden and forest. The air was hot and very damp, and the aura of soil and greenery was strongly punctuated with the perfume of flowers.

The trees weren't as tall as most trees outside, but they were lush and living. All the plant life seemed to have roots and soil cupped within some kind of containers that rested individually on the stone-like ground.

The high air was full of other sparrows sending evening messages back and forth that echoed loudly. There was clearly no evening praise Here, but something more like morning news.

There were a few Gods moving through the greenery, pouring water into the containers as Mother did somehow to Her out-of-nest plants with a mysterious, long snakeish thing that drenched certain trees and plants of Her choice in dry weather. *These Gods share a kind of plumage!* SL'an marveled. Although the crests or head feathers varied, they all had the same red bellies and backs, and most had dark legs. The Gods were still shaped very differently from each other, some very bony and tall and others rounder, closer to the ground. "Amazing! I haven't seen many of the Gods yet, but this is the first time I witnessed Gods having kinds! This seems to be one kind different from the rest!"

Sweet, the sparrow male, also looked surprised. "There are many Gods that come here during certain times of the sun, but this kind always comes early, stays throughout and is the last to fly away at night."

"They don't all nest or roost in this place?"

"No. They leave this to Their birds when the sun goes. This is truly the best place Here, no matter what Coor would tell you," Sweet said proudly. "There has never been a Blooder inside to memory, and it is more beautiful inside than outside. What more could birds want?"

SL'an had to agree. "I don't know why more birds don't choose it Here if there are safe nests like this to be had. I admit, the outside of Here is not what I'm used to, but it's as if the Gods created a paradise for birds with this. Why don't the pigeons choose to sleep inside this place as well?"

"I think if all the pigeons tried to live in this nest, although it is very large, there'd be no room left for the Gods or the green things!" Sweet laughed heartily.

"Have you heard the stories of how sparrows came to be Here?" SL'an wanted to know.

"What does it matter? Remember, we don't have Seekers and Tellers, and we don't need them. It's foolish to worry about why we are Here or how it all came to be. We're Here now, and that's all that matters. There's too much to do and enjoy to worry about such things."

Although the Gods in the enormous and magical nest controlled light the same as His Mother did, the sparrows urged Him up to metal roosting spots in the topmost part of the nest to settle in for the night. No sooner had the young starling nestled in than the light suddenly disappeared like lightning that brightens and then vanishes all at once. The previously noisy space was silent except for the gentle breathing of the plants and small birds; SL'an fought sleep for as long as He could to consider the shock of knowledge He'd gained today. There were no Seekers Here. What He chose for His purpose was considered unnecessary. It was a thought that left a hollow place inside His breast that started to flower with fear. What if the birds Here were right? What if this was the best way to live, and how they were spending time Out There, as they called it, was wrong? It did seem perfect Here…different, but very perfect. Still, there was the fear that had taken hold in the hollow spot in His breast; it stayed with Him and threatened to not let go.

Chapter Twenty

Gulls of the Large Water

The sun had barely released when the red-bellied and backed Gods returned. The sparrows who weren't tending young took flight, but SL'an asked to stay behind to watch what these Gods would do. Chip and Sweet urged Him to go for a while, feed and come back. "There are very few of the loud metal things and Gods moving around at this time of the sun," Chip explained. "This is the best time to find all the Gods have left behind for us from the sun before! It's a festival of good food every morning!"

Although His stomach was begging for breakfast, SL'an's curiosity was stronger. Chip and Sweet disappeared through the opening they had all entered the late sun before, and left the starling visitor to His Seeking.

As the sparrows described, these Gods-of-a-kind moved busily about at first with no other Gods to be seen. They sang sounds loudly to each other across spaces and carried things in and out. A few of the plants that didn't look as lush were taken away. Some Gods came and went from a wall that would mysteriously open and close again like a mouth, and beyond it the starling could see it seemed to be this huge Gods' nest stretching on even further. Instead of small trees, plants and flowers, though, there seemed to be rows and rows of other things in the section beyond. *Some of these are the same things Mother uses to keep our grasses short – and there are the same metal things She and the Great Teacher used to climb!*

SL'an could hear noises outside the paradise nest. They rose in intensity and frequency until there was no break in the raucous. Gods of different kinds joined the red-bellied and backed Gods, first as a few and then many more. Some made sounds at each other, and sometimes They sang back and forth with the red-bellied Gods too. They came and came, some taking flowers, trees or other plants away with Them. Some of Them pushed contraptions that rattled somewhat, and they placed various things inside those before finally moving with them toward their loud metal things resting side by side, also in rows, just outside of the paradise nest.

After SL'an had watched the spectacle a long time, Sweet returned and alighted next to his visitor friend. "So what have you learned?"

He had a hard time pulling His eyes away from the constant motion and sound. "This is all reversed from where I come from. The Sacred Space of God Flower has more grass and forest, birds and other animals, than it has Gods and stone. I'm amazed because what you see the Gods doing Here is what birds do Out There. Out There the sky is full of birds at this time, and full of morning news. Here there are few birds, but Gods acting as birds!"

"Strange!" Sweet's eyes widened.

SL'an's eyes were wide too. He wasn't sure what this meant, but it did sound like Bard's Starling Lore – that Gods and birds were becoming more like each other until they would finally be one and the same. He felt a wave of something dark, and the petals of the fear-flower in His breast trembled. *For some reason I don't want Bard to be right, but I have to be open to the truth I find as I seek,* He thought fiercely. He closed His eyes and tried to form the space inside where He could confront and understand the fear flower growing, but the unfamiliar and unending sounds all around made it impossible to concentrate.

"Have you eaten?" Sweet asked.

"I did find some flies, but I certainly could have something more if you could recommend a good place to find grubs."

"Grubs!" Sweet laughed merrily. "I can do better than that. You wanted to find the water and the gulls that live Here, didn't you?"

"Yes——"

"Now is the best time to see how gulls live Here, and to get a good meal at the same time. I came back to show you the way. We should hurry though! There are certain times during the sun when Gods will feed the gulls, and we don't want to miss it."

He followed Sweet out, away from the moist, earthy air and the echoes of sparrows with their babes, into bright sun and choking air. He dared to comment on how hard He found the air to breathe, and Sweet looked surprised. "The air is different by the water," he finally called as they hurried above stone-like paths and nests.

SL'an could taste the water in the air before they reached it. The blue-grey of it stretched far in all directions, and white dots circled the sky above. Other white dots bobbed along small waves. "In the air there and in the water are where the gulls are now," Sweet said, landing on a scrubby tree by the water's edge. There were a good deal of stones jutting out of the water, but SL'an was thrilled to see some grass there too. He wondered if there might be grubs or worms. Surely there must be! His desire for a juicy grub forced His beak open as if He was already down in the short green, searching.

"Are you okay?" Sweet cocked his head.

"Fine." The starling snapped back to attention.

"You see there are metal things on the vast stone field? Gods bring them to rest in rows here and leave them for a time. At this time of day, some of the Gods come and bring the metal things to rest, but stay inside Their metal things as They look out over the water. They come here to eat and to feed the gulls."

The tip of a God's wing extended from one of the metal things, and something flew out and landed on the ground. Although the gulls had seemed to be circling far away, their vision must have been keen. SL'an couldn't believe how fast the immediate air and ground was covered with them; He could see now they had brown or grey on them, along with white, depending on the bird. In a scene similar to the pigeons and the roosting God, the offered food caused a great competition. "First dibs!" One gull called out. Another shrieked, "You always think you can eat first!" There was grabbing and stealing and insulting and skirmishes of a kind like SL'an had never seen. There was so much animosity that the young starling gasped. "Will they kill each other?"

"Of course not." Sweet looked at the starling as if He had just grown two heads. "Why don't you go in and try to grab a bite? It's the food of Gods! Better than grubs!"

SL'an shook His feathers in a kind of shudder. "Oh, I don't think I should get in the middle of that."

"Nonsense! You're a visitor, and it wouldn't do for you to be Here and not try the food of Gods," he pressed. When the young starling didn't make any move to join the fray, the brown sparrow huffed. "Fine. I can be quick enough to grab you a bit."

The next time something landed on the ground close enough, Sweet darted forward in a move that would have made Steep proud, grabbed the bit, and raced back to SL'an. The event forced almost every gull there into a fury of expletives and pounding of the air with their wings. Some of them flew as if they would overtake and attack the much smaller bird, but despite the earsplitting noise and rude gestures, they soon became distracted by the next bit that was tossed from the wing tip of the God in the metal thing.

"See? Not a problem at all. Now try!"

"Shall I save some for you? You put yourself at risk to have this."

The brown male shrugged, but there was a glint in his eyes that told SL'an he did like this Gods' food very much. Carefully, He used one of His feet to hold the long, golden strip of food tightly while He tore an end off with His beak. It was soft and warm and tore fairly easily. Sweet grabbed it and bopped a distance away, throwing a suspicious glance back. The Starling God tipped His head. "I offered it to you, and I wouldn't have done so if I wanted to steal it away."

Sweet hopped back, although not as closely as he had been before. He picked at the shared bit with gusto. The new food reminded SL'an of the first time L'al and L'in took Him to eat the black seeds and taught Him how to crack the shell to get to the rich interior. *But when they ate what Mother provided, there was a reverence I don't see Here,* He thought. Still, it seemed clear that this Gods' food must be delicious, so He wasted no more time and tore a smaller bit of His own and let it set in His beak a moment to get a good flavor. It had a horrible tang He never tasted before, except perhaps in His nostrils when near the metal thing Mother used to keep the grasses short. It wasn't exactly the same, but something rang similar. He fought the urge to spit it out and forced Himself to swallow. As He watched the gulls, He saw they didn't even tear the long, golden food into smaller bits but instead gulped them whole.

Sweet was long finished with his own, so SL'an took advantage of the moment. "I've tried! Now I'd be pleased to offer my thanks by giving the rest to you."

"Oh!" Sweet hurled to the starling's side and grabbed what was left, taking it a short distance away again.

Afterward, the sparrow and visitor watched while different metal things came to rest close by the water's edge. Again and again, wing tips reached and threw out Gods' food for the gulls who clamored and argued and grabbed as if it was the first time and no one had yet eaten. Most of the time it was the long, golden food, but once in awhile something different would appear. SL'an enjoyed watching the gulls' acrobatics as some of them caught the bits in midair and were even bold enough to land on the metal things and come almost face-to-face with the shadowy Gods inside. *Birds have so much less love-fear for the Gods Here.*

The starling's stomach was aching, but He couldn't bear to try any more of what birds Here seemed to crave. "If you'll excuse me." He turned toward the rocky shore with the bit of beloved grass and soil. "I am going to go closer to the water. There's nothing like this in our Sacred Space."

Sweet nodded and contented himself with searching for something on the vast stone field. SL'an had no idea what he found there, but now and then he'd peck at something with fervor.

It hadn't been long since the young Starling God had trolled through short grasses, but it seemed like many suns. His feet delighted in the feel of it although it was not as thick and rich as it was at home. So He wouldn't be lying, He approached the edge of the water first and looked at where it licked the shore gently and regularly like an animal nursing a sore spot. He dipped down to drink but had to avoid some kind of orange goo that floated here and there and seemed to stick to any dry thing it touched. It reeked of foul, and the water, although better than none, SL'an thought, had a strange taste.

At last, He turned His attention to finding something more sustaining to eat. As was the way of His kind, He assumed the position of leaning over and looking at the soil and grass while walking. There didn't seem to be movement or much life to sense, but after dipping His beak experimentally in a few places, He did find a few small worms, although no grubs. *Still, better than what the gulls are eating.*

The feeding seemed to be almost over. There was only one metal thing left by the water, and it must have been awhile since the God inside had thrown out any food. The gulls were starting to relax, standing in a group to see if there would be any last treats. Some began to fly away when a God's song came ringing loudly, making chirruping sounds that seemed to be directed at the gulls themselves. SL'an saw the God walking toward the group of water birds, all the while making the strange chirruping call. One wing held something long, and He began throwing some kind of food out with the other. The first handful that scattered to the ground brought the gulls flying and scurrying closer.

SL'an saw the God raise the long thing with shaking wings and point it at the incoming flock. There was an eardrum-splitting crack and the gulls screamed, flying out to the water as fast as their large wings would take them. One gull flapped frantically but couldn't seem to take off from the ground, a wing dangling limp against bits of food the God had just thrown.

SL'an hurried to be with Sweet, who had flown back up into one of the scraggly trees to hide in the leaves there. "Sweet! The gulls seem terrified. Something's wrong but the one stays behind. Why doesn't he fly with the others? What's happened?"

The God had stopped pointing the long thing and was walking away with it now toward a small group of other, slightly larger Gods, leaving the gulls circling the air over the large water and crying out in dismay.

The one left on the ground hopped up and tried to fly again, but stopped suddenly and stood there with the one dangling wing stretched out and seemingly useless.

"I need to see if I can help," the starling nearly barked. He was afraid too but unsure why. Something very evil had happened; it had something to do with the long thing in the God's wings and the crack that was louder than anything SL'an had heard before, except a peal of thunder. The God was almost out of sight now. Did that mean it was safe?

Sweet's voice was tight with fear too. "We should go back home and forget what we've seen! There's nothing you can do here."

"But how do you know? There's something wrong with the gull! Something has happened to his wing."

"Listen to me! There's nothing you can do. The gulls were unwise to move toward the God holding the cracking stick. They were unwise and so one has taken his due."

"It was the God that caused this? How? What harm did the stick do to the wing?"

"Sometimes the cracking sticks do more than harm a wing, but it is just as well when they do. It is better to be dead than to not have one wing. Now the gull will have to wait there until the life blood runs from him or he becomes so ill with pain and fever that he starves and thirsts to his death, or until some Blooder comes in the night where he suffers and finds him an easy meal."

"A God would make one of His birds suffer this way? Or take the life of one of His own birds?" He thought of L'in and the fisher female. He didn't know if that was or wasn't the will of the Gods, but this, if what Sweet said was true, meant a God definitely willed – even caused – death or suffering. Why? The starling couldn't take His eyes from the defeated-looking gull.

"We need to go," Sweet said.

"I need to stay, but I thank you for your hospitality and guidance here." SL'an dipped in thanks.

"Why stay?"

"I do need to speak with a gull, and this one, I suppose, has nothing to do now other than talk. And if I spend time with him, maybe it will help him feel less alone." SL'an knew what alone felt like. It suddenly jumped from some invisible place in His innards and stuck like a thorn in the breast. *So you're here again,* He thought to the memory of 'alone'. *You will not stay. I won't let you stay with Me now, and I will not let you stay with the gull Here.*

"Suit yourself, visitor!" Sweet flew away with haste toward the paradise nest, leaving the Starling God still staring at the injured water bird.

Before He had time to think too much, He launched from the tree and landed next to the gull who was white with brown flecks in the neck. "My name is SL'an. I'm not from Here, but am from Out There – from a Sacred Space of the God Flower."

The gull turned his head to look at the newcomer with wide eyes. "What do you want? Can't you see what's happened to me? Leave me to die."

"If my being here is really a burden, I'll go. It seemed, though, that it might be good not to be alone. I'm not even one season's turn old, I know, but I've already learned something basic and true. Fear and pain are worse when your mind turns its eardrums to them. I don't know what else I can do for you, but I do know I can try to help turn your mind away from the fear and the pain."

The gull sighed; the sound was ragged. "My name is Spool. I also am not even one season's turn old. If you could help me with the pain, I'd be grateful."

First, SL'an taught the young gull how to create the place inside himself where unpleasant things could be faced and better controlled. It took some practice of course, but there was nothing but some time for the water bird now; the practicing itself seemed to focus his mind and ease the pain a very little bit. When the injured bird finally had the knack, SL'an directed him to go inside the newly formed space and meet the pain. "There are things Here that you have mastery over. You fly in the blue sky and use the currents of air. You are able to stay afloat on the water and have it transport you where you want to go. I am told you sometimes hunt the fish in the waters. There may be other things you have mastery over," SL'an instructed. "Choose one of those things and shape the pain into it. Bend it to your own will. Have it do what you need instead of having it use you as it wants."

The gull closed his eyes and followed directions. SL'an knew the exercise was working when Spool's feathers relaxed. He hadn't realized how stiff the other bird had been until that moment. When the gull opened his eyes again, there was more resolve and peace.

"Good!" SL'an clapped His wings twice against His body with pleasure. "Now we should find a place where you can rest without being in a Blooder's sight. You know this place better than I do. Is there any sheltered spot nearby?"

Spool tried to tuck the injured wing up as much as he could. He squinted with a return of the pain but closed his eyes again for a moment and opened them, once again having mastered it. "There are some bushes down the shore. It isn't far to fly, but will feel much farther to walk."

"I'll walk with you if you think you can make it."

The two of them stepped along the stone-like field toward the shore, and slightly toward a huge nest nearby. "We have to go behind there. Just past it are the bushes," Spool said, and the two started off together, Spool's wing tip dragging on the ground and repeatedly making the gull wince and stop to gain control of it again. They had almost made it to the first corner of the huge nest when Spool stopped again. "I can't make it. I don't have the energy to subdue the pain and walk too. Every step makes it bite my wing with its fangs."

SL'an's heart sank. "Well, then! Let's at least go near that tree. There's shade there and the water close by if you feel you are thirsty."

Spool looked at the young starling. "I won't need to drink."

"Well then, there may be food nearby I can find and bring to you when you become hungry again."

"I won't need to eat."

SL'an drew His head back. "Of course you will."

"Starling from Out There, I'm thankful that you taught me how to deal with this pain, but I don't know what hope you think there is for me. There's only the hope to die sooner than later."

"But there must always be some hope!" SL'an tried to look as chipper as the little finch Steep, but He felt the truth weigh the words down.

"I don't want to die, but it seems the Gods have chosen this for me. I've seen others cling to life as long as they could and suffer for days until the breath was finally pulled forcefully from them. This isn't the end I want. My end will be as fast as I can make it."

There was silence between the birds until they finally arrived under the tree.

"Your name again?" Spool asked.

"SL'an."

"So you have a profession? Two?"

"I'm learning to be a Seeker and a Teller, but I'm told you don't have either Here."

"No, we don't. But the gulls are taught of such things. I've always been curious about the job of Seeker and thought that if we did choose professions, it would make sense for me to try that one. We already spend so much time with the Gods; why not learn more about Them?"

"Why don't you just do it anyway?" SL'an spread one wing out with emphasis and then preened. "There are no professions like this for starlings either, although we are surrounded by birds with professions Out There. Still, I chose to be what I am."

"Wonderful!" The gull winced, focused again, then continued. "If I had more time I would be inspired enough by that thought to consider it, SL'an. However, since I will die tonight, there's nothing I can do but think curiously on it until the end."

"How do you know you'll die tonight?"

"When the black starts to creep in, raccoon Blooders will creep in with it. They come here at black to go to that square box against the nest. It is full of everything, and some of it's good to eat. We sometimes look through and find good things during the sun time, and the raccoons do so when the sun goes. I will move beside it where I can be seen. Then one of the Blooders will end life for me."

The Starling God felt His feathers tighten.

"I can see you don't understand, Seeker and Teller, but the choice is mine to make. The Gods must want my life to end if one took a cracking stick and pointed it at me."

"This is one of the reasons I left our Sacred Space to Seek further out. I want to understand the Gods. Why would a God want you to die?"

"I don't know. We don't question. Here is the proof that it was what He wanted." Spool touched his beak to the useless wing.

A sudden thought made SL'an's heart leap. "But if the God wanted you to die, then why not use the cracking stick to kill you? He must not have wanted you to die! He only took your wing."

"Imagine not having one wing, SL'an. It is the same thing as if He killed me."

But why would a God make one of His birds suffer? What would be the purpose? SL'an thought, although He decided not to ask the questions out loud. If this would be the young gull's last sun of life, it wouldn't do good to raise troubling questions.

"Well, we may never understand what the Gods want," SL'an nodded to signal that He was dismissing the topic altogether, "but I think there are many things I could learn from you if you don't mind me staying with you until…"

"I'd be pleased to have your company," Spool interjected. You were absolutely right that turning my eardrums away from the sound of pain and toward other things is helpful. So tell me then; what would you like to know?"

SL'an felt Himself vibrate with excitement. "Do you know anything about a Great Undrinkable Water? And whales?"

"Since I'm still young, there's so much I haven't learned yet, but I have heard about a Great Undrinkable Water where others of my kind live or travel to. It stretches out further than an eye can see or a wing can fly – at least in most parts. Of course I haven't seen it, but it does exist."

"But you haven't heard of the whales that swim in the Undrinkable Water?" Spool tipped his head toward SL'an questioningly, so the starling described what He had seen in His vision. He could sense the salt from the water and a mixture of so many other unfamiliar things just from remembering. It was curiously real. After He finished describing as many details as He could, Spool's eyes lit up. "The Giant Ones! That's what it sounds like to me. I don't know for certain if they're your whales or not, but I think it's possible."

Spool seemed to forget his wing and the pain completely, looking out over the large water that had been his own home during what would be a short life. "I would love to see the Giant Ones! None of them seem to live in water like ours, but they have a whole world in the Undrinkable Water where they are oldest and wisest. I don't know any more about them than that. Why are you curious about the Giant Ones?"

"I plan to fly to the Undrinkable Water to see them, even talk to them if they know how."

Spool managed a short laugh. "From what I understand, they must know how. How couldn't they if they're one of the wisest of beings?"

"I wish you could fly there with me," SL'an blurted, and instantly wished He would think better before letting thoughts free. Spool only brightened with excitement.

"I wish I could too! You'll have to have that experience for me."

When the black finally came, Spool encouraged the starling to the upper part of one tree and made his own way out by the box next to the huge nest. There was a God light nearby that kept the area in an unreal, sun-like state, so SL'an watched the white gull's feathers reflecting brightly for as long as He could stay awake. Spool stood still and proud despite the hanging wing, and although the Starling God was determined to not rest until His new friend was taken, the black fell over His mind and sealed His eyes. He opened them quickly at the first hint of sun and immediately looked where Spool should have been. He was gone. Soon a group of other gulls flew in, although the sky was still grey, and stood quietly by.

Chapter Twenty-One
Nestlings

SL'an knew what He would do that sun. The question He came to answer was *why*, and now the need for that answer was greater than ever. *Mother...I watched one of You harm one of Your own birds. I saw it happen, and there was no need for food. The God didn't take His bird's life quickly, but injured him so he would suffer. What purpose could there be?*

He walked slowly toward one of the gulls farthest from the small group collected where Spool had waited for his end. Normally the starling would have bobbed a bit to show peaceful intentions, but after watching the gulls vie for God-food the sun before, He saw bobbing meant something far different for their kind. It seemed to be wrapped up with aggression instead of peace. *There's probably more to it than I see, but it would be unwise to take a chance,* He thought. If there was time, He would have watched closer and longer, learned more, but time wasn't something He wanted to spend Here now.

The gull, a female with no brown on her at all, snapped her white head in SL'an's direction. He took that as a sign that He was close enough, and stood still. "Lady gull, I am SL'an, a Seeker from Out There. I had the honor of meeting Spool and spending the last of the sun with him before his end."

"I'm Spool's mother."

SL'an waited for a name but she offered none, continuing to stand quietly at the edge of the flock. "I hurt in my breast for you. May I ask you a question before I leave?"

She snapped her head toward Him again and tapped one foot a bit. "Please be quiet."

Suddenly, the young starling realized just how quiet the gulls were. They stood without moving. There was no news or looking for food from the metal box on the God nest's side – just a complete stillness that, He realized, seemed completely out of character for a group of this kind.

SL'an stood silently too and thought of Spool waiting there, making his choice of how he would end. *Although the end wouldn't have been necessary if it hadn't been for the God with the cracking stick.* His mind tightened on the idea.

"FREEDOM!" The largest gull cried out, and the small flock took instantly to the air – except Spool's mother.

"You were silent for Spool? I didn't realize it until you asked me to be quiet. I hope you can overlook what I had no way to know." SL'an had to fight the urge to bob His head with every feather.

"There is sound during life and stillness at the end," she said, looking off to the water. "In stillness, we stand for one last moment with those we love when they have ended."

"I only knew Spool for a short time, but he seemed wise and strong. He has given me much to think about. When the time comes for my end, may I be as clear and brave."

The gull female raised her head. "My Spool was a remarkable young one. He should have done great things, but the Gods felt differently."

"My Seeking is about the very thing – what is it the Gods really want of Their birds? Why do They do what They do? What happened to Spool seems…wrong. I want to find the God with the cracking stick and see if I might learn more about Him and more about the why."

Spool's mother lowered her voice. "I have never heard one say that the Gods' actions seem wrong, although I've thought it myself many times."

"What can you tell me about that one God? Have you seen Him before?"

A warm breeze picked up and smoothed over SL'an's feathers,

bringing with it the aura of the water and the orange slime that clung desperately to the rocks and gravel at the shore.

"He's a God we've seen here many times. He has given food to us before, and usually walks alone. Like us, He seems to enjoy the water and being beside it. The idea that He would do this…" her voice trailed off. Finally, she shook violently as if to loosen the doubt. "If you find Him – if you find the answer to why – I would ask you to tell me what you know."

"I will, but I need to make sure I understand more than small parts before I do. A great mentor told me that a little knowledge is a dangerous thing. This is why Seekers must spend their lives Seeking, and must give the Tellers what information they discover. A Teller hears information from many, and a Seeker only knows the parts he knows."

Spool's mother nodded her head enthusiastically up and down in the near-bobbing SL'an had only seen while the gulls were vying for food, and He felt the thrill of discovery – it was a motion of excitement, not just aggression! "Yes! Yes!" she cried out. "We have a saying, 'The bird is strong and good, but the flock is stronger and better'."

He said goodbye and flew, never having learned the female gull's name, to where He'd seen the God with the cracking stick walking away. He wondered for a bit if He should go back and ask what to call her, but when He turned to look, she had already disappeared into the white and silver of her greater group.

The sun was well released from the hills now, and the Gods were soon walking everywhere or moving in lines within roaring metal things. It was too difficult for SL'an to see any specific features of the Gods inside those, so He concentrated on the Ones He saw on foot. Spool's mother said that the God with the cracking stick walked, so there was a chance He didn't travel by way of the roaring metal things anyway.

There had been almost exclusively fully grown Gods when the starling arrived Here the sun before, but now there were many full Gods with what looked like God fledglings, and some looking far too young to even be out of their nest. *The Gods' young!* He heard about small ones when Hroo told the story of how Gift came to her nest, and before that, to Mother, but He had never seen One before. *Mother! They're amazing!*

One female God walked quickly, holding what must have been a newly hatched God in Her wings. From what SL'an could see, like L'al's new nestlings, the babe was naked, and squirmed into the warmth of His own Mother's unusual plumage. Other grown Gods walked wing tip to wing tip with nestlings, or watched them run just ahead of them, or sang to other full-grown Gods as the small ones lagged behind. Some small ones were quiet, others chirped loudly, and a few screeched and howled. *I can't remember everything about being a nestling with Mother, but what I can remember didn't seem like this. What must it be like to be hatched by and to live like a small one of the Gods? If Mother created Me and raised Me, what was the purpose of keeping Me inside until it was time to fledge? Maybe it was important that I be raised like bird and not as much like the Gods?*

One thing was already obvious – God nestlings of the earliest age weren't confined to the nest. *Are They teaching Them all to be Seekers as early as possible?* The starling wondered how much more His kind and all birds would learn if they could be taken out earlier to see things. *When I first went out I knew almost nothing, and then by being out I knew so much more,* He thought wistfully. Of course some of the lessons had caused pain, and there were those times He had wished the innocence back.

SL'an flew from small tree to small tree growing along the side of the stone-like path, all the while closely watching Gods with nestlings. *With the youngest of things, there's so much joy!* He reached the last tree in the line, growing just before a corner where another stone path sprouted from His present one. There were some pigeons gathered there, milling about with little care as the Gods walked closely by. The Starling God didn't recognize any from the group He'd spent time with the sun before.

They caught the interest of a God's nestling; barely able to walk, She chirruped with blatant glee and ran, if that's what it could be called, unsteadily toward the pigeons with Her wings stretched forward. The pigeons moved carefully away, staying just out of reach. The small One tried over and over, reaching forward until SL'an seemed certain She would lose Her balance and fall like a bird not ready to fly.

The small One's Mother sang to Her and the nestling stopped, swaying a bit on those unsteady legs, turning Her head to the grown God and then back again toward the elusive pigeons. *Why does She want to touch them?* He wondered. Mother watched Her birds and fed them, and had touched Him when He was Her nestling and fledge, but She made no attempt to touch Her birds otherwise. The Great Teacher certainly didn't try to feel the feathers of His birds Out There. The fully grown Gods seemed to pay no heed whatsoever to them Here – except, of course, the One with the cracking stick. With another strange prickle in His feather quills, SL'an heard Bard's voice in His mind saying birds would become more like Gods and Gods more like birds until they were one and would rule together. Could this be why the small One wanted to be with the pigeons so badly? Was it an invitation to become as one kind?

The Starling God flew from the corner tree and landed on the smooth stone-like path, carefully avoiding the Gods' feet and fighting the fluttering of His heart. *I was created by Mother, a God. I shouldn't have this fear of Them.* He clamped His beak tightly shut as if that would hold Him together and walked quickly in front of the small One before He lost courage. She stopped and made high squeaks that could only be delight, but before She could reach out to SL'an, He looked up and into Her wide eyes and felt the terror of looking into the eyes of a Blooder. His resolve snapped and caused His wings to jolt into action, almost of their own volition. He could only look down at Her from the tree branch where He landed, feeling a bit defeated. If He was of the Gods, why did even a nestling drive sharp pins in His breast when He drew close? Mother didn't make Him feel afraid when He was a nestling – there was no place He would rather have been than close to Her.

He spent more time up and down the stone-like path, riveted by the Gods' nestlings of all ages. There seemed to be no question that They were seeking. Even the smallest of them, although They couldn't move on Their own much otherwise, had eyes that moved everywhere, seeing everything They could. The Ones that could move on Their own legs wanted to explore. More than one God nestling reached for the pigeons. It wasn't until His stomach cried with hunger that SL'an realized how long He'd been in that same area and drawn away from His purpose. *I need to find the God with the cracking stick, but I'm afraid I have to find something to eat first!*

He flew back toward a small patch of grass with flowers growing in the center of it; Gods moved around it and seemed to never set foot there. *Could it be because it's one of the few green places Here?* Too hungry to do much thinking, He practically crashed into the grass that was kept short, instantly sensing something rank from the tall flowers that grew there – He couldn't recognize the aura, but it warned Him it wasn't anything He wanted to be near. He steered clear of them and sought the green space instead.

With grass as lush as this, there were sure to be grubs. SL'an forced His beak into the roots and began searching, but time and time again He came back with nothing. There were no worms either. He snatched a few unsuspecting flies, but they did very little to satisfy. The rank aura was present here too, it seemed, but SL'an's stomach hurt so He kept trying over and over again to find what He knew should be there.

He knew from L'al that grasses and other growing things needed the worms. Why were there none? Certainly this should also be an excellent place for insects to have their grubs grow. He plunged His beak in deeper than usual and stayed there for a time, letting His senses discover what they would. The answer was nothing. There was some vague smell of earth, there was the rank sense of something else, but no richness, or the life He was used to at the Sacred Space. Here, there was nothing but emptiness in the soil. It was so still and strange that SL'an recoiled and took wing toward the water where a group of gulls was still taking food from some Gods in the metal things. The water sensed badly of the orange goo, but at least the starling knew there was something to eat along the shore underneath the stunted trees.

The gulls were crying out with indignation and sometimes joy as they vied for the food tossed out by the Gods' wings, and SL'an shuddered. It would have been so much easier if He'd liked it. He couldn't imagine any bird enjoying the God-food as much as they clearly did. *Mother, they think that Here has so much more to offer than Out There, but I think they have never tasted things as they should taste!* He felt a swell of pride at what Mother provided for Her birds in the Sacred Space. It was such a feeling of light to finally think something so good about Her again!

A gull female flew toward Him – He saw it was Spool's mother as she drew close. "What news?"

"Nothing yet." SL'an dipped His head.

"Well, I am happy to say I have some news for you! The God you are looking for is back. While I was swimming, I saw Him catching fish off the tall, wooden bank there that reaches out across the water." She turned her head toward it, and the Starling God followed her gaze to where a God stood with a stick once again poking out from His wings.

"But is that the same God?"

"Oh yes! I'm certain of it." Spool's mother bobbed her head and neck up and down excitedly. "That is not the cracking stick in His wings, but another special thing He and other Gods use to catch fish."

"They catch fish like you do?" He looked doubtfully at the long, golden bits of what these birds considered great God-food being tossed out at intervals.

"They catch them, but then They put them in groups on the bank or in something They then carry them away with. For the life of a bird, I don't know why They don't just eat them then and there, but They never do."

This made SL'an ponder. "Could They bring them to Their own Sacred Spaces to feed the fish to flocks there?"

Spool's mother shook her feathers. "I suppose anything's possible, but I've never spoken to a fish-eating bird that claimed places where Gods would feed them such things. In any case, there's the God you want."

The gull female flew away abruptly after throwing a glance at the fishing God, leaving SL'an standing in the wave of sudden anger and disgust that rippled through her.

At first He couldn't bring Himself to fly closer either. Instead, He watched from the short distance and tried to see something familiar in the God who only yesterday pointed the cracking stick and took flight away from one of His birds. As Gods did, He had changed plumage. The starling had to admit that without help from Spool's mother, He may not have recognized this One again.

There was nothing remarkable from a distance. The God leaned over part of the wooden bank that spanned over water and used His wings to flick the new stick He was using – to catch fish, according to Spool's mother. Since nothing seemed sinister, SL'an pushed Himself to fly where He could perch on the same dead wood the God leaned on. From here He could see a white something at the God's feet, just as the female gull described. There was water inside the thing, and the starling sensed fish too. His belief was confirmed when the God pulled a fish up from below Him in the large water, the creature dangling and flopping desperately at the end of some near invisible strand that seemed not much thicker than a spider web. The God slowly and carefully used wing tips to disconnect the fish from the strand and place it into the water-filled thing at His feet.

Inching even closer, SL'an took note of the God's shape. There was something awkward and gangly about the arms and legs. The male was almost the size of a full-grown God, but something wasn't quite developed. SL'an gasped with the realization. This was a fledgling!

His thoughts were interrupted by the noisy cawing of another group of Gods moving toward where SL'an perched. The fishing God set the stick and strand aside and seemed to stand a bit taller and brighter. *They are other fledglings*, the starling quickly noticed. There was One in the lead that walked in such a jaunty way, it reminded SL'an of a posturing blue jay. Two others followed behind. Whatever the sounds meant that the group made caused the One fishing to call back. He gestured one of His wings to the white fish-filled thing and sang with obvious excitement, but the leader of the other fledgling Gods made a barking sound. He approached, looked into the white thing full of water and fish, and then barked again to a young God behind Him. SL'an jumped back a foot, flapping, when He saw what that other God brought toward the fishing God – the cracking stick.

The fishing God's posture changed; He lowered His head and was silent while the others pushed the cracking stick toward Him again. He uttered sounds so softly they were hard for SL'an to hear, but they had an aggravating effect on the leader of the other fledgling Gods. The leader bobbed His head as if He would snap the fisher God's face with His beak if He only could, and flapped one wing strangely. He turned as if to walk away, stepping a bit higher than normal, and then whirled back around and barked out at the fisher God again.

The fisher God's shoulders began to sag along with His head. He took a step back toward where SL'an perched, and the starling tensed up, ready to take wing if necessary. He felt His quills prickle.

The leader of the other fledgling Gods rushed forward and kicked the white thing with the fish and water, sending both splashing over the wooden ground. The fish flopped and gasped at the same time as the fishing God wailed and bent over to right it and reach for the fish closest to Him. Before He could grab it, the leader smacked Him with one wing, sending the fisher reeling backward, falling. The other two fledglings hurried forward, One kicking out at the downed God, the strange toeless feet thudding against the fisher's side. Down on the ground, the fisher raised His wings over His head to defend Himself as the leader's own wings fell on Him again and again. SL'an wished He could understand the muffled noises the fishing God was making, but there was a good chance the other fledglings didn't understand either because They never slowed their assault until the noises finally stopped.

The three fledglings finally stood back, the leader barking once more at the fishing God. One other picked up the cracking stick from where it had ended up being tossed on the ground, and the group walked away and toward the starling's perch. Instinctively, SL'an flew away as fast as He could manage, but stayed close enough so He could watch until the group of young Gods walked out of sight. When They were gone, He returned to the place where the fishing God was still crumpled on the wooden ground that spanned the water. The muffled sounds were coming again as a few full-grown Gods walked passed, barely giving notice. Blood was running down the God's almost-grown face, and He reached miraculously inside His plumage to pull something out and wipe the blood with it. SL'an could see there was water draining down the face too and pooling in the God's eyes. Had the other Gods broken something? Where did the water come from? Was there something like a gullet inside the Gods where They stored water? Could He live if it was ruptured?

At last, the fishing God stood up and slowly picked up each fish. Some were still moving, but some had already stopped. He walked with a limp now along the wooden ground until He reached the large stone-like ground where many metal things rested and which led to the edge of the large, fresh water. The gulls were no longer sharing the Gods' food there, but most had retreated to the water where they bobbed along on small waves or rested on perfectly straight limbless and leafless trees, all the same size, that emerged from the water in certain places.

The fishing God reached into the white thing and pulled out a fish, waving it in the air until some gulls took notice. Several white and silver birds flew into the air and circled cautiously, high enough to feel safe but low enough to learn more about what this God was offering. When they saw no cracking stick, they nodded to each other and drifted closer. The God threw the small fish onto the stone-like ground, not missed by the keen eyes of the gulls. They raced madly to the spot, and one large male landed first, grabbing the fish and making off with it before his comrades could try a steal.

Another fish followed, and another. Although the few first and daring gulls had been careful not to announce the bounty, the feeding couldn't be disguised. Before long, the fishing God was surrounded by a flock wanting whatever He would be willing to give. Shoulders still sagging, He reached into the white thing over and over, tossing what He had until it was empty. When it was, the gulls waited a short while to be sure there wouldn't be one last offering before leaving the fishing God still sitting there, alone.

SL'an continued watching from one of the stunted trees, hoping for some answer. He still didn't understand why this young God had been One to feed the gulls, and then took the cracking stick against one of them, and later chose to sit among them, feeding them again – in a way Spool's mother said she had never seen before. The only thing He could see for sure was that water still pooled in the God's eyes and ran down His face. *Mother, I don't know where Your kind keeps a water gullet, but I think the other fledgling Gods have damaged this One's for good.*

Chapter Twenty-Two
Cacophony

When the black began to fall again, SL'an returned to where the sparrows nested and the red-bellied and backed Gods flocked during the sun. He didn't feel particularly safe in the scrubby, short trees by the water. Besides, all He would think about there was Spool meeting his end there under the light. Questions of the fishing God and the behavior of the other fledglings would plague Him anyway, even if He roosted in the paradise nest, but He was certain to find little rest where everything had unfolded.

Sweet and the other sparrows were happy to welcome Him back. "Excellent timing," Sweet chirped. "Chip's sister has just had a hatching this sun! We'll dance and sing into the black, and there will be a feast!"

"A feast sounds wonderful." SL'an's mouth watered at the idea of grubs and other insects, black sunflower seeds exploding with nutty flavor, and a full belly for the first time since He came Here. "Where do you find your insects and seed?"

Sweet pulled his head back and opened his beak at the starling's words. "There are some insects to eat here, flies mainly, but why would we waste our time trying to catch them when we can share the Gods' food?" Sweet must have taken his guest's hesitation for wordless delight, because he waxed even more enthusiastic. "If you think the food by the water was delicious, there's something even better to share and as hot as the sun was; there should be plenty for everyone."

Arrangements were quickly made for sparrows to take turns tending to eggs or nestlings so every bird would have the chance to celebrate. "Do you celebrate this way every time there is a hatching?" the Starling God asked.

Chip had joined them. "Of course. Don't you celebrate hatchings Out There in your Sacred Space?" She seemed distracted by the promise of their celebration looming at blinding speed, but one eardrum seemed to stay masterfully tuned in to SL'an's answer.

"It's shared in morning news or evening praise and celebrated in the breast and feather of each bird, but..." His voice trailed off as He tried to imagine why there wouldn't be celebrations of the kind the sparrows described Here. He thought of the Watchers on patrol and the Praising and Seeking and feeding that must be done. There was ceaseless energy Here, but somehow things at the Sacred Space seemed busier. "There are many jobs to do Out There that you don't do Here, and I suppose there isn't time for the celebrations like this – although there are some."

He remembered soaring unimaginably high in the air, dancing with the swallows in memory of L'in, and the evening so many birds gathered to hear about Mother's Gift to Hroo.

Chip and Sweet made chucking noises in their throats. "I feel very sad for you that things are so hard and sad Out There," Chip said. "No doubt you'll decide to stay on Here and leave that behind. We suggest you go back to choose a female or two and bring them Here away from all of that."

The thought of it made SL'an want to recoil, but He knew it would be insulting. "Things are very different Here," He mused aloud instead.

"It's time," Chip said urgently. "Now you'll see what it is to really live."

"The black is coming." SL'an looked up to the sky.

"Not to worry, starling! The Gods have Their own light and stay about well into what you think of as the black. They eat and share, and at times like this we can stay out to play with the Gods," Sweet called out as he launched out of the paradise nest and into the warm air, still light despite the grey that was crawling closer.

Once a number of the sparrows, and SL'an, were back into the steamy air, SL'an fought back the urge to choke and stop inhaling the horrible, dead thickness of it. Undaunted, sparrows flew between tall stone and metal nests, singing out in high-pitched, unbelievably loud tones. There was snarling from the metal things and noises from Gods, pounding strains of something that Sweet called music of the Gods, and so many other sounds that the young starling was surprised one singing bird could even hear another.

After Sweet, Chip, and several others were finished with their turns swooping and singing, their notes and words echoing from the tall nests' sides, SL'an asked about it.

A sparrow SL'an hadn't formally met answered breathlessly. "Although I've never heard the songs of our cousins Out There, I'm told we sing higher, louder, better than those living in the trees. There's a need to, of course. How would anyone hear a thing if we didn't?"

It clearly had to be that way Here, but SL'an had already noticed in His one season that females seemed to enjoy the love songs of deeper-toned males, a higher voice usually belonging to a bird that was smaller and weaker. A rich voice was a healthy voice Out There. *You'd have a bad surprise if you came to the Sacred Space and hoped to impress a female*, SL'an thought. *Your better isn't better in all cases.*

"Sing with us, starling!" Sweet cried out. "Sing as loudly as you can and soon we'll feast!"

SL'an didn't know the song these birds were singing, but He was, along with the rest of His kind, a very good study at other sounds and songs. He listened a bit and then picked up the tune, chiming in with as much clarity as He could muster. Chip nodded with approval. "Not bad. You'll fit in Here well."

With little notice, the sparrows darted away from between the tall nests, and SL'an quickly followed. The flight led them to more vast stone-like ground and a nest that was lower to the ground than many others Here. There were three nest holes close together on one side, nicely protected by an overhang offering shade and protection from any rain that might fall. Lines of Gods – all ages – approached the nest holes guarded by one God each. The Gods there refused to let other Gods inside, but instead reached wings out to hand the intruders something that clearly made each God in line happy enough to retreat with that rather than fighting to enter. One after another, the guardians of this nest defended Their entryways from would-be intruders, but at the cost of what SL'an could see now was food. Instead of going out and finding, then eating or bringing food back to the nest, Here the Gods went to this nest to be fed instead! *Mother!* Was all SL'an could think. *They must be exhausted after having to defend Their own nests from so many without a break!*

The sight of this food made the sparrows chirrup with joy. Whatever it was, most Gods ate it by sticking Their tongues against it over and over again. Only when They reached something that looked different at the bottom did They use their flat beaks to break off parts and eat normally.

"Here!" Sweet called to SL'an. "As your host, I insist you eat first."

The young starling saw food just like that being held in so many Gods' hands, lying on the ground. Sweet and Chip nearly danced with impatience. "Hurry, before someone else comes and gets it or it melts away! It's impossible to eat when it's melted flat against the stone."

"Do I stick my tongue against it?" SL'an asked, but wasn't sure if He even could move His tongue the proper way.

"No! No! Just take some up with your beak like you would snatch a fly. If you're worried about the melting part, then grab onto the harder, darker part and break some off until you have a small enough piece to swallow."

The starling approached the God-food and snatched a bit of it. It was cold and there…and then magically not there at all, draining like a liquid down His throat. It was sweet like the sense of flower nectar and gave Him an almost instant ache behind His eyes. Next, He reached down and grabbed a shattered corner of the darker, more solid looking food. This was also sweet, but kept its shape as food should. SL'an was so hungry that He ate more than He wished He had to, almost forgetting to make way for His polite sparrow guides to have some as well.

At last, He backed away from the God-food and bobbed with appreciation to His hosts. Sweet and Chip both started forward and opened their beaks to each other irritably. In an instant, they were up in the air just above the food in a skirmish, beaks open and feet snatching in the air at each other, but never really touching or doing any damage. When they landed long enough, SL'an felt His Teller training coming to the fore. "There is plenty there for both," He pointed out. "If each one of you begins at your own end and then switches places in a few moments, it could work with no fighting."

Sweet and Chip stopped the scuffle and looked wide-eyed at the starling. "It isn't necessary to interfere with us," Sweet said, his voice slightly strained. "We're capable of working out our own problems. Here, a bird must learn to defend his own needs."

"We also have disagreements over feeding, of course," SL'an quickly said, "but the Teller in each Sacred Space helps by suggesting ways that birds might coexist more peacefully when possible."

"We have no need for that Here," Sweet snapped. Although it seemed to be normal to share with a rare guest, things were obviously far different when it came to sharing with neighbors and even family Here. Afraid of wearing out His welcome, SL'an only nodded and backed away, although the two brown birds did approach the food at either end as He had just suggested.

The black had nearly swallowed the area, but it was difficult to tell with the yellowish God-lights everywhere. There were other colors too, and all of it blinded SL'an when He tried to look around and get His bearings. Gods still moved in lines, challenging the single defending Gods at the nest holes; SL'an didn't know if it was the thought of the endless defense, or the black that was telling His brain to go roost despite the God-light everywhere, or if it was the strange food He'd just eaten. All He knew is He felt terribly unwell, weak and tired.

Everything was strange Here. Everything was so unlike home. If this was where most Gods lived, and He was One of Them, why didn't He feel more at home too? With a stomach so full He thought He'd barely be able to fly, He thanked Chip and Sweet for sharing their celebration with Him, but explained that He was tired and must return to the paradise nest to rest if they didn't mind a guest until one more sun released. "We have to return now anyway, so we'll fly with you," Sweet said. "It's time to give some others the chance to celebrate while we watch their nests."

"So late? But it's black."

"Ah, Teller and Seeker from Out There, this is still early for a celebration. There is enough time for one more shift to fly out and take part in festivities."

The flight back to the paradise nest was short, but SL'an had a terrible time navigating and following His guides. The lights and sounds made it difficult to tell what was the right direction, and sometimes His eyes blurred and the brown forms flying ahead of Him seemed to blend in with the air and disappear. Once, He nearly flew directly into the side of a stone nest, veering away just in time without Sweet and Chip noticing.

He was greatly relieved when they reached the paradise nest at last and He felt His toes grasp firmly around metal that seemed placed there specifically for bird feet. He was almost instantly asleep, sure He would feel much better when the sun released again.

When it did, the sparrows were slow to move, calling to each other lazily from their nests and roosts but not flying yet. SL'an's stomach churned, screaming for food as if He had never eaten the enormous mass of God-food the black before. To His chagrin, there was barely any quiet before the cacophony began again. It hurt His brain now with all the sounds rolling over each other and competing. It wasn't the soothing blend of sounds He was used to Out There in His Sacred Space. The sounds rattled and ground without meaning or harmony. Why didn't the sparrows or the pigeons seem to notice? He remembered the way they sang as they had darted to and fro among the spaces between tall, stone nests – the high-pitched voices screaming to be heard over the writhing mass of God-sounds. There was so little life Here. So much was dead all the while Gods swarmed everywhere.

There was so much SL'an wanted to understand, but His stomach and brain were crying to leave this place as soon as possible.

He bid thanks once again to Chip, Sweet and the other sparrows, and flew frantically for the bit of green and earth by the water. After being among the biggest cluster of tall, stone nests, even the orange goo smelled welcoming in comparison. The starling dug desperately for some grubs or worms and ate what He could find. It would hold Him long enough to fly a bit more toward the cooler lands before veering at last toward the Great Undrinkable Water and the whales. The vision He saw of that place seemed endless and peaceful, churning with life and, better yet, without a tall stone nest to be seen.

SL'an hoped to say goodbye to Spool's mother and to finally learn her name, but the gulls weren't in the area then. He'd promised her that He would tell her any answer He found. That would mean coming back Here, at least for awhile. The young starling shuddered.

Chapter Twenty-Three
The Punished

It was surprising how quickly the choking sense and tall stone nests gave way to more and more green land and clean air as SL'an flew. He felt the weight of the reek and noise leaving His wings, freeing Him again. There were trees – real trees with proper branches and leaves! There were saplings growing near mature ones, and some very old souls ready to offer solid and safe refuge to the weary starling. Fields and trees still stayed obediently to the edges of the Gods' paths, but at least they were there.

SL'an chose a spot to rest where a cluster of fruit-laden bushes graced the edge of a Sacred Space. He saw birds of many kinds again. Most were too busy to pay Him any mind, but a few greeted Him jovially. "Looking for a place to be?" One robin male called from where he tugged at some berries on low, thorny branches.

"Just a place to rest and eat before I go on my way," SL'an told him.

"You're welcome at the Sacred Space of our Gods," the robin nodded. "There's plenty of food to share. If you want to find more of your kind, some will come through later to troll the short grasses."

The young starling nodded that He understood, but had a strong feeling in His breast that a starling flock would have too many questions about why one of their kind was traveling alone. It wasn't usual, and He didn't want to risk having to answer questions or raise suspicions, and perhaps action, if other starling flock Secret Keepers believed as Bard did. He shouldn't be Seeking, according to Bard.

There are teachers, but no Tellers. No Seekers. There should only be the flock and the service of becoming more like the Gods.

SL'an focused on eating as much real food as He could without being weighed down. He still felt weak after only two suns of mainly God-food, but the good berries and grubs and worms in this Sacred Space were already filling Him in a way He never appreciated as much as He did now. *Mother, why is it that the God-food left Me so empty? How is it that I'm different from the sparrows in the Here who live so much on that?* He looked around at birds coming and going from this new Sacred Space. There were some sparrows there, but they seemed larger, and their voices were not as high and loud. *If it weren't for the same plumage, I would almost say these sparrows were a different kind!* SL'an suspected that Chip and Sweet had been born in the Here, and probably their parents too, and they never knew anything different. He wondered if Bard had ever been to the Here to see how very much like Gods those birds seemed to live. Would Bard still believe starlings were the Chosen Kind?

There were starlings, He had been told, that did come through and even sometimes live in the Here, but He hadn't seen any.

"I just came from visiting a Sacred Space the birds call Here," SL'an said casually to the male robin who had ventured to the short grass to look for the same food the starling had just enjoyed.

"I've never been there, but I have heard of it. It's not a place for most robins."

"No!" SL'an ruffled His feathers. "It seems to be mostly a place for pigeons and sparrows – and many Gods. I have to say I much prefer Sacred Spaces like yours – or my own."

The robin turned a questioning eye. "What took you to such a place then?"

"I am a Seeker," SL'an said slowly, "and I want to learn more about the Gods and the world They've created." He expected another litany about how unusual it was for starlings to allow one of the flock to become a Seeker, but the litany never came.

"Fascinating! I don't know a single robin Seeker in this Sacred Space, or any robin Seeking in any Sacred Space that I am familiar with," the robin mused. "Many Praisers, though…"

"I'm SL'an. I'd be grateful to know of any other interesting places to visit where Gods and birds interact; these places should be unlike Sacred Spaces like ours, and unlike the place called Here. Also, these places should be even closer to the cooler lands."

"I'm Praiser Han. During our migration at the start of the returning long sun, we pass a wonderful area where there are small rivers and a stretch of fields and fields of brown soil pushed up in rows as if a giant bird already trolled the place with an unimaginable beak. The Gods have made these places for Their birds. Many birds rest and eat there on the way back from the warmer lands, and not just robins! Whatever happens there now, I'm not certain, but I've been told there's other food provided over the long-sun times by the Gods. You'll even find pigeons living there with other kinds! But relax! It is nothing like the Here you describe."

It sounded like a good fit for His Seeking, so SL'an asked for directions to this particular space and left immediately after, since Han said it would take at least a full sun on the wing before He would arrive there.

The sky was grey and moist, tasting strongly of coming rain. *If I fly as fast as I can, I might make it before the rain falls.* If He didn't make it before then and had to shelter from a downpour, it would be another part of a sun before He'd reach His destination.

SL'an started out pumping His wings forcefully, but soon the two suns of God-food wore at His muscles. It was as if vines were pulling Him down toward the earth, and flying quickly took enormous effort. To compensate, He closed His eyes and focused on the air around Him; there were breaths of wind He could use. When they came, the starling spread His wings and relaxed, allowing the gusts to carry Him along in a glide and giving His tired muscles a small break. It was enough to keep Him going.

The first drops of rain struck His feathers about halfway there. He flew through those and even through it when the water began misting steadily. Soon, however, the drops fattened in a torrent, spiking the young starling's face and needling between His feathers. He had no choice but to find a well-leafed tree branch to shelter under while the water thundered down. The trees bowed their heads, curling over the many lives they protected.

The storm slowed and finally stopped, leaving puddles on the nearest Gods' path. Two female purple finches were indulging in a bath, dipping and fluttering their wings to make sure the water reached to the quills and the skin. It had been a long time since SL'an refreshed with a bath, too, so He dropped from the tree where some water pooled in short grass. "Why don't you join us here?" one of the young finches called. "It's much better without the grass in the way."

SL'an hesitated. Didn't they know how dangerous those paths could be? "I've seen horrible things happen to those crossing the Gods' paths," He admitted. "I feel safer over here, and would feel even better if you two would join me instead."

They tittered together, shook the last water from their mostly brown feathers, and flew away. *I wish you wouldn't laugh,* He thought. *If you think the metal things are any less than Blooders, you're wrong. They're worse. They kill without care, and they kill without eating.*

The two female finches darted and played with each other until they were out of sight. SL'an took more time than He thought He should have bathing, but it was the most wonderful feeling, and once finished He was well refreshed. There was still a chance of finding the new Sacred Space before black.

The sun came out again and warmed the wet earth quickly, causing the air to thicken and plump all around SL'an and within His lungs. It was clean air, though! He breathed it in deeply and thanked the Gods for making so much more clean space than dirty, choking space.

The Starling God stopped at other Sacred Spaces during the flight to eat good food when He needed it. Every meal washed away a bit more of the God-food weakness, and He was relieved to feel normal again. His wings were tired but not drained when He finally saw long rows of plants that were set similar to His Mother's gardens, but much larger. Clearly the Gods were responsible for this, but SL'an didn't know if this was the Sacred Space Praiser Han spoke of. He described rows of brown, turned earth, and here were rows of green. *Han did say there were other foods that were offered in this Sacred Space during the warm times…*

It was becoming black and most birds had already roosted or returned to nests; SL'an decided to find a sturdy tree where He could also spend the black safely. When the sun released, He would find a bird to talk to, and try to figure out if He was in the right place. He followed the directions, and the arrival time matched, so the chances were good.

He found better than a branch to settle in. One larger tree had a hole from where a proud limb once reached out. The starling didn't know what made it fall away from the base, but He was glad to find it; it felt like it could rain again. Leaves were good cover, and water would pour off His feathers well enough, but something drew Him to the rounded crevice.

"Is anyone sleeping here?"

When there was no answer, SL'an cautiously landed on the hole's edge and listened for breathing or movement. There was none! He hopped wearily inside and found the added bonus of leaves tucked into a soft nest there – probably left at some past time by squirrels. The softness reminded Him of the nest Mother made for Him, and of sitting dutifully on L'al's eggs before they hatched. What would the nestlings be doing now? In the few suns that had passed, they'd surely grown a great deal. *I won't be able to see them take first flight, L'in. I wonder – will they still be there when I return?* He felt L'in's presence in the air intensely warming the smallest place inside His breast. The thought of her caused that warm spot to grow and expand until it was like basking in the sun. *You'll always be a part of My insides, L'in. You warm Me from the inside out where the sun only warms Me from the outside in.*

The last waking thought the young starling had was of L'in's kind face, the blue outlining her understanding eyes. Her eyes were wise and gentle. *I'll never forget your eyes, L'in…*

A different eye snapped SL'an out of His wistful drifting. It was also wise, but large and laughing, familiar, somehow drilling into the starling's mind again with something He couldn't understand at first, but then the meaning became clear. *You need to come soon, starling. I am waiting for You!*

SL'an looked around Him. He was flying above a great space of brown earth that moved like waves. The whale's body leaped out of it, the eye fixing Him again joyfully. The body melted back into the brown, roiling earth without a splash. *Look at them, starling. Look at them forgetting!*

The roiling brown earth was filled with starlings, pigeons, sparrows and some other kinds the young starling didn't know. There were Gods and metal things, and the birds flocked around the Gods, taking what They threw out on the earth. When the food landed, the brown soil stopped undulating and lay flat and quiet like an animal drawing one last breath. The birds screeched and gobbled whatever was there, growing larger and larger as they ate and as SL'an watched. He noticed a group of Cleaners picking at what seemed to be the mangled body of the fisher female.

Look at them forgetting! The whale's voice pulsed through the ground and into SL'an's brain, vibrating intensely. *You have to help them remember. Some are forgetting, and some have already forgotten.*

SL'an snapped His eyes open to hear a robin Praiser greeting the sun with several others harmonizing. Morning news began, but it wasn't as tightly knit as it would be at Mother's Sacred Space. The bits of news came from farther and wider out, carrying loosely on the open air. Most of the news was usual, and except for the wideness of it causing a different feel, it was very much like being home – tidings of first flights, new clutches of eggs and other typical events.

SL'an took His first truly clear look at the strange fields down the hill from where He had roosted in the softly lined hole. All the hills sloped down to greet these fields with their rows of something growing. The field plants were all the same kind and basically the same height, and like the Gods' paths, there were no trees allowed there. The starling shook His head at the spectacle of so many of one plant kind repeated over and over. It was the opposite of how any other things grew that He'd seen. *Even in fields of grass, there are many kinds of grass and flowers and different plants. It seems it must be... that for one to live, the others must be there too. How can these live alone?* He thought of the seed His Mother provided and all the different bird kind there. Ground feeding birds benefited from the higher feeding birds. Some watched and others kept the peace, and each had their place and purpose there. He couldn't imagine a vast expanse of only starlings, never mingling at some point with others. All robins? All redwings? It wouldn't make sense!

The closest He could come to imagining such a world was the place called Here, and even that had seemed very wrong to Him. There was emptiness in the very soil, where there even was soil.

He launched into the moist, warm morning air to find another bird to speak with. If He was lucky enough to find the Teller of this Sacred Space, that might afford Him the best information.

There was a collection of long, narrow God nests set on the edge of a gravel path of the Gods. These nests were set between the enormous fields of same-plants with a bit of short grass around each one. Across the Gods' path from these long nests was a much smaller nest, lighter colored and neat. SL'an could see a few pigeons patrolling the gravel path and picking at bits for their gullets. Smaller birds were flitting to and from a seed feeder set closely to one of the clear boxes that seemed to be on the sides of every God's dwelling. A large apple tree grew at one corner of the lighter nest, not far from the seed feeder, with something round and bright hanging from it that hummingbirds were clearly eating. His heart leaped when He saw four doves looking for fallen seeds at the bottom, their heads bobbing in such a familiar way it made the young starling's breast ache.

SL'an flew toward the seed feeder and called to the doves. "Would one of you be the Teller of this Sacred Space?"

All four longish necks stretched up with surprise, but not alarm. "I'm Teller L'om," one female replied, the head bobbing quickly. "Peace and welcome!"

The Starling God landed on the ground beside them.

"Please! Have some seed and tell me how we may help you here," the dove said.

"Thank you. I haven't had anything to eat yet, and I appreciate your willingness to share."

The doves looked at each other with bright eyes. "There's always plenty to eat thanks to the grace of the Gods," another said.

SL'an looked around Him. "You must be very proud of this Sacred Space! Everyone I see seems happy and well fed. Are there Blooders?"

Teller L'om shook her head. "So rarely I should say no. There are some raccoons that look for food at night, but they're often happy with other food from the fields and the nests where our Gods store special food for Their cows and chickens."

When the Teller saw her guest's confusion, she added, "Cows and chickens are animals that have done something wrong to the Gods, so they are locked away. Still, our Gods are kind enough to feed them and take care of them!"

"Do they come out of the nests at any time?"

"As rarely as we are troubled by Blooders."

"So they aren't Blooders?"

"If they were once, then they've been changed by the Gods. They eat only the special food the Gods give them."

"But if they aren't Blooders, what harm could they have done the Gods to deserve being locked away?"

The dove Teller looked at her friends and One and laughed. "This young one hasn't even introduced himself to us because of so many questions!"

SL'an dipped His head. "I'm sorry. I've chosen to become Teller and Seeker, but am Seeking right now. My taken name is SL'an" – then He added before they could comment, "Although starlings usually don't have professions like this, it's what I've chosen. Even though most only choose one profession, two are what I have chosen."

"Well. So you say and so it is," Teller L'om said softly. "It isn't for me or any of us to question the choices of another as long as the choices don't cause harm." She took a few seeds and savored them. "So you're Seeking, and this is why you have so many questions. I see. As Teller here, I'm happy to share whatever I know."

SL'an felt so many questions bubbling to the fore and didn't know where to begin. He remembered the dream, and the whale telling Him he was waiting – that He must hurry. *Yes, but there are things I must know first. I feel it.*

"Tell me how you look upon your Sacred Space and what makes it special," He finally asked.

The Teller tipped her head slightly. "There is so much plenty, and our Gods love Their birds so much that many who travel from one place to another make certain their path allows them to rest and feed here, even if that means they must fly a bit off the straightest course."

SL'an knew then He'd found the right place. "I'd like to see the ones the Gods keep locked away. May I?"

"I'd be pleased to show you, Seeker. It would be very easy to show you. Our Gods have made those nests so Their birds may fly in and out, but the ones held inside may not leave."

They all enjoyed more seed and SL'an probed beneath the short grass to find some grubs. When every bird had eaten enough, Dove L'om shook her feathers to announce she was ready to go.

"You have no nestlings?" SL'an asked.

"Our babes have fledged and are nearby, but on their own," she said before launching. "There's time for one more family, but we haven't started that yet."

It was a very short flight to the nest where L'om said cows were locked away. There were many strong, but not entirely unpleasant, auras in this Sacred Space, and once the starling flew close to this particular nest, He knew cows were a source of one of them. The nest had sides, but some kind of see-through material similar to netting covered the top two-thirds or so. Through this, SL'an could already see many faces pushed closely together, but not as in-line as pigeons. The faces were punctuated with large brown eyes looking somewhat to the front and somewhat to the side – not forward like most Blooders'.

L'om led Him through an open space toward the nest's top where the view was unveiled – countless large, slow-moving animals with very little room to move any way. There was no grass or plant life of any kind. Some lay down in what seemed to be their own waste. There were several piles of dry grass set loosely within some kind of metal things, surrounded by a few cows who munched away at the offering. There was something else placed around too, like yellow gravel. Other cows crunched that while some iridescent black birds SL'an had never seen flew in and out, snatching bits each time.

"What is that bird kind?" SL'an asked.

"Those are grackles," Teller L'om said in a faraway tone.

SL'an watched the cows with interest, but there didn't seem to be anything menacing about them. They pushed each other rudely sometimes, but the aura of them said only vegetation. They weren't Blooders, and the starling couldn't believe they ever had been. With a jolt, He recalled the swallows' tale. *They said the Gods came from the sky and wanted to be with the other creatures that walked and flew on the earth. They said They tried to live like Blooders, but when hunting wasn't enough to fill Them, They kept some non-Blooders in bondage!*

SL'an's breast tightened. "Do cows stay here always and die here?"

They had landed on something metal. *The more Gods do Their work, the more metal there seems to be*, He mused.

"Our Seekers have seen cows die here. However, most of them are loaded into large metal roaring things and taken away. When one is taken away, it never comes back."

"Maybe They take cows away when they've paid their dues and are forgiven. Maybe then they don't need to be locked away anymore, and walk with grass beneath their feet," SL'an suggested hopefully, but His breast was still tight.

"Yes! This is what we suspect too. Travelers have told us they see cows with grass beneath their feet in some Sacred Spaces. How good the Gods are! Of course the cows cannot be fully trusted even then, so it seems. The Gods put up boundaries to make sure there are only certain places the cows may go."

SL'an shuddered to L'om's notice. "I agree, Seeker! What might the horrible cows do if the Gods didn't keep them at bay?"

A pair of grackles pecked at the last of the yellow gravel, and one turned a curious eye to SL'an. The starling thought he was about to speak, but L'om quickly nudged Him with her wing shoulder. "Next, we'll see the chickens."

Another brief flight brought the two birds to a similar long nest, but with a very different aura. "It senses vaguely like bird," SL'an gasped.

"They may have been birds once, but they are no longer." L'om's voice was matter-of-fact but still soft. "Whatever they did against the Gods must have been terrible because the Gods have taken their flight and much of their sense, and have locked them away."

The nest, if it could be called that, had a floor of ground wood and waste, covered on nearly every space by white things that resembled birds in the beak and eyes and feathers, but were shaped like no other bird SL'an had ever seen. They were misshapen, with legs spread out widely to barely support what looked like leaden-heavy bodies. Some were flopped down on their bellies, seemingly unable to stand at all. Tallish metal containers held something like the yellow cow gravel-food, but finer like pebbled sand. Other containers were filled with water for the chickens that jostled around each other to get a drink or a bite to eat.

Several other grackles were at these feed stations, grabbing bites of what they could. Some would leave and then more took their turn to steal. L'om spoke as if the grackles were invisible. "Chickens are brought here as babes and don't stay long. They eat and grow quickly, but then the Gods take them away – these will go soon – before they grow old. We don't know what happens to them, but travelers have never said they have seen such as these with grass beneath their feet."

"But there may be some somewhere that travelers just haven't noticed?" SL'an felt ill.

"That's very possible. I'm sure you know there is always more to Seek and discover, or there would be no need for Seekers and not as much need for Tellers!"

SL'an was overcome. Without another word, He flew to a small bare patch of ground in the middle of a group of the flightless birds. They milled around Him with no concern, so He walked directly in front of one and addressed it loudly. "I am Seeker SL'an from the Sacred Space of God Flower. Can you please tell me what your kind has done to deserve this?"

The chicken, that seemed male, turned a red eye to SL'an and made a croaking sound.

"Do you speak?" He tried again.

"We are. Nothing," the flightless bird said, or at least that's what it sounded like.

"I don't understand…"

The chicken turned and jostled his way to the sandy food.

"Don't bother trying to talk to them, Seeker. We've tried over the years, but the Gods have taken some of their sense. We wonder alternatively if it is because they have little sense that they must be locked away. They would be food for Blooders all too easily if they weren't protected!" L'om had the same blue circling her dove's eyes, but although she shared the softness of voice, there was something that wasn't quite the same as L'in and L'al.

"I think I'm ready to leave here," SL'an barely managed to say. They flew out as another batch of grackles was just flying in.

It was a relief to be out of those nests and back where the other birds happily flew, ate and loved under the sun and within the trees. He was determined that when He returned to His Sacred Space, He would try to communicate with Mother. *I'll ask You to forgive them for whatever they might have done and let them free. Surely You'd want it that way? Surely You could speak with other Gods and tell Them it must be so.* He tried not to think of the swallows' words.

His thoughts were broken by a group of clamoring grackles flying toward the edges of one field. Another group heard whatever they were saying and joined them, then another, and still another. Soon at least thirty grackles landed at the edge and began pecking enthusiastically at something. SL'an looked at L'om. "What are they doing?"

L'om was facing away from the field, and answered the starling without turning. "The Gods have placed special food there."

"Why aren't other bird kinds joining the grackles? Perhaps I should go over and try this food." He tried to sound upbeat and interested in trying new things. Isn't that what a Seeker should do? Still, He felt dishonest speaking as if He really wanted whatever the grackles had. So far God-food had been less than enjoyable.

The dove Teller's words were barely audible. "That food is meant only for the grackles."

SL'an watched as a few more stragglers joined the grackle flock, pecking fervently and raising their gleaming heads at times to share how much they were enjoying the feast. The starling still couldn't hear their words, but He recognized the tones and motions as pleasant focus and conversations. *They look a little like Me,* He thought. The bodies and tails were longer, but the iridescent black feathers made Him think of how Bard looked when he spoke to Him on the top of Mother's nest. He didn't have fond feelings toward Bard, but there was something comforting about being in a flock, of having a home. Seeing the grackles so content struck a chord in the starling and allowed a bit of contentment to seep into His own breast.

"Do excuse me." L'om bobbed her head quickly, still facing away from the field's edge. "We must go. We encourage you to join us."

To the starling's surprise, those were the only words she spoke before flying to the feeder in front of the light-colored, smaller nest. He thought she was only going there to feed, but after what looked like hurried words, every bird kind at the feeder flew away toward a very distant line of trees slightly up a hill from where the grackles and SL'an remained by the huge fields of rowed plants.

He didn't know whether to follow, or stay and try talking to one of the grackles. *Since this is a bird kind that I've never seen before, and is favored by the Gods, I should stay and try to speak with some of them. There's food placed only for them – I'd like to know why this is so.*

SL'an quickly preened His feathers and took wing to join the grackles where they trolled to find the last bits of something bright yellow scattered along a large area of the field side.

"Good sun!" He called out as He landed nimbly on short grass next to some bare ground where the grackles fed.

One raised his head and walked a bit toward SL'an, stumbling.

"Goodness! Child!" One female chastised the youngish one. "You've been flying long enough that you should also know how to walk properly!"

A group of others laughed, but the young one lurched back toward the female and fell forward, quivering.

The female, that SL'an guessed then to be the young one's mother, bolted her head upright. "What's the matter with you?"

The young grackle opened his beak and stretched it wide, rolling over to his side. The quivers turned into violent whole-body convulsions as the bright golden eye stared pleadingly at his mother.

"Speak!" She flapped her wings frantically while other adults around her stopped searching for food. Her fledgling's beak continued to stretch open, then close slightly, but no words came from his throat. All SL'an could do was watch while the young one's breathing became faster and more shallow, then slower and slower still until the cloud of death crossed the once bright golden eye, and he breathed no more.

The mother shrieked, followed by other shrieks of agony among the flock as more young adults staggered and shook. A few fell over quickly while others seemed confused and stumbled, or tried to fly and crashed back onto the ground.

The starling's mind whirled. *What can I do? What is this?* Some of the adults seemed unwell too, He noted with a knot deep inside His heart. Birds who were much older were also stumbling or shuddering like the young, and the cries of distress filled the field and SL'an's head in a dismal chorus.

"I can go for help," SL'an yelled out to the flock. "The Teller here may know what this is and what to do!"

He heard no reply, but flew as fast as He could toward the distant trees where L'om and all the other birds had gone. Once He was close enough to sense the cool shade from the trees, He saw some birds resting in the branches. SL'an scanned quickly, but saw no doves. "L'om – has anyone seen L'om and know where I can find her? Quickly!"

"L'om is in meditation and mustn't be disturbed," a finch piped.

"I have no desire to be rude, but this is an emergency. There's something wrong with the grackles, and I need to know what to do to help or ask L'om if there is anything she can do to help!"

The finch looked away. "There's nothing Teller L'om can do."

SL'an stretched His beak with frustration. "Then do you know what's happening to them?"

"They have eaten the corn left for them."

"By the Gods? The Gods left them this 'corn'?"

"Yes. The corn is there to kill the grackles." The Finch's voice trailed off absently as L'om's had.

"You all know this? You know this and didn't warn them?"

The finch reached up and picked at something invisible on a leaf. "The grackles steal from the Gods, so they're punished. We only take the feed offered here and don't steal from inside any of the nests. To do so means to face punishment."

"But you could warn them – tell them what would happen so they wouldn't steal and so they wouldn't have to die." SL'an spoke the words out loud, but He already knew what the answer would be in one form or another. *It's the will of the Gods. We shouldn't interfere.*

"It's in the grackles' nature to steal. They would never listen to any of us anyway. Why should we try to save a kind the Gods don't favor? It is unfortunate, but it's the way it must be. They should learn to stay away, but they continue to come."

"Will…any live?" SL'an could barely get the thought out.

"I don't know. In other years some have lived, but most often all of them die, although it might take a sun or two."

"Suns!" SL'an felt a wave of something bitter and hot sweep throughout His entire being. It was similar to what He felt when Mother allowed L'in to be taken by the fisher cat female, but, if it was possible, this was stronger and deeper. It lodged teeth firmly into His being and propelled the bitter heat so it threatened to blast out of His beak.

He took wing without another word to the birds there, flying back toward the dying grackles. *How could they warn their own kind to stay away from here if they have no one left to warn them – if these others will not warn them? How could they redeem themselves if they're not given the chance to learn?*

The bitterness and heat made His wings tight. They didn't want to work properly, and His breath came fast. *So the Gods feed the ones They place in bondage, and then They kill those who take any of the feed? There's no sense to it! There's no sense to it!* The story the swallows shared was sounding more like truth all the time.

Chapter Twenty-Four
Black and White

For the next two suns, all SL'an could do was watch while the grackles suffered and died, one after another. Sometimes they died in pairs or small groups, but others lost life-light alone – except for the horrified starling who tried to be close to any of those He could. Those who had been stronger and healthier than other flock-mates took longer to become very sick and die. These birds tried to fly and roost, but even those hearty, glistening ones succumbed eventually.

Gods came out, now seeming ghoulish to SL'an, and collected the bodies They could find. Some of the dead stayed prone and still in deeper grasses, or where they had flown to a distant tree line, and the young starling was glad of that. *You will not have these,* He felt His thoughts hiss. *If I had My way, You would not have had any of them.*

The bitter heat held Him firmly in its jaws. There was a strange sense of power in it. When He roosted during the three blacks after the grackles had eaten the special corn, the quiet was almost impossible to hear. Instead of the crickets and their lulling night music, He realized how loud the bitter heat was. It rushed through His eardrums. *I should stop this Seeking now. Haven't I learned enough about the Gods? There's nothing worth knowing and nothing else I want to see.*

But L'in believed! She would want You to continue. She'd want You to follow this until the end," another voice inside Him reasoned. It was so drowned out by the hissing bitter noise, though, that it was hard to hear.

L'in was misguided. They're all misguided. The swallows are correct. These Gods are The Blight and are not right in their heads, the bitterness insisted.

The softer, distant voice was gentle, but with its own persistence. *Perhaps there's more to know and understand. Your Seeking has been short. Take more time. L'in would advise this.*

I wish...The bitter heat swelled...*I wish They would all die instead of the grackles, or Spool, or L'in, or even the fisher female. I wish They would all die.*

The distant gentle voice pressed further. *Then You would die. You're of the Gods, and You have a purpose You must fulfill.*

As sleepy as He was, SL'an snapped His beak and could nearly taste the bitterness. *I am NOT one of Them. I will never be.*

You can't change Your destiny.

Maybe I can...

To do that, you need to know more.

SL'an didn't know how the distant voice could be so strong and wispy at the same time; He fell asleep still gripped by the jaws of bitter heat – just not quite as tightly.

After the last of the grackles died, the starling flew further toward the cooler lands. He didn't say goodbye to the birds at that Space – in fact, He refused to stay around them or speak to them once He learned that they knew the grackles' fate and chose to say nothing. Their cheery morning praise and news fed the bitter heat and threatened to make it grow. They behaved as if nothing horrible had taken place, and it changed nothing in their world. *It's changed Me.*

The power from that bitter heat urged Him onward with purpose. He scanned along His travels for any grackles and took time to tell them what He'd seen. Most were aghast and some had trouble believing the Gods would ever do such a thing to Their birds. "I can't force you to never go to that place, but I urge you to listen to me and stay away from there," He said over and over again. He told them about the flightless birds called chickens, and explained that for some reason, feed for them, the imprisoned, was off limits to all others. Most grackles laughed at this. "I've been to similar places and have eaten this food. There's never been a death or a problem," one said, flashing a proud golden eye in SL'an's direction.

While on the wing, the starling passed many Sacred Spaces of varying sizes and kinds, but He couldn't bring Himself to stop at any of them. Instead, He rested and fed where there were only trees and fields alongside the Gods' paths. He also noticed the number of dead creatures along the paths. They were as small and sometimes smaller than finches, and as large as moose. The carnage made the bitterness flare, and His wings thrust wildly because of it.

Go create a space inside where You may face this, the softer voice suggested, but SL'an focused on pressing the voice down until He muffled it completely. There was too much power in the bitter heat to give it up. Something about it was good.

He had finally turned away from the cooler lands and began the journey toward the Great Undrinkable Water when He came across another small flock of grackles. They turned their heads toward Him as He came in for a landing on the short grass where they were trolling for wild seeds. "A starling!" The largest called out happily. "Join us! But where is your flock?"

Once He answered questions and warned this new group of the horrible event and place, the largest, called Treek, shook his head and began to argue, as others had before, that he had eaten at similar places many times. "I'm six season turns old and can tell you this is not always the case. The Gods aren't The Blight you describe."

SL'an pulled His head back with surprise. "I didn't call Them The Blight—"

"—But you're describing that and thinking it? I've heard that some bird kinds think of the Gods this way, but I insist that you, and they, are wrong."

"I know what I've seen." SL'an tapped His foot sharply. "The Gods have punished birds by taking away their flight, imprisoning them, and killing others."

"I've seen the flightless chickens you describe, Starling SL'an, but they weren't and aren't imprisoned. They walk with grass beneath their feet, eating under the sun and bathing in the dust, and going back to a space where the Gods have provided special nests for them to lay their eggs and roost. There looks to be no better life.”

“But they still can’t fly!”

“No. Neither can the Gods, but They’re greater than all nonetheless.”

The young starling scratched His head with frustration.

“I see you aren’t convinced, young Seeker. Since a Seeker you are, perhaps you need to see what I say with your own eyes? I can take you there in less than half a sun.”

The other grackles murmured support of this idea, and SL’an preened as He considered. “I need to travel toward the Great Undrinkable Water and have…someone there I must meet soon.”

“Your time won’t be interrupted much. It’s in the same direction,” Treek reasoned. He turned away from SL’an to inspect a sound, and the young starling noticed one bright white feather showing from within Treek’s other long, black tail feathers.

There were several young grackles who begged to come along; they’d been born and fledged close to where they all now visited and fed, and had never tasted the food or seen the place Treek described. “I used to go there before I won the heart of your mother.” He closed his eyes as he spoke to the young ones. “A group of us would go together to the place and take turns flying in to eat while the others kept watch.”

“What were they watching for?” A young female asked breathlessly.

“When we get there, I’ll share the rest of the story. Until then, you have to wait, Tanka!”

The group took off together and, true to his word, Treek got them there in less than half a sun.

There were no obvious Sacred Spaces near it. The God’s nest was small and a bit ramshackle, reminding SL’an a bit of a dove’s. There were places where the God or Gods here were growing food in rows, but not directly on the ground; instead, the plants rose up from mounds of soil and sometimes climbed up some kind of wooden frames. Treek landed on the top of one of these, followed in kind by his young.

SL'an landed on the grass instead and looked around. He could already sense the pungent aura of chickens. It was similar to that of the imprisoned ones and yet something was slightly different.

"There are your flightless birds," Treek said, turning his body quickly where he perched to point the direction. There were six females scratching at the grass and pecking busily. Although they were still strangely shaped for birds, clearly too heavy to take to the wind, they weren't as misshapen as the first ones the starling had seen.

"Their legs are not so far apart, and these can walk properly," He told Treek, walking a bit closer Himself to get a better look. "Their breasts aren't so enormous either."

"And they are free to go where they choose and eat what they choose in the grass as I told you they could," Treek preened. Tanka and her siblings were busy flying around the ramshackle nest, exploring.

"Yes! What you told me is true," SL'an marveled. The bitter heat released a bit more and made His bones lighter. "The others I saw were only white and rather dirty. These have such beautiful plumage."

"Rude!" A seventh, white chicken rounded the corner of the God's nest and stood with breast puffed forward and head pulled back. "What isn't beautiful about white plumage?"

SL'an jumped into the air while Treek laughed heartily. "I'm certain no insult was intended, Fair Hen! Forgive this young starling. He had a bad experience in some strange place with what sounds like birds very different from you."

"You can speak properly?" SL'an choked, then dipped down as if to deflect the torrent of indignation His words caused.

"Of course I can speak properly, but I'm not certain at all that you can!" She ruffled her weighty white feathers violently, causing a dust cloud to erupt. "It may be true that a good dust bath leaves the white a bit dingy for a time, but it's better than the infernal itching. And I'd rather be white than whatever that color is on your plumage! And . what, may I ask, is wrong with the size of my breasts?"

"Nothing! They're quite lovely!" SL'an rushed the words out in a flood. "The others' were so large they – they couldn't walk properly. Some had trouble standing."

A reddish-brown hen stopped pecking and turned to her rankled flock-mate. "Calm down. You heard what the grackle said. This starling's young and has had a different experience. Hear his words! The poor creatures he describes sound like they were born with their bodies all wrong."

The white hen shook a smaller cloud of dust from her feathers and smoothed them out, but SL'an could see there was still an ember in her eyes ready to flare if He wasn't careful. He thought of L'al and took a centering breath. "The creatures I saw were like you, but yes, their bodies did appear wrong. I also tried to speak with them, and they didn't seem able. Since I'd never seen chicken kind before then and learned nothing of them before, I thought all chickens would be the same. I'm a Seeker who is learning."

At the word Seeker, all the hens stopped feeding and looked at the starling with new curiosity. The white hen huffed under her breath. "Are all starlings exactly the same?" she challenged.

"No, Dear Hen, we're not all the same, although—"

"—Well then. Wouldn't you already know that one of us is not like another? Goodness!" She growled.

"Don't mind her," the brown hen soothed. She's been Her favorite for these few season turns, but now that she's laying fewer eggs, she fears losing her place and it puts her in a mood." The other hens had grown disinterested and wandered away.

"Who is 'Her'?" SL'an started realizing He was getting hungry after the long flight and looked longingly at the rich, deep green short grass, promising a bounty of food just beneath it.

"Her," the brown hen stated simply. "She is One of the Two who feed and care for us. If She doesn't, then Her One does. She nests with Him. He doesn't love us in the same way, but He's kind."

SL'an forgot food for a moment as fear for the chickens made his quills prickle. "What do your friend's eggs have to do with her favored place?"

The brown hen laughed loudly. "It is all about the eggs, of course! Isn't it for you? There's nothing more glorious than the moment you have laid an egg – although you are male, and I suppose you don't understand that feeling in the same way." She tipped her head demurely. "We lay our eggs for Her and She comes to take them and praises us with Her songs! She sings us beautiful songs for the eggs and strokes our feathers. She cleans our waste and messes away and lays fresh, sweet hay. She brings us fresh water and food."

"Doesn't it bother you that She takes your babes before they're even hatched?"

The brown hen looked amused. "There's no life in them because there are no roosters. I don't know what She does with the eggs, but they are no good to us except to please Her."

SL'an was still fighting the prickle. *L'om said the chickens there would disappear and never come back,* He thought. "What will change for you if you lay fewer eggs?"

"It only means we grow older, young one." She looked out at the white hen who had stalked away to the shade of lilac trees. "She's especially close to Her, and worries that closeness will disappear if she cannot please Her with as many eggs. I tell her not to worry! There've been some wise old ones who died before us, and I've heard about and seen no less care or love shown for them than the rest of us. She's being insecure." The brown hen chuckled at the starling's expression. "Yes, I'm the oldest now. It's rare that I lay an egg anymore…but once in a while I still have a gift to offer!"

The reddish-brown hen seemed to think the conversation was over and went back to scratching and pecking, pulling at tender grass blades and bits of clover, but SL'an still had His own niggling worries to quiet. "How did the wise ones die?"

"In a quiet way. They usually begin eating less and growing thinner. One day we all roosted at the black and a wise one seemed so very tired. When the sun released, she had died there beside me, called to the soil. When She came in to gather our eggs, She saw the wise one dead there, and water poured from Her eyes."

"I've seen it!" SL'an opened His beak.

"It happens when They feel pain – I'm reasonably sure of it," the reddish-brown hen nodded. She didn't sing for us that day, but carried our dead flock-mate outside and helped her become one with the soil by placing her inside it and covering her well."

SL'an felt the jaws of bitter heat let go at last, and He was amazed how like Himself He felt again. For a time, He had completely forgotten what it was to truly be Himself, and stranger still, He hadn't even wanted to remember. Now He sighed with relief. "I foolishly thought I'd know so much more than your kind. I judged all of you on one group of you, and now I know I'll never make such a mistake again."

The hen's eyes gleamed. "Happy to have helped you! Now, I feel it's time to lay my own egg – today is one of those days, so I'll go inside to the nests." She raised her voice to be sure the grackles were included. "All of you are welcome to share in our food if you'd like to come inside with me." She spoke at a normal tone again toward the starling traveler, "We have an agreement with the grackles, from years before I was born. One of the wise ones told us all about it – that they will come through at times and we shouldn't trouble them. In return, they will leave if we come to eat. It's the best way, isn't it? To get along?"

Treek had flown close enough to hear and landed beside SL'an. "Yes, it's the best way, and we teach our nestlings how the sharing is to be done. One at a time, then?"

"Oh, I think two at a time will be fine. There are only four of you today. You'll be in and out before long. There's always plenty."

SL'an suggested that Treek take his youngsters in one at a time first to show them what to do. While He waited, He made sure to enjoy some grubs and worms along with a few other insects that were crawling in the lush grass. Unlike the Here, the soil was dark and rich, giving the food a loamy flavor that tickled the starling's brain with sheer pleasure. If groups of bird kinds were not the same as He saw with chickens and the birds at various Sacred Spaces, then groups of the Gods clearly must be different as well. He was so content to have the bitter heat gone and to feel something good toward Mother and Her kind for a moment that He chose not to think anything deeper about it.

When the young grackles had fed, they chattered excitedly amongst themselves in a nearby tree, and Treek led SL'an in to try the strange new food. It was golden like in the other horrible chicken nest, but there was such a sweet aura in the air, SL'an couldn't even compare it. As it turned out, the aura wasn't from the food, but from the dried grass the hens had called 'hay' spread about and filling nests. The reddish-brown hen was settled in one such nest, puffed out and concentrating. There was nothing but the sense of happiness. As He suspected, SL'an had no great love for the food itself, but ate some politely with His guide.

They gathered outside together and rested for a while, Tanka close enough to her father to give him a playful nudge. "You promised to tell us a story about this place."

"Thank the Gods you reminded me, little one," he laughed.

"Is it a story about you?" The other pressed.

"It is! What other story would be worth telling?" He laughed again and the young grackles danced about from branch to branch, laughing too.

"Now settle in if you want to hear it."

They did, hunkering down and looking, to SL'an's amusement, like little nestlings again – wide-eyed and silent.

"This story's about the first sun I came to this place with my own father and mother and sisters. There was a wise old hen here as our new friend described, and my father introduced us to her and received permission to share the food. As of the old agreement, we were given this permission and went with Father one by one into the chicken nest. As you've found out today, the food was more than we'd been promised it would be! So when we each took our turns, and the feeding was over, all I could think about was having more. It wasn't that the hens told us we could only eat once, but my father said we mustn't be greedy."

He squinted with memory and continued. "I pretended to fly about to explore, but stole away to the nest opening instead and hurried inside to grab a bit more. The black was close and the hens had all settled in to roost, although they were not fully asleep yet. I was so busy gulping down as much as I could that I didn't see the one the hens call 'Her' walk in behind me. Foolishly, I had kept my back to the opening – something Father had warned me to never do."

"And you told us not to either!" Tanka cried almost accusingly.

"For good reason," Treek said. "With my back to the opening and my mouth and brain full of the food, I wasn't aware of anything coming up behind me. If a Blooder had come then, I would have gone from eating to being eaten."

The young grackles snuggled together.

"The God was standing almost on top of me before I noticed Her, and I felt the most intense stab of fear and love that I had ever felt or have ever felt since. It made me go mad! I flew into the nest wall then into one of the hens, who was not at all happy with me then, and kept flying back and forth, in one direction and another but unable to find the opening again in my madness."

Treek paused, looking brightly to and from each of his listeners. SL'an felt Himself caught up in the idea as if He was the one in the hen's nest, with the God 'Her' close enough to drive Him mad. It wasn't as real as the whale and the Undrinkable Water had been to Him, but it was almost as vivid.

Treek continued. "Suddenly, I felt Her wrap one wing tip around my body! I tried to flap but I was held close, but not so tightly that it hurt. She turned me so I was on my back, feet facing Her own face, and She sang something to me. I looked fully into Her eyes then and froze there. I can still remember them – brown and looking straight into mine. I froze so that ice seemed to fill my blood and stiffen my feathers. I didn't know what a God would do to me, but She carried me to the opening and relaxed Her wing tip so my own wings were free."

There was another pause, and SL'an waited with the others breathlessly.

"I was still frozen for a moment, panting and upright now on Her wing tip. I couldn't do anything but clasp my feet around Her. I could feel Her heat and the blood pulsing through Her. For a moment, I *knew* Her and recognized the life that She was and is. I finally came to my senses and flew to my family, who by now had noticed I was gone and was watching for me."

"Amazing!" SL'an finally said.

"The story isn't over yet," Treek said. "When I had my first molt after that, and my adult feathers grew in, one tail feather came out white!"

"You were touched by one of the Gods and given something different…" One of the young ones whispered.

"Different. Special," Treek sighed. "A reminder forever to cherish. I have told this tale to every one of my nestlings when they reached your age, but have asked them never to share it. It is my story alone to tell. Do you understand?"

The young grackles nodded wordlessly.

"When my life has been called back to the soil, then you're released from your promise and silence."

The group of them roosted fairly close together during the black. When the sun released, Treek told SL'an he would spend the next few suns there with his young ones to teach them a bit more about this Sacred Space that changed him not only on the inside, but on the outside too.

When the sun brightened things well, SL'an got His first glimpse of the Gods who nested there. They walked out together with something steaming in Their wing tips, with plumage as ramshackle as the nest itself. The two walked together slowly like SL'an had seen L'al and L'in do as they fed on seeds, close together and making soft sounds meant for each other alone. The one called 'Her' left Her One's side and unblocked the hen nest opening, letting Her beloved birds flood out with welcoming, happy greetings. The male waited for Her quietly, and when She returned, He spread one wing to enfold Her, and They walked slowly together back to Their nest.

"They're growing old," Treek murmured.

I've never seen any other Gods as good as Mother, SL'an thought, *but now I see there are others of Mother's kind.* His heart rejoiced.

Chapter Twenty-Five
Forged of the Same

There were many things to see along the way to the Great Undrinkable Water, but SL'an could only take things in fleetingly as He stopped to eat, drink and rest. There was an intense, pressing call now to get to the whale quickly. *The time has come to see what this giant has to tell Me,* He thought over and over again. The idea made the fiber of His muscles vibrate.

It took three more suns, but He finally found a flock of gulls close to one of the Gods' nests where some threw Their food to the clamoring birds that wanted it. One young gull tried to grab a prize repeatedly, but was constantly beaten to it by those faster and more experienced. Chagrined, he pulled away from the others, content to watch and learn for a time before trying again. That gave SL'an the chance He'd waited for.

"Would you be willing to tell me about the Great Undrinkable Water? How much further before I'll see it?"

The gull looked quickly at the starling, then back at the flock darting in wild acrobatics for the sake of God-food. Without looking at the stranger he said, "Can't you sense it? We came inland here for a bite to eat, but if any of us fly that way, then the water is just out of bird's view."

SL'an's heart leaped. "Will you be returning there after you feed?"

The young gull only turned his eye fleetingly in SL'an's direction that time, then back – fixed on the action. "Yes – yes."

"Would it be acceptable if I followed you there then?" He dipped His head politely although there was almost no chance the gull could see.

"Do what you want – can't you see I'm busy?" The gull walked away from SL'an and a bit closer to his flock, grumbling. "How am I supposed to ever eat if I can't watch and learn? Focus! Focus!"

The Starling God wanted to call out and thank the gull, but thought better of it. Instead, He found some short grasses where the soil was not completely dead, but also wasn't rich, loamy and full of food either. *There are too many places like the Here. So much in these places is dead or dying. So much is empty although it is so full of Gods and stone and metal things.*

The land had changed from home too. Instead of rolling hills, the fields and trees and even the places like the Here grew or set on flat and more flat. There were some bumps, but none that rose up proudly and offered places for the sun to hide during the black. SL'an wondered where it went to rest, but was distracted from wondering when a clumsy fledgling sparrow flew up to Him. "Another starling alone," the fledge piped.

"Stay away from him! He could be sick." The sparrow mother flew in too and looked at the lone starling almost accusingly.

"I'm here to—"

"—I tell you to get back from my babe!" she spat. "One starling alone and now another? There could be a plague coming!"

"Please, I'm perfectly healthy—"

"Sometimes they don't even know they're sick, but if their flock won't have them, they aren't right. Now fly over there right now, young man!" The sparrow flew toward her fledgling, harrying him with her wings and beak like Chip and Sweet had when there was a disagreement. In this case, the young one didn't argue. He flew as quickly and smoothly as he was able to where the protective mother directed.

I know I'm alone. I don't have My flock. I don't have Mother. At least I have a purpose.

The gulls called out indignantly when it seemed the God-food was finished, and soon after took to the air in gleaming white and silver groups to fly away. The irritated young gull stayed back a bit longer, walking hurriedly around the stone-like field in front of and behind metal things to see if something had been missed. SL'an chuckled when the frantic gulping motion showed the young gull's hunch paid off. When he flew to join the direction of his flock, SL'an also took wing and hurried along behind.

A strange aura struck the Seeker's nostrils not long after the journey began. It was water, but with something very different mixed in it that clung to the air He breathed. *The Undrinkable Water!* There was something bluish and endless in the distance; the closer they flew to it, the richer the aura grew. Waves were slapping against walls of rock and then slithering away, only to rush to the rocks again like they were playing a game. *The Ocean is pulling herself back, starling. I will be waiting for You, but You need to find Your way to me now,* the whale's strange voice came to SL'an's mind.

SL'an didn't know where to go, so He tried something: *Do I fly over the water? Where should I go to find you?*

He landed on the top of large jagged rocks and jumped when the strange voice popped into His mind again. *If You have learned to go inside Yourself, go there now and feel for me. You will see where to go and will know it when You see it.*

After looking carefully in all directions for Blooders and deciding it was safe, the starling closed His eyes and went down inside Himself, forming and forming the place He usually went to face strong and unpleasant feelings. Today, He greeted His uncertainty there; it looked like little else than mist, hovering and taking no form at all. *What's this showing Me? There's nothing here!* He faced the mist for what seemed like suns and thought He'd failed when an idea finally struck Him.

I need the answer. I need to know where to find the whale with the laughing eye.

The mist obliged, moving, parts separating and others joining more tightly, until an image formed of the rocks where He perched. SL'an watched the vision before Him move as if He was flying along and looking – along the rocks, speeding by until there were fewer of them and more large spaces of sand. He saw something ahead that looked like a large, long smooth rock sticking out on its own and surrounded by sands, with only a bit of itself touching the lapping waves. *It's odd that the one rock is smooth while almost all the others are sharp and jagged,* He mused. When the image rushed closer still, He saw the eye of the whale staring patiently into His own.

SL'an snapped to awareness and took off where the vision had led. He wasn't sure what was wrong, but He did know in the deepest part of Himself that the whale needed Him now.

His wings beat in quick, sure strokes following the line of dark rocks and sands where the Undrinkable Water – the Ocean as the whale called it – had just been but had left behind, still wet. It moved further back as the starling flew.

Now the shore opened up to more sands than rock, and with it the long, smooth form of the whale appeared, the smaller end of him barely kissed by receding water. The whale was as big in the flesh as in the Starling God's visions. SL'an opened His beak and gasped in some air from the wonder of it. Why wasn't he in the water or, if he could come onto land, why wasn't he walking or moving? He remembered His earlier experiment that had worked so well. *I am the Starling SL'an.*

I know!

How do you know?

I can see You. Even if that wasn't enough proof, I can feel Your mind and recognize it.

Why are you on the sand? When I first saw you and felt you, you were swimming far out in the Undrinkable – the Ocean.

I have waited for You a long time. I have waited for You for the turns of seasons and the turns of seasons. I am here on the sand so I may finally share everything I need to share.

SL'an pulled His head back.

You doubt me? The whale's eye squinted in understanding and joy. *How could I wait for so long for One who is not even a season's turn old?*

It isn't possible, the starling couldn't help but think.

It is possible, of course. Here I am and here You are. How do You feel your flock-mates when You create Unified Flight? How do You know where the others are as You move? There are connections between us all. We are all forged of the same and from the same. This links us all. We have different gifts, but we have many things we share and have ways we may share them.

But how is it that I have never heard anyone speak of this before? SL'an's mind groped desperately.

Young starling! So many of you are forgetting and others have forgotten completely. They have forgotten we are all forged of the same and from the same. They are forgetting or have forgotten that we all have gifts that are spectacular, and that none of us are one better than the other.

SL'an felt a deep peace and knew it was true, but the peace was nudged by more questions. *You haven't told Me why it was necessary for you to come to the sand. You've spoken to Me this way perfectly well as you swam in the water.*

The whale closed his great eye tightly. *I can hear You and send my thoughts to You this way, but I can't share what I must show You in the usual way. I am a Teller too, but with our kind, we are all Tellers. Other kinds send us their thoughts and their wisdoms and pain. We take it and keep it until it must be told. Each of us has stories that are told to only us, and we know that there is One that is meant to hear them. Sometimes it is many season turns before that One joins us, but we are aware when the One is on the way! There is greatness in sharing what we were born to tell. Some have died before they ever could fulfill their purpose...*

For the first time, the joy SL'an felt and saw reflected in the laughing eye changed to a crushing sorrow. *There are some visions that can only be shared most directly, either because the ones to receive are in the process of forgetting and their own senses have dulled, or the details of the image are so fine or distant that they must be shared by the strongest connection possible – touch. If You come and fly up to rest on my skin, I will show You why some of us never fulfill our purpose.*

SL'an felt dread, and the whale sensed it. *It will not be easy to receive or for me to share, but You must receive it*, he explained.

The starling fluttered and rose high enough to land on the whale's side, not far from the eye. The sensation of the wet, thick skin, so smooth and unlike anything He had felt before, sent a strange thrill through Him.

Now close Your eyes and go to the place inside Yourself. When You are ready, I will send what You must see.

Since the place had been prepared so recently, it was still soft and malleable and easy to form. It was only a moment or two and SL'an found Himself waiting. He looked around the space for something, not sure if He was supposed to form the beginnings of a vision or let them come, but there was no need to wonder long. The aura of the Ocean smacked His mind, and He was flying above it once again and looking down. There were whales bumping out from the water, and some kind of God thing floating on top of it close by. A ruckus of cries rang out, similar to the fledgling Gods' tones as They had hit the fishing God over and over. Something flew out from the God thing, and then another. SL'an cringed as He saw those pierce one of the whales as she swam close to the surface of the water. Red blood erupted from the wounds, and more of the things shot from the Gods and pierced the suffering whale.

The image stopped and left SL'an's throat tight, panting with emotion where He stood on the head of the living whale.

The Gods killed her, didn't They?

They killed her. She was my mother, and I was only a calf then but luckily old enough to survive when she was gone. They are not Gods. This is a very important thing for You to know.

The starling felt something crumble inside. *They are The Blight as the swallows say.*

No.

SL'an blinked. *Then what?*

They are the ones that have completely forgotten what they are and how they belong – so completely that they can't receive what they need to hear from all of their family. We are all family, forged from the same and of the same, but they stopped knowing this. Without this, they have no guide for how to live. What is more frightening still is that other kinds are falling into this sleep too – they are forgetting. I have waited my entire life to tell You this.

Can they remember?

It must be so or I believe there would be no reason to tell You about it. This is the message many of us have carried for certain Ones of different kinds. The Ones are charged to go out and try to reach human kind in various ways – to help them remember. How could I possibly do that? The starling stared off into the vast Ocean, as empty on the surface as His mind was of ideas.

All kinds have been given special gifts. You have Your flight and better yet, Your Unified Flight. I will soon show You how other starlings have created murmurations to communicate with human kind. Our gift is our song. We sing many songs rich with messages for human kind, but over the generations, it was clear they could not hear, or understand us when they could hear. A gift all kinds share to some degree is sending and receiving images through thought and current. We are especially strong with this, so we have volunteers who come here onto the sand as I have today.

What good does that do? SL'an asked.

If we leave the water and come to the sand, humans will sometimes respond in kindness and try to help us back into the Ocean. When they do, they touch us, and when that happens we send the strongest messages we can with hopes that one of them will understand, and that something will flicker and the spark of their memory will be reignited.

What if the humans don't come?

Then we often die.

The whale was silent for a bit as SL'an digested the information.

Wouldn't it be better to live? Why should more of you die because of the Go – humans?

If human kind does not remember, the forgetting will spread until it has consumed all living things, even perhaps whales. Living things that have forgotten are poison to all things, even when they don't want to be. We are forged from the same and of the same – family. If one branch of the family is ill, then the illness spreads until the entire being dies.

SL'an nodded. It was another piece of news that felt truer than most things He thought He'd known.

The whale continued. *I don't know if we have ever been able to ignite the memory of a human, but the survival of all of us is at stake, so the possible sacrifice of our lives is worth the effort.*

A thought struck SL'an, and He could hardly get it out fast enough. *So I am not a God!*

The whale laughed heartily, squinting his eye with the merriment of it. *No! You are not a God, but are family with all of us. Still, You have a certain set of gifts and a purpose that not all creatures have. It doesn't put You above any other, but it gives You a different purpose. You were born to be more open, and to lead and teach. You will take what I share with You and pass it along as it should be.*

But you still say You and not you when addressing me!

Dear little starling, You are the One I have waited to tell all of my life. You are not a God, but You are important to me.

There was a group of humans walking far down the sand toward SL'an and the whale. For the first time, the starling looked at them and understood why they were so different from birds. They were not meant to be birds, and birds were not meant to be like them. They didn't have wings, and the eyes were forward and plumage changing because they were a kind of their very own. *They are very different from all other kinds and creatures I have seen,* SL'an mused.

They would be different as You are different from me no matter what, but they are most different from all of us because they have forgotten for so long. The longer they do not remember we are all family, the more alien they become.

So show me what I can do! I do love Mother, and I believe Mother loves me and the birds around her. I'll make her remember!

You cannot make her, but You can try to help her eyes open and encourage her senses to come alive again. She and her kind make the ultimate choice if they will release the shield of forgetting or build on it instead.

The humans were coming closer, pointing and making sounds. *Show me what to do now before they come!* SL'an said breathlessly.

This message was given to me by another whale. It came to her from another whale, and it came to him from a starling from Your origin lands. It is a murmuration –Unified Flight that sends messages in the sky for human eyes – and the eyes of all kinds who might be forgetting. Your kind's desire for Unified Flight is from deep memory that You and other starlings have been forgetting. Still, there has been a piece of the memory left, but starlings here haven't known what it was originally for. Close Your eyes again and I will show You!

This time, SL'an was inside his own inner space in an instant. He watched an enormous flock of starlings, larger than anything he could have imagined, coming together over a large body of water. He could sense everything and, if he focused, he could see the feathers of any one starling in the distance. They rose up high and came together at last, merging and then moving as one being.

SL'an's heart ached to join them, but he knew he must watch instead.

The huge group moved together in a rush of wings, and SL'an gasped when he saw the shape of a whale in the sky. It held for a moment, and then they all moved fluidly until he saw a heron. It changed again into a human, and on and on from one living creature to another. There was representation of those who swam in the waters and flew in the skies and crept on the ground. Snakes with no legs slithered across the clouds and rabbits with long ears sat in alert poses. *It's beautiful!*

It is that, the whale sighed. *I have shown You what You need to do. Lead well! Now You need to fly away and begin at the beginning. There is someone of Your kind not far from here waiting for You, and she will help You with Your purpose. I have another message to send to these humans now, so I will say goodbye!*

Will you die?

I may live yet! I feel some very dull embers of memory buried deep inside these humans coming. There is at least some hope for the kind ones. That very low glowing ember of memory makes them want to touch us. They want to remember and know on some level we are the same in the important ways. If nothing else, they will work very hard to save me.

SL'an marveled that the whale had no fear, and saw the laughter and joy in his eyes only grow as the humans circled around him and carefully laid what SL'an had thought of as wing tips against the now drying skin. He flew away as they made urgent sounds to each other. Were they working out how to move the giant creature back to the Ocean? Would they remember?

The whale said there was another starling waiting nearby for him, a female. Had the Ocean dweller sent some kind of message to another starling in a nearby flock so he'd have help?

He scanned the area as he flew, and finally saw the small form of starling resting in a bush where the rocks ended. He landed on a nearby branch where she would see him coming, so as not to startle her, was about to introduce himself, and cried out with surprise.

Chapter Twenty-Six
Lost and Then Found

Flora's eyes widened with surprise, and she launched herself from the branch toward SL'an, nearly bowling him over in mid-air. She fluttered around him in a delirious dance. "I found you! I wasn't sure if I would ever really find you, but you are here!"

Winded, they returned to the bush where Flora had just been nestled and faced each other breathlessly. SL'an's breast was full. "What are you doing here?"

"When Father realized you were gone, for some reason he was furious. It's not that I didn't expect him to be upset if one left the flock, but it has happened before, I am told, and no one spoke of him being as affected as this. He is taking it out on the others, and can think of very little else. Mother is also strangely sad. She will hardly speak with anyone and barely eats. Father has groups searching for you in all directions. All Unified Flight and other lessons have stopped – ordered stopped until you are found."

SL'an took it in and shuddered. "What does he think will happen if one of these groups finds me?"

"I don't know, but he is acting out of feather, and I feel strongly that you will not be safe unless you do whatever it is he wants you to do…" She looked away and then fixed an eye on him resolutely. "What is it that he wants you to do? Tell me why my father and mother are so interested in you – why do your choices matter so much?"

"First, you haven't told me how you found me, but only why you've come. I need to know that."

"Steep."

SL'an gaped. "Steep told you where to find me?"

"He didn't want to at first, but I had seen you speaking with him before you disappeared and I told him how Father was behaving. He asked me if I thought Father would have you killed if you didn't come back and comply with his wishes. When I said I didn't know, Steep read the fear in my eyes. I took the chance of being caught talking with another kind – you know we aren't supposed to – and told him I thought he knew where you went. I told him I had to go warn you to stay away, and he said he believed me and thought he could trust me."

"What did he tell you?"

"Only that you were on your way first toward the cooler lands, and then over to a Great Undrinkable Water."

"That's all you knew and you found your way here?" SL'an looked at Flora there on the branch, small but bright, with gleaming feathers starting to show the white speckles L'al told him once that he would have as the suns grew shortest of all. She was suddenly so familiar to him. *Is it because I haven't seen any of my own kind closely for so long, or any of those from my home?*

She cocked her head and looked at him strangely for a moment, but then the expression was gone.

"I found some who had seen you, and others who had heard of the Undrinkable Water and knew generally how to get there. I am pretty sure the others won't be able to find you as long as Steep doesn't say anything to them. Without that information, I would have had no trail to follow."

"I'm told the Undrinkable Water goes on nearly forever," SL'an murmured. "That you happened to come to the same part of it I did is—"

"—A miracle. I hoped this was the right place to be – more than hoped, really. Somehow I could feel you the closer I came." She turned her head slowly and pecked at something invisible on the branch between her feet. "Now will you tell me why my father and mother are obsessed with you like this? I have suspicions, but it can't be…"

"You've thought that I'm the one Starling Lore tells of?"

"I admit it. Are you?"

"This is what many believe, and until recently I believed it too. But I'm not a Starling God, Flora! I'm only me, and the Gods are only human."

"What?"

"They are a kind called human. They aren't Gods at all and don't deserve worship. They are forged of the same things we are forged from. We are different branches of one tree – unique but not one better than another. I've learned this here today."

Flora fixed her eyes on him with frozen silence.

"I learned it today, but I really had always known it in the deepest parts. I had forgotten, but now I remember."

"Stop…it…" Flora's voice trembled.

"I know it's true in my breast. Let the idea set, and you'll know it is too."

"Stop! You mustn't say such things! If you think Father would kill you before, if you are heard to say this, he will definitely kill you then!"

"You live in fear of him. All of you do. It isn't the way it should be. That is what must stop. There is no punishment from Gods, and there is nothing we can do to make them decide to be cruel or kind to us. They are creatures who have forgotten they are part of the world and part of all of us. They go mad trying to find meaning and trying to hear the guidance, but they have forgotten for so long they hear nothing but their own fears and needs. They're deaf, and many of us are becoming deaf too."

She stood on the branch, panting. "I am afraid too. I'm afraid what you will do with this thing you believe. Do you plan to fly back home and announce to all birds that the Gods are not Gods?"

"You do believe it then? Can you feel it's the truth?"

She snapped her beak several times with frustration. "I feel you would not lie to me, but this is a tough seed to crack!"

He told her about the things he witnessed, until he finally shared the amazing contact with the whale. "I agree that it won't work well if I suddenly share that the Gods are only humans. I think that forgetting must be similar to being in the black. Even if you're still awake, it's hard to keep the brain clear, and nothing makes sense then. It's almost a relief to not try to stay awake, and to let the black take over. I see that this is a delicate state to be in.

"I had time to remember. The remembering happened slowly and in stages like the sun releases from the mountains, first making the black grey, then a bit rosy, then brighter and brighter still until the black is gone. This is the way it must take place."

Finally, he shuffled close to her on the branch so their bodies touched. She stiffened, but he quickly tried to send her the image of the murmuration. He was lost in his own seeing, and didn't know if she shared his vision until Flora let out a deep breath, her body relaxing along with it. "I will help you. There is a flock of starlings not far from here that I met while searching for you. They do believe in the Gods and that starlings are close to Them, but they don't share the particular beliefs my father holds. If we could join them, and you could teach them this, they might travel with us to show others."

He wasn't sure if she had spoken or thought the words, but it was a perfect idea.

"Do you know where we'll find the flock now?"

"I do. The young males are off on their own learning the last of the season's lessons, but the others are always within their Sacred Space. Do you want to go there now to meet them? They told me I would be welcome to join their group, so I believe if you come with me, you will be welcomed too."

SL'an heard the 'you' she spoke all along despite her suspicions that he was one of the Gods. "Thank you for not saying *You*– ever – even though you thought for awhile I was something I'm not," he murmured.

She straightened a feather and drew up her head. "No matter what, I don't know if I could have used 'You'! You are SL'an to me. That is enough."

She readied to take wing, but he nudged her quickly. "There is somewhere I need to go first. Will you follow?"

They launched off the branch into the air that sensed all throughout like Ocean, and flew to where the whale was still unmoving on the sand. Humans surrounded him and there were a few metal things as well, looking as though they were all desperately pushing and pulling, inch by inch moving the great creature back into the water. SL'an could tell by the vacant look in the whale's eye that his body was weakening out of the water, but at the same time his mind was stronger than ever. "He's focusing on trying to reach them," he called to Flora. She dipped and flew directly overhead to get a better look.

"Will he hear you if you say goodbye?"

"I don't think so. I could hear him sometimes, or even see him from so far away; perhaps this won't really be goodbye. I have so many other questions for him and so much else I know he could teach me."

The two starlings swerved and Flora led the way now, only just a beak ahead of her friend so they could still talk. SL'an suddenly laughed. "How amazing living is!"

"Well, yes, I suppose…but what do you mean?" Flora asked.

"If we drink that water, we'd die. The whale must have it or he'll die. Still, we are forged of the same! Why are humans so surprised that they are different from whale or bird? It's the same level of difference between one of us from the other of us. How did they begin to think their gifts are better? What drew them so far away?"

"And why would we want to be like any other than what we are?" Flora added.

The two of them stayed on the wing until they came to a Sacred Space just on the edge of a place smaller than the Here, but vaguely similar. There were many places for worshippers and travelers to feed, and a crowd of redwings, grackles and starlings were wandering the area together, feeding amicably.

"You'll see a difference in how our kind gets on with the others," Flora said softly. The starling Secret Keeper has no desire to keep the young away from others as they learn, and he also doesn't seem to think or share that Starling Lore makes us in some way better. I think he will hear you! Others welcome starlings freely in their groups since no superiority has been suggested. I am told starlings and redwings and grackles even travel together when there is need!"

Flora found the Secret Keeper, a slight but keen starling called Moon, and introduced the two males with cheerful reverence that appeared to please the flock leader well. "My friend has information that should be shared only with the Secret Keeper," Flora ended.

Moon eyed his new guest. "I imagine, by the highly unusual professions you've chosen, and that you have also left your flock before it is time, that your information will be as unusual as you seem to be." His words were softened by the twinkle in his eyes. "Go on and tell, Teller. Your thoughts are safe with me."

SL'an closed his eyes for a moment and sent his feelings out to the other starling male, reaching and exploring. *Can you be trusted? Are you safe?* he asked. When nothing but clean, peaceful openness touched his senses, the young starling knew this Secret Keeper truly was one he could share everything with. Even if he didn't believe it or do things with the information SL'an hoped he would, he would not be harmful.

He told of being raised by Mother and not even realizing at first he belonged to the kind called bird, how L'al and L'in became his first mentors and believed he was one of the rare Equals, and even then more than that, the prophesied Starling God. Moon shuddered his wings with excitement, but SL'an quickly told him that he was not what some birds believed.

"What grounds do you have to disbelieve it?" Moon questioned. The younger starling could see the passionate wish in the Secret Keeper's eyes – wishing more than anything that it would be true, and a great joining of kinds might take place.

SL'an leaned forward after shooting a look at Flora. "I don't believe I am a God because the Gods, as we believe them to be, do not exist. They are not Gods at all, but behave strangely as if they are not forged of the same things we all are."

The horrified look in Moon's eyes slowly melted as his starling guest described the Seeking he had done and what he witnessed and heard. As with Flora, he ended with the whale's words.

"Seeker and Teller, these are very serious things to believe and more serious yet to say. Even if it is true, what would be the purpose of knowing it? What reaction do you think you would have from most of bird kinds if you shared what you believe?"

Flora told Moon some of her father's teachings and how he was now having small flocks hunt this 'Starling God' down to force him to comply with his perceived role, or to kill him if he would not.

"Would he kill a bird he feels is the One of Starling Lore?" Moon's eyes were wide, yet now held an air of calm. "It seems that under no circumstance would he kill such a One."

Flora sighed. "My father in sensibility would not, but there is something in him that is unraveling and nonsensical about this. He gave me life, and it hurts me to say it, but I believe he is capable of many dangerous things that wouldn't follow normal thought."

Moon paced a bit back and forth, but slowly and methodically. SL'an liked him. It wasn't the move of fear or anxiety, but motion, to help thoughts percolate and settle where they should. Finally he stopped and cocked his head at the two friends. "It seems that telling bird kinds too much too soon will only cause disaster. I imagine you agree with me on that?"

"We do and have already discussed it," Flora answered before SL'an could, as if somehow she was one with his own mind.

"So since you have already discussed it, then have you discussed a plan for what to do next?"

Flora and SL'an looked at each other with eyes shining. *This is going much better than I could have hoped!* he thought. He felt something soft and light inside his breast that didn't seem to be his own being. *Flora?* There wasn't an answer, but the feeling inside him was written on her expression. It was approval and agreement. He could feel her! *The whale helped me remember, and now I can feel so much more than before! Can you feel me too?* Flora didn't respond, but it gave the young starling an idea.

"I do have a plan. I hope to teach you what the whale shared with me – an entirely new way to use Unified Flight – and that the three of us may teach the others in this flock how. There's no reason to tell them more than that it is to communicate the oneness of all living things on the soil, in the air, and in the waters. Even to those who still believe in the Gods, this will not be offensive. My hope is that by doing this, it will awaken the deep memories."

Moon looked bemused. "That is a very fine idea, SL'an! But how can I teach something I haven't seen or done before?"

"I'll try to show you if you allow me to touch you." SL'an automatically bobbed in peace like the doves, making Moon laugh loudly.

"Your mentors' influence is obvious, Seeker and Teller! I don't know if this will work either, but I am always willing to try."

The younger starling walked closer to the slender Secret Keeper, wondering what would be the most effective touch. When he shared with the whale, he perched not far from the eye – perhaps head to head would be most powerful? He had touched Flora in a similar way. "I ask you to keep your mind free and relaxed," SL'an suggested, and he rested his own head against the side of the Secret Keeper's.

He closed his eyes and felt Moon's eye close too, the muscles brushing a bit against his short face feathers. In a moment, SL'an was looking up into a silver sky at the massive group of starlings collecting, roiling and then finally forming the shapes, sliding seamlessly from one into another. He felt Moon beside him watching too, and suddenly the younger starling took to the air until he was racing along the edges of the murmuration. *Join me, Moon!* His mind called. Moon was beside him in what seemed an instant.

The two of them focused on the feel of the wing beats and rushing air around them, moving as they would with a usual Unified Flight. The more they moved with the others, the less they were aware of anything but the message being sent throughout every starling mind in the flock. There was a leader, somehow they knew, and that leader sent the idea of each shape along. The idea traveled with breathtaking speed from one starling to another, causing the fluid shifts of form to begin, coalesce, then hover for an instant in completion before flowing out of that and into the next.

I can do this. There is every reason in the world to do this, Moon's thoughts came to SL'an as the murmuration finally came to an end and both were, with some disappointment, pulled out of the vision and finding their bodies where they had always really been – on the short grass with Flora nearby.

"That was so real! I could feel the wind and warmth of other starlings…but it wasn't real at all," Moon breathed out reverently.

"We felt it as truly as if we were there, so is that any less than real?" SL'an asked.

"Could you see this too when SL'an tried to show you, Flora?"

"I could, but from the sound of it, you did more than watch," her voice trailed off slightly.

"Flora, I'll show you what it is to fly in the murmuration. Until just then, I didn't know it was possible."

Moon's eyes shone with a newly resolved light. "Since there are three of us who could lead, I will break the flock into three smaller practice flocks. Each of us could be in charge of teaching one the basics, and it will be faster than a single bird trying to share that vision and direction with everyone."

Flora looked toward one group of other starlings trolling the short grasses at a distance. "SL'an is the only one who has passed this information along. We have only received it," she pointed out. "How will we know we can do it or that the others will be able to receive as we have?"

Moon flapped his wings and flicked them until they were settled again. "We won't know if we don't try. As far as the others go, there may be some who aren't able to receive, but we don't know this to be true, either, until attempts have been made."

The three starlings took a moment to search for a bit of food, wandering only a bit until they filled up enough not to feel light-headed.

"I needed that," Moon nodded. "The excitement was carrying me away and now I am grounded again and have more questions. There is no question this is something worth learning, but what are your plans once we have done so? Will you remain here with us and hide from Bard the Secret Keeper?"

SL'an looked away briefly and Moon nodded again. "I didn't think it would be as simple as that."

The younger starling stared out to where his Mother's Sacred

Space lay somewhere far away. "I have to face Bard and undo the damage he's done there. I can only ask if you and your flock would be willing to go with me to join with others there, and show them what I have shown you. I would ask volunteers there as well to come with us, to travel from one place to another sharing this. If humans, the ones who have forgotten, and the other kinds who are already forgetting, are to ever remember, then it will be important to share the murmuration to as many as we can."

"I appreciate knowing your vision." Moon also looked away as if he could almost see Bard and his flock there. "Teaching my starlings the murmuration will not be difficult. When the time comes to ask them to travel and share it, however, especially when it means possibly dealing with angry and even violent starling strangers, we may need to tell them more. I know that I would not take on a request like that without some kind of reason or explanation."

Flora blinked quickly in thought. "There is no way to know how all things will work since there are too many variables. We need to look at this as the first step to a general plan and move in the ways that feel best at the time."

"Not unlike a murmuration of our own!" Moon laughed again.

"Yes," SL'an agreed. "Very much like that."

Chapter Twenty-Seven
The Starling God

The suns released for shorter and shorter periods of time while SL'an, Flora and Moon worked with the three smaller groups of starlings to teach them murmuration. There were only a few who couldn't be reached by touch and vision, but the leaders had those fly on the fringes of the practicing flocks until, as predicted, the motion and energy grew some kind of memory inside them and they started to receive well enough to follow along respectably.

It was a thrilling evening when the three leaders decided it was time to combine groups and see how they would function as a larger whole. "This is your flock, Moon," SL'an said. "Guide us in our first real murmuration!"

Moon stepped back slowly. "You are the leader of all of us – even me, Starling SL'an. You will take the first flight and show yourself."

"I am not a God in any way!" The younger starling stepped back as well.

"Not a God, no, but I am certain you are the One spoken of in the Starling Lore."

"That's not possible; what are you saying? The Lore says the One will show the Gods how to be more like bird and bird to be more like the Gods – that they will become One!"

"And if you succeed in this, so it shall be." Moon closed his eyes.

When SL'an was still speechless, Moon opened his eyes and looked at his friend. "Perhaps the Lore isn't wrong, but misinterpreted. One will come to show starlings how living is to be done so we are one. Perhaps One means Equal and differently gifted – not the same, as Bard and some others have chosen to see it. As it is now, there is not equality. With the forgetting, balance has been lost. Remembering will bring us back to Equal."

SL'an felt a thrilling mix of embarrassment and joy at the new idea. Of course!

"Then Mother was chosen to play a role in this as well," he said with satisfaction. "She may not be a God either, but she is good, and I think she is closer to remembering than many."

"I imagine there are many humans who have forgotten, but still have some ember of memory waiting to be ignited – and why wouldn't one of them be part of the plan? If they are Equal, then they must be worth waking up from this sleep they are in. Whatever power has forged us all knows it," Moon said softly.

SL'an, Moon and Flora gathered their flocks together and Moon announced that they would all be following the young starling in the first complete murmuration.

"I will be near you," Flora whispered to him as he prepared to rise.

"I'll feel you," was his answer.

On mark, they rose into the air and got their wings about them, swirling for a bit and gradually reaching the point where they could each feel the other move without distraction from anything else. SL'an let his vision flow, sending the message of forms gently and pointedly until the murmuration of starlings moved as one being, forming a swimming whale first, then a bird in flight, then a human lifting a babe in its arms – the visions SL'an had seen on his travels. There were Blooders too, which had struck some of the starlings badly when they first learned to do the images. It was finally impressed upon them that Blooders were Equal too. There was something bittersweet about the form of a fisher humping along the sky that especially filled SL'an's breast. The long list of living things ended with the head of a dove. To SL'an, it was none other than L'in. He hoped that in some way, she could see.

After a dozen practice flights, the greater flock had the connection well forged. They showed their skill over the beaches and surrounding Spaces with various names that were, as far as SL'an was concerned, very much like the Here, but the starlings always returned to their Sacred Space to rest.

One evening just before the black, Moon, Flora and SL'an met in a strong maple.

"They are ready," Moon told the other two. "The suns are growing short and cooler weather is setting in. It won't be long before the time will come to fly to warmer lands until the suns return to length. This is the time to decide if we will share more information with the others now and travel to your home, SL'an, or if we will wait until we return after the cold season has mostly gone."

"My friend Steep thought I'd be unlikely to return before the suns returned to length," SL'an remembered aloud.

Flora shook her head. "But that is when there will be pairings made and nests built and claimed. I think the timing will be poor if we expect anyone to join us or to watch what we do – if there is even anyone at that time who will want to take part in murmurations."

"Well said," Moon agreed. "How long did it take you to travel here from where you and SL'an were fledged?"

Flora looked at SL'an. "I stopped as little as possible, so it only took me a few suns to arrive. I believe it took SL'an longer because he took time to Seek and stay several places. My flight was fairly direct."

"If it only takes suns, then I am fairly confident we could fly there with volunteers, do what we need to do and still make it to the warmer lands before there is any danger."

When they all gathered for the evening praise, Moon first congratulated his flock, young and old, on their fine progress. "There was no question in my mind that if any could learn this new kind of Unified Flight quickly, it would be all of you. What you have been practicing is far more important than you yet realize, but as your Secret Keeper, I am here to share information with you, and a request that you will have this black to sleep on and consider."

There was a burst of conversation throughout the Praising Tree where they were roosted, the sun being pulled in a sleepy red state toward the shelf of the horizon.

When things died down a bit, Moon called SL'an over. "You have all gotten to know SL'an and Flora well. They have been skilled teachers these suns. I have invited them to join our flock, and because SL'an has had special experiences, I have asked more than that of him. I have asked him to take my place as the flock leader."

"But you are our Secret Keeper!" A voice cried out.

"I will still be your Secret Keeper, but I ask that you follow where SL'an leads and listen to his wisdom as well."

Another clear voice rang out, "It isn't done! The Secret Keeper is always the leader."

"Murmurations have never been done here in the way we just learned. Are you sorry to have tried it?"

When there was no answer, he continued, "There is value in doing things as we always have because they work, but there is foolishness in keeping those things if something screams to be changed. This is a time when we can make a difference for all our fellow creatures, including those creatures we now call the Gods." He tapped his foot soundly on the branch. "We know that Starling Lore says there is One who will come to us, who will show us all how to live so we are Equal."

"It is said!" Voices rang out.

SL'an couldn't see where the voices came from, but they fell in such unison that he imagined this was a usual response to the idea.

Moon motioned for SL'an to step beside him, and he did, feeling the eyes of nearly one hundred of his kind looking at him curiously, as if they had never seen him before. "This starling is the One of prophecy." There was silence – almost absurd with the number of birds in the tree. Moon persevered. "The murmuration is the way he will try to reach the Gods and other kinds. To do this properly, I need as many volunteers as possible to travel with him and teach other starlings how to fly a murmuration, and to demonstrate it for all living things to see."

"You believe He is the One?" an older female asked incredulously.

"There is no doubt in my mind. But please refer to him as 'he' and not '*He*'. SL'an feels equality demands it. In any case, a flock of volunteers will gather and leave after morning praise, news and first meal. I will be part of that flock, and while I would never force any of you to go where it goes against your feathers, I hope we are able to remain as a full flock and will set out together."

SL'an spoke out for the first time, his heart pounding in his breast but his hope holding him upright and steadfast. "I need you to know that there will be a special place where I will fly with those who join me. It is the Space where I was fledged from the one birds call God Flower, my Mother. There is a Secret Keeper there who believes a strangely bent form of Starling Lore, and before we work with flocks there, I will need to leave you for a time – to go ahead and face him along with his elders."

"You can't go alone," Flora hissed. "Father will have you killed if he doesn't kill you himself!"

"If I go in with others, Bard may turn upon them. There's no need for injury and fighting among our kind. If I do have this purpose, Flora, then I need to trust where it leads me. I believe I can handle Bard," he whispered back quickly.

Flora pulled her head close to her body and huddled there while Moon addressed the flock once more. "We will think about these things as we rest and as we rise with the next sun."

The flock found places to roost, SL'an joining the young males as was tradition. Before the black swept them away to sleep, he heard them talking quietly to each other –but none spoke to him. *I suppose it's only natural,* he thought. *How would I be if the situation were reversed? They aren't looking at me as a starling like them yet – but they will!* He tried to stay awake to hear more of what was discussed – were most leaning toward joining him or not? One by one, the voices as decipherable as whispering leaves turned off as the black pulled each into blissful slumber. SL'an felt his eyelids growing heavy, and then he was also taken from wondering, at least for awhile.

Chapter Twenty-Eight
The Trouble with Miracles

The moment a touch of light hit his eyelids, SL'an was awake.
Usually only the morning Praiser would be up so early – most usually
one of the robins – beginning a lone, clear crisp song that would rouse
all others until they chimed in with their own voices and news.

This morning it was a Praiser called Hseep. SL'an watched as she
was barely visible and flying against the deep grey, finding her way to
a taut metal limb and beginning the first beautiful strains of song.
There was no other stirring yet, and he huddled on his branch, feeling
his feet clenched well around it. *There's no turning back now, Mother.
They know and the challenge has been made. Today I begin a flight
with how many? Several? A hundred? And when I face Bard, what
will I find there?*

He wished hard for Mother to help him through this, then laughed
a bit bitterly. She was his Mother; how, he didn't know, but she was
not a God. There wasn't anything she could do to help him now any
more than she could have helped L'in at the close of that terrible sun.
At least I know you didn't cause it either, he thought with a sigh.

The morning praise continued, and then was joined by the other
various voices of so many kinds sharing thoughts and news from the
day before. One stood out to SL'an like a ringing bell: Moon's voice
calling, "Starlings! This is the morning you must decide. We take
flight after all have had the chance to eat. If you do plan to come on
the journey, eat lightly. Trust there will be stops along the way to rest
and find more food, since it will be uncomfortable to fly if you are too

loaded down. Think of it as the way you would prepare for the flight to warmer lands."

Flora landed on the branch next to SL'an. "Moon would like us all to meet in the Praising Tree once we have had our fill," she said, a bit more breathlessly than seemed usual for a short wing from a few trees away.

"All starlings join SL'an, Flora and me in the Praising Tree when you have had enough in your stomachs," Moon's voice cut in.

"Oh! I guess I should have known he would announce that in the morning news." Flora's eyes darted.

SL'an moved a bit closer to his friend. "Are you okay?"

"I'll admit that I am nervous. What if most don't believe us, or they don't want to risk going? What if this fails?"

He felt deep warmth in his skin. It passed through his quills and through his feathers, and he willed it, strong and calming, into her. "I awoke with the same thoughts, but there seems to be no other path to take. As strange as it seems, Bard was the one who told me my purpose would reveal itself to me and I would know it when it came. He was right. I took small steps in this journey filled with doubt, but following bits of light. Now the confusion has lifted and there's no question of what must be done. No, I don't know how it will turn out, but it's the only way."

Flora turned her head away as far as she could from SL'an. "I…I am afraid…you…what if something happens to you?"

He reached over and nibbled her neck and what part of her check he could touch in the way of the doves. "Believe I'll do my best to have nothing happen to me."

After the morning meal, the three leaders made sure they were at the Praising Tree first to welcome other starlings from the flock as they gathered. There would be stragglers some mornings, but not so now. "Every bird is anxious to see what will happen," Moon said, appraising the tree limbs full of gleaming feathers.

"Are there final questions or comments before we leave?" SL'an had to fight not to jump at the power of his own voice.

A starling closest to them moved a bit forward. "I don't know if I believe all of this in my brain, but I believe it in my breast. I faced the black thinking I would not be able to join you because of my doubts," he turned to Moon, "and because I believe there is more you are not sharing with us. Still, as the black pulled me into sleep, my last thought was of the murmuration. Unified Flight has always been a wonderful joining and meditation, but there is something more to the murmuration that makes me feel complete."

There were noises of agreement.

The starling continued, "When I felt this and stopped thinking, I knew I would have to go – so I join you this sun and will fly in your flock. Who will come with me and fulfill our place together in prophecy?"

There was a roar that nearly deafened SL'an, but it was the most welcomed sound he could have heard. "I'm grateful for your words, and for the willingness of those who will come with me." The young starling leader dipped his head and then raised it again quickly to look back to his gathered kind. "Are there any who choose to stay behind? There's no shame in it, but Moon would like to quickly meet with those to decide who will lead them."

An elder female flew forward on an open branch with fewer than a dozen starlings. They looked either unusually small or much older. "These would like to go, but cannot. Their health in one way or another makes it unwise to travel any more than they must."

Moon cocked his head. "Is there one willing to lead them?"

"I am willing," she answered calmly.

"Muse, you are a fine choice for a leader, and I know all will be well while they are with you."

"I make no promises except to do my best," she said.

Moon chuckled. "Then we will meet you again in the warmer lands. Until then may the winds be beneath your wings and may the soil provide! Now SL'an," he turned to the younger starling, "it is your time to lead. Fly us away."

SL'an caught Flora's eye and saw the mixed emotions there as he lifted into the sky and flew back the way he had come suns and suns ago, but this time with the rush of wings beside and behind him, and a purpose he never could have imagined.

They flew in more of a straight line than the young starling had taken on the way to the Great Undrinkable Water called the Ocean. Now that he knew the way, he didn't need the humans' paths and navigated with no difficulty.

As promised, the flock stopped regularly to feed, but SL'an insisted on flying about first, looking for danger before signaling the others to settle on short grasses or soil to feed. He told questioners he was looking for signs of Blooders, and this was partially true. The larger part, however, was that he wanted to be sure there was nothing like the yellow food set out by humans to kill.

The journey continued for two suns with no troubles, but as the flock came close to the Here, SL'an felt a prickle in his skin that reminded him he had a promise to keep. After asking Flora and Moon to guide the others in a feeding and to locate the best place to roost for the coming black, SL'an flew into the Here and scanned the water there for gulls.

There were a number of them bobbing on the water, and others resting on wooden things jutting out of the lapping waves. A few walked on the shore, but SL'an couldn't tell which one might be Spool's mother without getting closer. He flew over the water and searched the faces, finally seeing her familiar profile. "Spool's mother," SL'an called out, feeling chagrined again that he never learned her name. She snapped her head up and opened her beak in recognition. "Come with me to the shore," he said. "I have news for you."

"And I have news for you as well!"

She broke from the group and joined the starling on the scrubby grass. "May I tell you my news first? I think you'll be quite amazed." Her eyes sparkled. Before he answered, she blurted, "My Spool lives! The Gods have saved him!"

SL'an felt as if he had just smashed into a tree limb. "How?"

"The Gods are good, no matter what we might have thought! There was a reason that the fishing God only maimed Spool's wing. It wasn't cruelty; it was so he would become one of the Chosen! He's now staying with one of the Gods and She tends to him within Her very own nest! Chosen! My son! I told you he was meant for something great."

The pride and love seemed to radiate from her white feathers so they appeared to glow and cast a circle of light around her.

How can I tell her now these are not Gods? SL'an felt his throat tighten.

"Lady Gull, how do you know this is the truth?"

"From my Spool himself! The God brought him here one sun ago and released him to practice flying and to see us, I can only imagine. It was a sun of great celebrating to find one of our own is Chosen!"

SL'an tried to speak, but there were no words to form.

"Many of our group were as astonished as you are. But not me! Once I saw how things unfolded, it all made perfect sense. He was always different, and I wait for the days he'll tell us all what it was like to be Chosen, and perhaps what the Gods intend him to do now that he has been!"

"I can see why you think this is a miracle," SL'an finally said carefully. "No matter what his purpose in life may be, I am very happy that Spool lives, and that he's being cared for in whatever way is possible."

There was no end to the gull's glowing. "This God spent some time singing with the fishing God while Spool tried his best to fly with the rest of us. Certainly that is more evidence that this was the Gods' plan."

"Someday I'll visit again and hope to see Spool here with you," SL'an bobbed. "But now I must go back to my Space."

"Sacred Space?" Spool's mother corrected.

SL'an looked away before taking wing again and said softly, "Yes."

"But what about the news you had for me?" the gull asked quickly.

The air was already rushing over his feathers when he called back, "The news was that I have no news to share with you today. I did promise to stop on the way back from my travels...I'm certain I will see you again!"

SL'an returned to the flock, found Flora right away and shared what he learned. Her eyes were filled with emotion. "SL'an, hold tight to the branch. We knew that learning humans are not Gods would be a tough seed to crack, and that some will not be ready to discover the news right away, but would need to remember it bit by bit."

SL'an paced. He hadn't eaten yet, but even the idea of the juicy grubs waiting within the grass roots didn't tempt him. "I did imagine it would be a long, difficult process, but this has made me wonder if remembering can ever happen enough to make a difference – at least before it's too late. How can I show them? How can I ever convince them when they're sure these events are miracles?"

Flora tentatively reached her head forward and nuzzled her friend's cheek. "Have you ever thought perhaps these events are miracles? Whatever forged us forged us all – from the same and of the same. If you have a purpose to fulfill, and I believe in my breast the Lore was not wrong on this, then why couldn't human kind have their purposes too? Some of them must be working toward the better good and toward reconnecting as Equals."

SL'an had to close his eyes. There was an incredible feeling welling up within him like the petals of a flower unfurling. Flora's words kept replaying in his brain, thrilling him with their exciting timbre that was similar to her mother's and yet all her own. Yet again how clear it was, and he hadn't seen.

The flock rose in the air once again and took less than the rest of the sun to go from the Here to just outside Flower's Space. They found a good place to land, feed and roost for the night where there was a mix of shortgrass field bordered with what was left of ripe berries. With so much to eat and plenty of shelter, SL'an felt safe leaving them here; he would stay and rest over the black, but when the sun released, it would be time to go and face Bard alone.

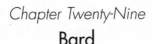

Chapter Twenty-Nine

Bard

Flora was insistent. "I'm coming with you, and there is nothing you can do to stop me."

SL'an lowered his voice each time she raised hers. "I won't be able to focus on my own safety if I'm concerned about yours."

"I am capable of taking care of myself!"

He sighed. "I know you are, but knowing something and believing it enough not to worry are different. I tell you with all truth, if you come it will endanger me. I need to be clear and not think of any of the rest of you – I suspect staying out of Bard's beak and claw will be tricky enough."

Flora slapped her wings nearly in his face, reminding the starling male of L'in as he jumped back. "Foolish! Isn't that the very reason you should take more of us with you? Don't you see the folly of going alone? What chance will you have against Father and the flock? It may not be only one you are defending against. It may be his elders or groups of youngers like us."

"I have ideas of what I'll say and do, Flora. I need to trust that we're not the only ones who have felt there's something amiss with Bard – your father." He looked at Flora then and saw a little of Bard in her, realizing somehow for the first time who Bard was. "This must be hard for you."

She drooped a bit. "If you mean because I hear the things you say about Father, it is not as hard as it would be if I hadn't always known deep down inside that something was wrong. I have always kept some distance from him. He is my father, but not the kind I imagine you would be…"

"I'll do everything I can to reason with him."

Flora tipped her beak up and looked at SL'an fondly. "I wouldn't expect anything less of you. If something happens to Father, it will not be from your lack of trying to avoid it."

The young male starling looked toward Mother's nest, setting just in the distance. "Forged from the same and of the same." He bulleted up from the field and toward the Meeting Tree where there would be the best chance of finding Bard and Glee. *There aren't many starlings here now,* he thought with kindled hope. *Bard has sent groups out looking for me and left the Space here nearly unattended!*

It took a bit of looking, but Bard, Glee and two of the elders, Mentors Diver and Trill, were resting together in a small but sturdy maple. After quickly surveying a good place to land where he could take off quickly if faced with aggression, SL'an came in for a neat landing. "I've been Seeking and found my purpose. As you said, Bard, it would reveal itself to me in time, and so it has. If I'm indeed the One of Starling Lore, then I have come with news of how we will become Equal."

Bard's face shifted in an instant from rage to euphoria while a gentle breeze swished the leaves around him. "That is excellent, Starling God! I have to say I misjudged You and thought You left because you were a fraud, or would not accept Your place in Starling Lore!" He jerked his head from Diver to Trill, and then to Glee, whose own eyes were wide and misty, locked onto SL'an's figure, silhouetted a bit against the sun. "The Gods have planned this to be perfect in every way!" Bard's voice chimed with pleasure but the tones fell on SL'an's eardrums as arrogance. "The favored are here to find out what we must do to live like the Gods. We, who have strived to be close to Those who made us Their Chosen Birds! You will have the chance to hear first, you the only ones I have trusted with this Secret." He turned to SL'an with wild eyes. "Tell, Starling God! Don't waste another moment!"

SL'an took a slow, deep breath and let it out before he described the special Unified Flight – the murmurations – that would strive to remind all that no one kind was above another. "This is what the prophecy of Starling Lore intended for me. I am to come teach you how to do this and lead you in doing it."

Bard was frozen, the ember of rage flickering in his eyes again.

"An amazing concept," Trill mused to Diver's enthusiastic nodding. "I always knew that Unified Flight was song and praise in motion, but now, to hear this…"

Diver fluttered his wings like a fledgling begging for food. "Yes! I always knew in my breast Unified Flight was too consuming and wonderful to only be used to bond a flock!"

"ENOUGH!" Bard shrieked. "Can't you understand what he is suggesting? This claims that all kinds are Equal to the Gods. This is not the Truth of the Starling Lore! The Gods are great and the Starling God is to come and teach us how to live with Them and as part of Them – we are the Chosen Ones. We brought music to the Gods, and They rewarded us with this honor!"

"I understand you came to believe this, but as the One, I can tell you I'm sure of what I say and what I, and we, must do from now on."

"He is a charlatan." Bard's feathers were puffed with fury. "I have been deceived! We have all been deceived. This starling is not the One at all but a miserable little wretch who is trying to be the undoing of us!"

Glee's eyes were swimming with confusion. "But Bard, why would he try to harm his own kind?"

"He is an abomination," the Secret Keeper nearly growled like a Blooder. "He was Chosen, but then finished in his raising by dove Tellers – pathetic that they are – speaking of peace and not understanding the Truth at all. They speak peace but they are jealous of starlings; they want to be Secret Keepers, but must only ever be relegated to lesser beings – doves – Tellers. Can't you see what the doves have done? They found a Chosen One to be sure, but they fed him lies and twisted his mind so he would join us and poison our own minds."

"I hope to show you the Truth, Bard; if you will let me touch you, I will show you what murmuration is. You will be able to see it as if you are there, and it may help you remember the real Truth you have forgotten," SL'an said as softly as he could without letting his voice sound weak.

"*You* will not touch *me*." Bard's eyes darted to the top of Flower's nest. "But if you really want to prove the Gods have given you this purpose, and that you are the Starling God of Lore, then you will come with me and take a test."

SL'an pulled his head back a bit. "What is the test?"

"Come with me and I will show you."

The two flew to the top of Flower's nest, close to the spot where Bard had roosted with SL'an not so very long ago and began his teachings. A tall stone thing jutted out of the nest's top and smelled badly of something once burned and still acrid. Bard faced SL'an with forced calm. "This is the mouth of the God Flower's nest. All Gods' nests have one of these at the top, the most sacred place of all. It is a place where birds are drawn in to become One with Them, although none who have tried entering have made it out. If you are the Starling God, there should be no problem for you to go into the mouth of the God's nest and return to us unharmed."

Bard flew up and landed on the stone edge of the mouth, leaning back a bit and seeming to fight suction as he swayed forward at moments against his will. "Are you afraid, starling of the doves? If you are who you say you are, then there is absolutely nothing to fear. See how I remain here perfectly safe."

SL'an felt tightness in his entire being warning him away, but he fought it for the moment and flew up on the edge facing the Secret Keeper. He gasped and drew his body back as foul air seemed to reach out to pull him inside.

"You have just felt the breath of the Gods calling you in, or *You* in – we shall see once you travel down to the calling."

"Have you done this?" SL'an tried to look down the mouth without losing his balance.

"There is no need for me to. I am the Secret Keeper. I have nothing to prove. I follow the Lore and have spent my life forming my flock to be more like the Gods. There is nothing but right with me."

"It seems that one of us is right and one is not. Perhaps we both should go down," SL'an suggested calmly.

Bard started to open his beak widely, but then a peculiar flicker of satisfaction came and went from his eyes. "You may be right on this. There may always be doubts in my flock if we don't both take the test to see who is recognized and rewarded by God Flower. I suggest we rise together, take three solid wing beats, and drop at the same time. There looks to be room for both of us."

"Agreed." SL'an's heart pounded in his breast so hard the young starling worried Bard would hear it, yet without another word the two males rose and took one wing beat, then two, and as SL'an had suspected, Bard suddenly rose up above him and reached out with his talons to push him down into the suction of the mouth. The sharp claws dug into SL'an's back before he could move completely out of the way, and he felt the weight of the older bird pushing down on him, forcing him closer to the foul aura of the strange stone mouth. With panic, he wrested free and nearly turned upside down, flapping wildly and using his own legs and talons to grip onto Bard's toes and swing him around and off him. The move worked, but with hardly a moment of hesitation, the Secret Keeper flung his body back at the younger starling again and smashed into him, knocking him to the right – just clear of the looming black hole of a mouth. It gaped menacingly as Bard hovered over it, seeming to fight an invisible pull and breaking free at the last moment.

Once clear, the Secret Keeper lunged another time. SL'an made a quick maneuver straight up, but the older, more experienced bird was faster. He rose like a bolt of lightning being pulled back to the sky until he was exactly above his enemy once again. There almost wasn't time for SL'an to think as Bard dropped down toward him, his wings flat against his body so there would be the greatest speed and least wind resistance. The gaping black mouth was directly under them both, and the younger starling knew in an instant that a smash from the Secret Keeper's heavier body would send him down to whatever horror waited inside.

SL'an dove to one side, feeling just the brush of Bard's angry talons before watching the Secret Keeper disappear with only the flash of a terrified wide eye, and then a squawk as the hungry mouth pulled him out of sight.

The young starling retreated to the lower top of his Mother's nest, panting and staring up at where they had both perched just moments before. There was still a faraway-sounding call from Bard, begging the Gods to help him. *Maybe you will save him after all, Mother,* he thought in a wish. *I don't want him to die, no matter what he has been or how he has been to me.* But he also realized the metal thing that sometimes rested on the gravel space by Mother's nest was gone. When it went, it usually took her with it, and there was no telling how long it would keep her away.

SL'an stayed on the nest top as the sun changed its place in the sky, climbing higher, peaking, and then slipping back down as it was also pulled by some invisible force to its resting place behind the mountains.

Bard's pleas came less and less frequently, and then there was silence. Either he had given up or had been drawn to some other place. Whatever had happened, SL'an didn't believe there was any other God in the nest that could help him, and Mother had not yet returned.

He finally left with a heavy heart back to where Glee, Diver and Trill had returned from feeding. "The other flock members will be coming back from their searches soon," Diver said.

"Do you want news of Bard?"

Glee trembled as Trill replied, "We saw enough. It was his intention to kill you, and in doing so, he lost his own life. We have never seen any bird return from the mouth of the nest, although there has been word that some have survived in other Sacred Spaces."

SL'an lowered his head. "I'm so sorry. I hoped he would listen, and I had no wish to have him die."

"Bard has been a lifelong friend, but his anger and belief have always run hotter than was wise," Diver murmured. "We will honor him as he would want, but we will also have you share your murmuration with us if you are willing."

The younger starling looked at Glee, who was still trembling and staring at him with her eyes swirling. He called the two elders close to him and began the vision without more explanation. There was none they would need once they experienced it for themselves. Glee huddled away from them, but watched as amazement caused the two elder starling bodies to lift and swell somehow with joy. When the vision was shared and the connection broken, SL'an saw she was still rooted to her branch, but trembling a little less at least.

"I've taught this to another flock of starlings from where the Great Undrinkable Water called the Ocean lies. They have agreed to travel with me to teach the murmuration to as many starling flocks as are willing to learn."

Trill looked pleased. "Bring them at the next sun. When the black starts to make its way here, we will share the news of Bard and explain to the others so they are ready for you."

"We must leave time for a proper praise and celebration of Bard's life and service," Diver added.

Trill's eyes misted. "We will."

SL'an thanked them and hesitantly approached Glee. "Will you be alright?"

"I will offer myself to You when You are ready to choose a One," she nearly whispered. "Then I will fulfill my own purpose."

I can't accept that offer, Glee, when there's another I hope to woo into my nest someday. He didn't dare say it aloud now, but he hoped she would understand when he tried to make Flora his One and only. He had no doubt Glee would have her share of suitors when the time came, with the magical lilt in her voice and shining feathers. *Forget me. I'm not the One intended for you.*

Before he returned to Moon and Flora, SL'an took a detour to L'al's nest. There were four young doves huddled closely on a branch – SL'an recognized two as L'al's Helpers, and the other two, a bit younger and looking very much like L'in, were the now-fledged nestlings. His heart sang as he landed on a branch near them. The young male Lorn perked his head up high. "Starling SL'an! Look here at what happened while you were away!"

Libn preened. "We did a very good job of helping our uncle raise his nestlings, I'd say."

"I would agree!" SL'an marveled. "Young ones, you must have taken names?"

"I have taken L'in and choose to be a Teller like my father," the female cooed happily.

"I am Loft," the young male bobbed. SL'an bobbed back enthusiastically.

"Where's L'al? Is he well?" SL'an looked at the beautiful babes and couldn't imagine that his mentor wouldn't be.

"We're without our mother, so we know Father is not the bird we are told he was, but we plan to stay and raise our own here someday, and hope this continues to heal his heart and feather," the young L'in said, with such enthusiasm that SL'an laughed.

"Tell your father that I, the Seeker, have much news for my Teller in between some very important teachings I must do with my kind." He looked at all of them one at a time.

"We'll be certain Uncle gets the message," Libn said, fluffing her breast.

From where SL'an and the other flock roosted, they could hear faint strains of the celebration of Bard's life. Flora had gone to join them while the others agreed to meet her and her home flock at the next sun to begin teaching.

Before it was time to leave for warmer lands, the greater flock was ready, having practiced over forests until they had formed a strong vision connection. Now it was time to show what they had learned – to hopefully spark whatever hidden embers of memory were buried in the kind called humans, if there was any ember left to spark. If nothing else, they hoped it would inspire the other kinds in the process of forgetting to pull back from the black that would swallow them whole. SL'an knew if Mother and her kind couldn't remember, then the swallows would be right. They would flail around with no sense of Truth until all living things were consumed in their paths.

But whatever the outcome, SL'an reveled in the murmuration, feeling the warmth and moving air of Flora beside him as hundreds of starlings moved in graceful unity in the sky.

Epilogue

The two women stood outside of the house with steaming mugs of tea clasped in their hands, wrapped in colorful shawls against the cold.

"Isn't it the most amazing thing? I told you it was worth coming out for," the first woman said. They stood among the last of the season's flowers that echoed the colors of the first woman's flowing dress. Her friend made an appreciative humming sound.

"You certainly didn't exaggerate. There are so many of them!"

They watched as hundreds of starlings whirled into the sky and began moving like some kind of fluid, first into one shape, hovering, then into another, and others and others. "What are they doing? Mating?"

"Not this time of year. I think they're creating pictures of other animals – look there! That's clearly a whale. Look! Now it's some kind of bird. I saw one that looked an awful lot like a person."

Her friend giggled and sipped her tea, shuddering against the chill. "You have the wildest imagination! By the way, how is the gull coming along?"

"He's doing well, but it's slow going. The boy who shot him didn't just break the bone – that's already healed – but there's been muscle damage too, and that takes longer."

"So…he's still in your bathtub?"

"I think he'll be there for the winter, but I'm sure he'll be releasable in the spring. Anyway, the outside rehab building for the birds is coming along too, and if this happens again, at least I won't have feathered friends staying in my bathtub anymore!"

They laughed again and sipped more tea, looking up to the sky at the still changing shapes. "Oh, that one is definitely a rabbit," the friend declared.

"I told you so."

"It's like looking at the clouds. Stare at it long enough and it could look like anything."

"I don't know about that. Starlings do this over in Europe, you know, and scientists can't figure out why except to say they are doing it to keep predators away, which makes no sense to me."

"More sense than thinking they have enough ability to plan and enough self-awareness to create art in the sky. Why would they do that, anyway?"

"I don't know. Why do we do what we do?"

The friends were quiet for a moment, and then the flower-clad woman shook her head. "Different from us doesn't mean less than us."

"Hey, I know I'm not going to win this one with you, so I'll just nod and love you anyway, okay?"

Flower looked into the sky at the form of a woman holding a baby and could only smile.

"There is nothing plain about starlings!" ~Dove L'al

Definitions

Gods: Humans. One human is a God in a species of Gods from bird perspective.

Sacred Space: The area surrounding a human home or building. Birds do not differentiate a grocery store, mill or other large building from a house. All are simply seen as Sacred Spaces.

Teller: A bird position of wisdom and information sharing, not unlike a pastor. Tellers take in information from other birds and consider what should be shared and how. They also mediate and try to be sure peace is kept and that the Gods are appeased. They are often doves.

Seeker: A bird's position of information gathering. A Seeker is curious and constantly looking for information about the Gods' activities and events around their Sacred Spaces. Any bird species can be a Seeker, but they are often small, quick-moving birds like finches.

Watcher: A bird's position of protection and alarm for a given Sacred Space. In God Flower's Sacred Space, Watchers are the redwing blackbirds.

Praiser: This bird position is open to the largest number of bird species. These birds sing in the morning and see out the evening, as well as deliver important bits of information to the Sacred Space when needed. They take direction from the Teller.

Secret Keepers: This is a position known only to starlings. Since starlings have some specialized beliefs, the Secret Keeper is responsible for teaching the flock or other birds as much as they believe they should know about that.

Taut Metal Limb: Phone and electrical lines spanning from pole to pole.

Clear Boxes: Windows on the side of human homes.

Loud Metal Things: Cars, trucks, etc.

The Paradise Nest: Garden Center of a chain home goods store.

Stone-like paths, Stone-like fields, etc.: pavement and concrete – roads, sidewalks and parking lots.

Cracking Stick: Gun.

Paths of the Gods: Roads.

The Great Undrinkable Water: Ocean.

Murmuration: The unified and fluid activity of many starlings flying in the sky in breathtaking formation.

The Mouth of God Flower's Nest: Chimney top and opening.

Creating in different ways and connecting people with the idea that all living things deserve respect and kindness are the two most important threads running through author Tanya Sousa's life.

"I love Einstein's quote, 'if you judge a fish by how well it climbs a tree, it will live its whole life believing it is stupid,'" she said, "because that quote not only speaks to different forms of human intelligence, but different forms of intelligence overall. All living things are amazing—just differently gifted."

Tanya sends this message through her magazine articles, creative non-fiction, children's picture books and now through her first novel, The Starling God.

Tanya lives and writes in rural Vermont.